CAMP MURDERFACE

DOOM IN THE DEEP

CAMP MURDERFACE

DOOM IN THE DEEP

BY JOSH BERK & SAUNDRA MITCHELL

MASTERS OF DISGUISE

HARPER

An Imprint of HarperCollinsPublishers

Library of Congress Control Number: 2021933213
ISBN 978-0-06-287166-4

Typography by Corina Lupp
21 22 23 24 25   PC/LSCH   10 9 8 7 6 5 4 3 2 1
❖
First Edition

Saundra: I dedicate this book to Josh Berk.

Josh: I also dedicate this book to me.

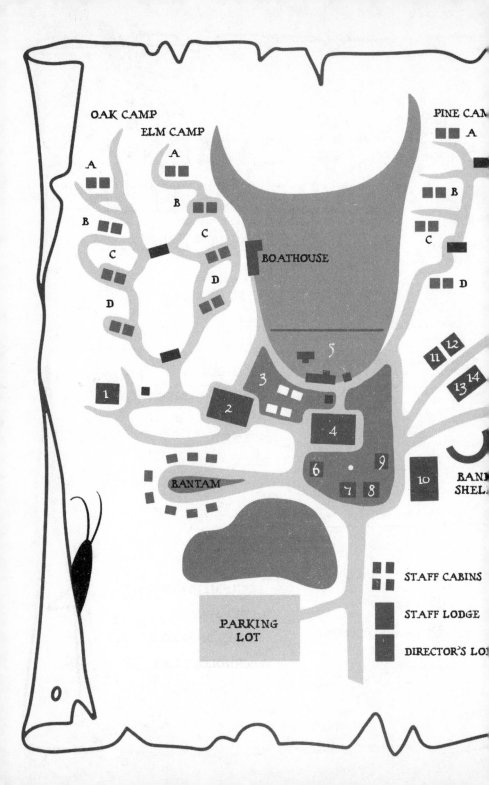

RIFLE
RANGE

ARCHERY
RANGE

EST. **CAMP** 1863

SWEETWATER

Abyssus Abyssum invocat

1   ARTS + CRAFTS

2   REC BARN

3   TENNIS/VOLLEYBALL/
    ATHLETICS

4   GREAT HALL

5   DOCK + DIVING

6   CANTEEN

LAWN   7   INFIRMARY

WATER   8   LAUNDRY

CAMP BUILDING 9   LIBRARY

CABIN   10 EQUIPMENT/STORAGE

SHOWER/LATRINE 11 RADIO STATION

              12 PHOTO/DARKROOM

              13 TECHNOLOGY LAB

1
Wake 'em Up!

Tez

There's a new normal at Camp Sweetwater, and that normal is *normal*.

Ghosts don't appear in our bonfires now, screaming for justice. All the lifeguards at the lake are actually alive. There are no cryptic French whispers at night. And *extremely* important: shower curtains, towels, razors, and blackened wood just sit there, not doing anything.

Corryn Quinn, my best friend, and I made sure of that.

She and I vanquished the evil. We helped three missing campers go home—metaphysically, anyway. Sure, we had to find them in a bone pit of doom, and nearly die ourselves. But we did it. Together. And now the worst thing that happens here is Scrap Dinner Thursdays.

Don't ask. It's indescribable.

Gavin, our counselor in the Oak Camp boys' cabin (we're technically Oak Camp, Group A, subsidiary to Camp Sweetwater, but I'm learning to be more casual), throws open the door and greets us with a rattling belch. His sandy hair falls in his eyes. I think he's going for a pompadour. It makes him look like a confused rooster.

"Get your kit on, you tossers!" he shouts, his British accent thick enough to spread on toast. I'm not sure why most of the counselors here are from Europe. I'm also not sure how Gavin and Scary Mary—the girls' camp counselor—keep their jobs.

But! Their neglect and incompetence are *normal*.

Knees rolls off the top bunk across from me. That's his new action-hero trick. So far, he's managed to land on his feet exactly no times. He doesn't let that dissuade him, though.

I, on the other hand, use the ladder to climb down very slowly. No three-point hero landings in my future, nope. Tez Jones is the brains of the operation, not the brawn.

Nudging past me, Bowl Cut (who remains sadly shorn, although he's starting to show a little bit of ginger peach-fuzz) grabs his bathroom bag from the cubby. He's quiet; he even seems thoughtful.

It's hard to believe he's the same kid who flashed us a full moon and farted into our fan as an introduction. But I guess getting your glorious mop shorn by an unseen evil can do that to a guy.

"Hey," Nostrils says, stripped down to tighty-whities and standing without shame in the middle of the cabin. He drums on his scrawny chest, throwing his head around like he's a lion. His black bangs quiver with anticipation. "Chickenlips, gimme one of those wake-'em-up drops!"

Ah yes, Chickenlips. The camp name Gavin bestowed on me, despite the fact that chickens have no lips. He threatened to do worse, so I accepted it. I've even, kind of, started to like it. And I secretly love that Nostrils insists on calling my sweet li hing mui "wake-'em-up drops."

They're salted plums that my grandmother Nani sends us from Guam. They're about the size of a grape, dehydrated in salt, then coated in a sweet-and-sour powder. I shared them with the cabin *once*, and now Nostrils is addicted. He's never had candy with flavor, I guess.

Since I'm running low, I hand one precious plum to him. I lick the delicious, tangy dust from my fingers. Then I fold the bag and put it back in my cubby. Mom hasn't sent a care package in a while, so I need to ration.

Nostrils pops the plum into his mouth. "Yeahhhh," he says, because the plums start out sweet. Then he groans, flapping his arms and slapping his own chest. When the sour kicks in, he stomps his feet. The cabin shakes a little, and everybody gets out of his way. We know what comes next.

Windmilling in the space between our bunks, Nostrils bounces off both beds, one wall, then ricochets past us. He jumps over the box fan. No, he tries to jump over it but knocks it on the floor. Plaintive, the fan whumps as Nostrils bursts out the front door and into the sunlight.

Still in his tighty-whities.

Okay, that part was new! Two angry Brits yell; Nostrils disappears from sight. Laughter fills our cabin. Knees doubles over with it. Bowl Cut shakes his head and snickers. And I slap a hand to my forehead.

"He ran outside," Bowl Cut says in disbelief.

Knees gasps out, "Did you see that?"

"He hit the door running," I exclaim.

"He's crazy," Knees says.

Bowl Cut creeps to the door to peek out. When he sticks his head into the sun, it shines like a beacon. "I think he's running to the latrines!"

"If he jumps in, he's banned from the cabin for life," Knees says firmly.

"He'll be legendary, though," I say.

"Oh yeah," Knees agrees, and Bowl Cut nods. "Totally."

I take a deep, fresh breath of cabin funk and put on my camp shirt. Carefully, I tuck it into my khaki shorts. Then I pull on the tube socks with teal stripes at the top. They go all the way up to my knees, nice. Tennis shoes, double knotted, and I run a comb through my hair.

All that's left is a stop at the shower house to brush our teeth before breakfast, and voilà!

I'm ready for another great unhurried, unhaunted, de-eviled day at Camp Sweetwater! Oh yeah!

2
Happy Camper

Corryn

Hairspray lets out a primal scream.

Nobody in the shower house looks twice. The damp, mildewy walls trap the sound of her cry, and it's not like the Oak Camp girls' cabin hasn't heard this about fifty times this week.

She wails, "It's empty!" then shakes her can of Aqua Net hairspray. Beads inside it rattle furiously, but nope. They're not mixing up any more bang glue for the buck. That can has shooshed its last shoosh.

We'd hold a funeral, but eh. If we started holding funerals for stuff that dies at Camp Murderface, we wouldn't do anything else. There would be no time for lanyards, no time for Scrap Dinner Thursdays. Now, if we were allowed to set the Aqua Net on fire . . .

"Are we done?" I ask, because I've been done for a while now. All I had to do was polish the ol' chompers. My hair does what it wants. We have an agreement: it does its thing, I do mine. The two zits I have don't need toothpaste on them, and I'll bite anybody who comes at me with a mascara wand. It looks too much like a bug. No thank you.

Dumping her stuff into her bag, Ew says, "I'm done. We can drop this back at the cabin and head to breakfast if you want?"

"Rad," I say, and we head out together.

The shortest out of all of us, Ew is also the nicest out of all of us—me included. And since she was the one most directly touched by the evil in camp, I feel protective of her. The rest of the cabin is all right, I guess. They believe freaky stuff happened. They're on the *team*. Still, they're not on alert like me and Ew.

Because, see, I know me and Tez helped those missing camper girls go home. Like, home-home. To the great beyond in the sky. Heaven. Nirvana. Whatever your tradition happens to call it. But Tez thinks now that they're saved, it's over.

I do not agree. I think this is intermission.

Tez keeps pointing out how normal everything is, and I'm happy for the kid, really. He has a bad heart, and I guess his parents keep him in a cage full of books most of the time. Camp Sweetwater is the most freedom he's ever had.

But I have my spying eye tuned to high alert. I'm ready to notice anything out of place. And yeah, nothing has been out of place since the night the police came and took away the "remains" (HUMAN BONES!) we found in the giant pit (FILLED WITH A MEGA TON OF REMAINS!).

But come on. We uncovered the truth about some crazy cursed French guys who tainted a whole lake for *hundreds of years*, and we're supposed to think they're done because we sent three of their victims into the light?

Pshhyeah, right.

"I think they're supposed to do activity sign-ups today," Ew says after we toss our kits onto our bunks and make our way down the path to the Great Hall. "I wonder if we're going to do a camp play."

I hold out my arms a little to balance when the path gets narrow near the C cabins. "You're into that?"

Ew nods with a little smile, her wispy blond hair

floating in the wind. "Yeah. I got to play an angry elf in our school Christmas play last year. It was tons of fun."

With a laugh, I try to imagine her as an angry anything. I can't get the picture in my mind. All I end up with is Ew in a green tunic and those swirly-toed shoes. "Cool. So let's ask about the camp play."

"Awesome," she says decisively.

And even though we're talking and walking and it's a beautiful morning to be outside, we've got our heads on a swivel. Ew covers her side of the path and the canopy of trees above us. I cover mine and all the dark places underneath. It's a system. To keep us safe.

In my field, there are lots of pine cones and pine needles, branches and mushrooms. I bet if I told Tez I was gonna eat one, he'd give a two-hour lecture about poisonous mushrooms. And I'd sit through it, just so I could say, "I just thought you would be a fungi to hang with." *Then* I'd explain the joke to him. *Fun guy! Fungi!*

"There's a garter snake," Ew says.

We slow and, yup, sure enough, a little green danger noodle squiggles back into the brush. We get too close, and he beats a serpenty retreat. I lean over to try to catch one more glimpse, but he's gone.

"We've been seeing a lot of snakes, huh?" I say.

Ew splays her fingers out and counts. Then she nods at me. "Yeah, like eight since the weekend."

"At least we're seeing them *outside*."

"Seriously." People would notice the screaming from our cabin if a snake got in. But now that Ew mentions it . . .

Are snakes like cicadas? Do they have a season? Huh. I wonder what my dad would say. I miss all the camping and hiking and outdoor stuff he knows. I miss leaning against his shoulder, roasting marshmallows on a little fire in the middle of nowhere.

I wonder how much more of that I'm gonna miss, since my parents are obviously getting a divorce. They sent me here to distract me from everything that I *know* is going on. Meanwhile Tez and I are slaying *vampire devils* at camp.

Ew shudders. Her bangs ruffle, and she nods. "Ew. No snakes in the cabin, please."

Definitely. No murderfacing snakes in the murder-facing cabins, thank you.

"Ooh, get the good table!" Ew exclaims as the Great Hall comes into view. Seniors pour out of it, most of them trudging behind their counselors.

Yes! We're here just the right amount of early! See, there's a meal schedule that we have to stick to. The seniors eat first, then clear out to start their day. Then Oak Camp eats—that's us—followed by Elm Camp. Finally, the diaper babies in Bantam Camp get to eat.

If we get to the Great Hall too early, the lunch ladies (who also serve breakfast and dinner—does that make them meal ladies?) send us back to our camp group to wait. If we get there too late, all the good tables are taken.

Here's a good table: one by the giant fireplace they never light. There's air from the outside coming in, so you don't have to smell everybody, and the meal ladies can't see what you're doing. Perfect.

The bad tables are the ones crammed back by the kitchen. They're constantly under observation, and they smell like camper sweat and canned chicken. They also have this slightly greasy film all over them. You can spill a whole glass of water, and it just beads up and rolls onto the wooden floor.

Thanks to me and Ew, we have the best table waiting when the rest of the crew rolls in. Knees and Nostrils appear first, karate-chopping each other the whole way.

For all the practice they get in, the only thing they've ever managed to break with their kung fu grip is Tez's nose.

Knees slides in next to Ew and says, "Heyyy."

She stares at him, kind of like he's from another planet, and says nothing.

Before it turns into a thing, the rest of the gang piles in. It's nice to see Bowl Cut getting a little color on his bare head, and it looks like Hairspray managed to coax one more desperate shoosh from the can into her hair. The bangs are standing, just not as mightily as usual.

Braids practically sits on top of Nostrils, forcing him to move down. And that leaves just enough room for Tez to slide in next to me.

"Morning," he says brightly. "It's another gorgeous day at Camp Sweetwater!"

I mean, look at that beautiful nerd. Just look at him. *So* full of optimism. I don't wanna break his spirit or anything. But I do kinda want to remind him that the camp tried to kill us. Like, just a couple of weeks ago? That thought squirms in my guts like a handful of earthworms. There's evil here. It might try to kill us again. We don't really know. Cursed camps don't come with a guidebook!

But man, Tez has had the cheer button turned to ultra since the ghost girls disappeared. Reaching for the orange juice, he smiles. Tearing open a mini-box of Frosted Flakes, he beams. As Knees describes Nostrils breaking free and streaking down the camp, Tez chews and grins at the same time.

He's the smartest kid I know, but jeez.

That doofus is literally a happy camper.

3
Minefield and Soft Shoes

Tez

Breakfast was so invigorating that I walk expeditiously to Arts & Crafts.

The sun beats down, bright and clear, from a sky that is exquisitely cloudless. The gentlest breeze threads through the woods, so there's a soft hush everywhere I go. It's almost conversational, like the forest is talking to the sky.

I take this walk on my own. This is a secret part of my day; even Corryn remains in the dark about it. When everybody else in Oak Camp is doing Confidence Course or Tree Climb Race or . . . basically anything super physical, I help with the Bantam campers. Corryn affectionately calls them Diaper Babies, but you know what? These little guys are awesome!

When I open the door to the A&C building, the Bantam campers are already sitting in their places. Well. They're already squirming in their places. They remind me of my little sister, Hypatia, Hi for short. She has too much energy for her tiny little self, so it comes out in wiggles and squiggles and sometimes random shrieking.

And just like Hi, these baby campers are all six and seven; they also have the attention span of one half-Nostrils, so the place is buzzing!

I smile when Soft Shoes (real name: Seok Jin) almost falls off his stool waving at me. He's the tallest kid in Bantam, and his black hair is cut into a killer baby Mohawk.

My smile is big and genuine; I wave back.

Picking up a craft packet, I circle the table and sit down between Soft Shoes and Minefield (real name: Tasha). I get *hugs*. They're excited to see me, and they actually want me to sit next to them!

The beads on the ends of Minefield's black braids chatter as she moves. She has her own percussion section wherever she goes! Her brown eyes sparkle, like she's always having the best time ever.

And you know what? I love that Minefield almost knocks me off my stool and always talks right into my ear. It's part of her charm.

Puffed up, I make sure that I spread myself around so nobody feels left out.

"All right, what are we making today?" I ask out loud, opening the craft packet. It contains a paper tube, a baggie of beans and popcorn kernels, some construction paper, and a small bamboo stick. I don't need instructions to figure this one out. Or any of them, really.

All their crafts are big and easy to make. They decorate the Bantam shelves: lots of messy yarn God's eyes and friendship bracelets, strings of fat uneven beads they rolled from clay, brilliantly bright castanets made from cardboard and bottle caps.

"Can you guess? Are we making a telescope?" I put the tube to my eye and peer at Soft Shoes and then Minefield through it.

"NOOOOOOOO!" Soft Shoes shouts.

"WAIN STICK!" Minefield yells at the same time. She waves the tube at me. Somehow, even though we just started, she's already sticky.

Soft Shoes watches me with big brown eyes. He's

16

usually pretty noisy, but I can tell he's super curious about everything, too. So I like to tell him little facts while we work on the craft of the day.

"Do you know what a rain stick is?" I ask.

He shakes his head, and Minefield leans across me. She's practically in my lap again. She yells even though she doesn't have to. "WE'RE GONNA MAKE MUSIC WIF IT. IT GOES—"

And then she demonstrates, shushing the loudest shush I've ever heard (and kind of spitting on everybody as well). She's missing her two top teeth; she sprays everything in a three-foot radius.

Soft Shoes leans back, but he's still grinning. Then he leans into Minefield's face and shushes her in return.

The saliva is everywhere! Glad I'm getting a shower later!

After they dissolve into giggle-spittle silliness, I separate them gently. "Awesome! You guys got it! Now, we need to get started or we won't get to hear our rain stick today, okay? Take your tube!"

I thrust it forward in one hand, brandishing it like Excalibur.

Soft Shoes and Minefield do the same.

"Now," I say, glancing at the instruction sheet, "take the pick!"

The pick is a precut bamboo spear with one sharpish end. I watch and make sure my kids are following along, and then I say, "Now we're gonna *poke* it."

I demonstrate, holding the tube just so, and using the pick to pierce the sides. Immediately, Minefield beats her tube flat with her bamboo pick. It's like a tiny slasher movie, without the blood. Yet. I reach over to catch her hand and say, "Gently, like this."

She gets it, more or less. She just wants to wreck it first. I turn, reaching over to hold the tube for Soft Shoes. My voice is strong. Encouraging. "You can do this, Soft Shoes. It might help if you turn the pick a little, like a drill— Oh, you got it! Good job!"

Minefield leans in, waving her tube. "What about mine?"

"You did a great job, too," I tell her.

I mean it. They're all working hard, and they care. They *want* to do a good job, and they glow when you tell them they did! I bet I could teach them to make about anything. Well, as long as each part took only twenty minutes.

They're smart and determined. And when I think of

what could have happened if Corryn and I hadn't totally defeated the evil . . .

I shudder. Thankfully, we *did* defeat it. Hit the road, Jack. Don't you come back.

Like, ever.

4
WMIA: The Voice of Camp Murderface

Corryn

"You are listening to WMIA, the voice of Camp Murderface," Hairspray says. She's using her hairbrush as a microphone, pretending the mirror in our bunk is her radio station audience, I guess. Ew is still combing leaves and twigs out of her hair. When we play King of the Mountain at this place, we play for keeps.

And Ew, even though she's the tiniest girl in both Oak *and* Elm Camps, is a Tasmanian weasel when she gets to the top of the hill. She whales on me with the pugil stick, knocking me down first thing. Then she takes out three boys from Elm without blinking. I don't know if there used to be such thing as a pugil-stick ninja, but there is now.

Quickly, I strip off my dirty shirt and pull another one on as fast as I can. I'm ignoring the white cotton training bras in the bottom of my suitcase. Mom wrote my name in those, too. It's like the woman is trying to humiliate me. I don't know what they're supposed to train, but they can stay folded up with my extra socks.

Hairspray swans over with the brush and thrusts it in my face. She says, "WMIA!" like a weird robot.

I take in a deep breath and sigh. Then I reply dryly, "Oh yeah, I get it. MIA, like Missing in Action?"

"No," she says with a laugh. A very specific laugh that calls me a big old silly-willy. "W-M-I-A. Get it?"

I blink at her.

"Her name is Mia, you goof," Braids says. "M-I-A. Did you think her actual name was Hairspray?"

"I . . . don't . . . know?" I mumble.

"Ohmigosh! Do you think *my* name is *Braids*?"

Her disappointment hangs in the cabin like her Love's Baby Soft perfume. Why does she put on perfume at camp? I'm not about to ask. I offer an empty guess. "Could've been short for, uh, Braidsabella. Or, like, Braidsifer."

Taken aback, Braids gets a little testy. "Seriously,

you *do* know what my name is, right? We've been living together for like *a month*."

There's this heavy weight settling on my shoulders. A girl-shaped one. Everybody in here kind of sucked at the beginning. They were mean to me in an easily identifiable way. So I kind of . . . wrote them off. Decided not to care. After Tez and I discovered the bone pit and saved everyone's butts, they started warming up. I know.

Most of their questions since then are nice, but . . . maybe they're not? I mean, they just seem weird.

Is it because they really are? Or maybe because I don't know how to ask them the right kinds of questions in return. I mean, girls are cool, but sometimes, I feel like I'm the *wrong* kind of girl. At home, the word *tomboy* got thrown around a few of times. Until I bloodied a couple of noses, that is.

Still, Hairspray's and Braids' eyes remain on me. They mirror each other perfectly, leaning in at the exact same angle, their nostrils flared the exact same amount. They're waiting for me to cough up Braids' name, and my brain is busy wondering what's for lunch.

"I know things about you . . . ," I stammer. "You, uh, play tennis."

"We all play tennis," Braids says. "This is summer

camp. Tennis is mandatory."

"You enjoy mandatory activities," I say. "There. That's a thing you enjoy. And you, your name is Jenny," I offer.

Whew! Clutch play, brain, spotting the sign written above Jenny's bunk in bubble letters.

"Last name?"

"Settle down," I say. "We're not that close."

"You're *such* a weirdo," Braids says with a laugh. But she smiles and shakes her head, like she's amused by me. Like my weirdo-ness is charming or something. (I THINK?) At the same time, Hairspray giggles and goes back to grooming/broadcasting.

She belts out a Blondie song, and you know what? She has a pretty nice voice! But then she changes the lyric to "Call Knees!" and starts throwing herself around the cabin like she's onstage.

I have to admit, it's a little funny. And it gives me an idea for a question to ask! Finally!

"Do you like Knees?" I ask.

The singing instantly stops. "Oh my god, shut uuuuuup," Hairspray bleats.

Braids gloms on to her with a hug that looks suspiciously like a wrestling hold. "You doooooooo!"

"Noooooooooooo! It's not truuuuuuuue!"

For approximately six years, Hairspray and Braids yarp at each other about whether Knees is or isn't the bee's. I'm not sure what tips the balance in this epic meeting of minds. But finally, Hairspray flops back on her bunk, grabs a pillow, and strangles it to death. "I mean, *what's not to like?*"

"Well, he has nice knees. I'll give you that," I say. "His legs certainly . . . bend." Everyone has dumb nicknames around here, but besides mine, Knees has to be the worst. I take that back: I forgot about Nostrils.

"You want to make out with his knees," Braids says. She mimes French-kissing Knees' knees. Everybody laughs, even me.

I glance around at this place we've called home. After the weeks we've spent here, the inside of our cabin has started to resemble the inside of our brains. Totally jumbled up.

In the beginning, our bunks were neat, our walls were bare, and everybody was stiff. Now, though, there are pictures from magazines taped to the walls, drawings of hearts, lots of hair products. I even put up my own extra picture of BMX champion Danny Stark

24

catching awesome air, but that's only because Braids sat on me until I would. Apparently, pictures of bikes aren't personal enough, or so she claimed.

"So many activities to choose from. I'm probably not really going to do radio, though," Hairspray announces from her exhausted sprawl on Braids' bunk. "Maybe archery!"

"Go on with your bad Robin Hood self," I say. Then I add, "I'm definitely doing radio, and I'm definitely going to call it 'the voice of Camp Murderface' on the air."

"Nuh-uh!"

"Yuh-huh!"

Hairspray suddenly says, "Ooh, you have to play a song for me, *for Knees*!"

It's cute, I guess, the way they're excited about Hairspray's dramatic gesture to declare her love for Knees. And I guess that's their right, being excited. Thinking summer romance is possible. It's not their fault the camp has other ideas.

"Guess it's just me in the DJ booth," I force myself to say. They smile. I grab the microphone/hairbrush and put on my best radio voice. "You're listening to DJ CQ, your host with the most, rocking the hits from coast to coast."

"What coast?" Braids asks with a chuckle.

"The coast of Lake Sweetwater," I say. "Duh."

"Lake *Murderface*," they all say together.

Murderface. If only they knew how not funny it is.

If only they knew that the evil isn't gone. It's climbing the charts. And it's about to rocket right to number one.

5
Ditto

Tez

As we leave lunch, the counselors gather their campers in little sweaty knots outside the Great Hall. With the sun directly overhead and not a cloud to provide shade, everybody's slightly damp and slightly rank. I try to stand closer to Corryn and Ew, because they don't funk up the place like Bowl Cut, Nostrils, and Knees.

Gavin and Scary Mary slump sullenly against the building. They get that way a lot when they have to do their jobs, I've noticed. Something else I notice, glancing around, is that there are a lot of new faces.

We don't see the counselors for the other camps very often. Mostly in passing, at mealtime or swim time. But

I'm pretty sure there are at least four new ones. They almost glisten; that's how new they are.

One of them rounds up the Bantams as they leave the Rec Barn; another one plays goalie as the senior camp spills from their side of the lake.

Their country-club precision sets them apart from everyone else. Their polos are crisp, their shorts ironed, and useless sweaters are neatly knotted around their shoulders.

"Have you ever seen that guy before?" I ask Corryn, pointing out the goalie.

Corryn squints and stares at him. Then, clipped, she says, "No."

She's kind of grumpy now that all the evil drained out of Camp Sweetwater, and she has to enjoy herself. Her parents are breaking up at home. I don't blame her for being upset. But, I mean, we're here, right? We may as well have some fun.

"Get over here, you little—" Gavin cuts himself off when Camp Director Gladys Winchelhauser passes by. Plastering a (frankly frightening) smile to his face, Gavin finishes in a singsong tone with, "Nutters, and get the sign-up sheet."

Then he reaches out and tousles Bowl Cut's nonhair.

28

His smile lasts until Mrs. Winchelhauser is out of range. Once she's gone, he wipes his hand off on his crumpled jeans.

Scary Mary doesn't let go of the sheets in her hands. Instead she fans herself with them. Looking down her nose at us, she says, "All right, you spoiled gits. There's three choices, so it's not bloody hard. Archery, radio, photography. You're going to pick one. ONE. No changes, no take-backs, no complaints. Mark it, and turn it in after break."

A furrow crosses Corryn's brow. "What break?"

"The break you're getting right now," Scary Mary says irritably, and for once, it doesn't seem like she's irritated with us. She keeps glaring at the sheets, and then, I think, at Mrs. Winchelhauser's back.

But that can't be right. The two constants in a camp full of variables are these: our British counselors loathe us, and they wish they were anywhere else. Actually, there's a third constant, too. We don't get breaks. It's back-to-back activities, interrupted only by meals and nightfall.

But! My mom says just because something is different doesn't mean it's bad. They have to release the info sheets now, and as soon as they hit our hands, it's chaos.

The papers are limp and slightly damp. The paragraphs describing each activity are purple, outlined with little ghosts of the letters in lavender. An appreciative murmur ripples through the girls.

"Dittos!" Nostrils yelps.

Knees punches the air. "Yesssss!"

Both of them instantly plaster the papers against their faces and take deep breaths. They do it again, hugging the papers with so much gusto, it's almost embarrassing. It's perfectly possible to enjoy the smell the methanol and isopropanol leave behind when you make copies on the ditto machine, without *huffing*.

In fact, the aroma lasts longer if you don't handle the papers too much. The more Knees and Nostrils wave the papers, the more they dry. Goodbye, addictive ditto smell. So basically, they're ruining their own fun. (I wouldn't call myself a connoisseur of reproductive technology, but I can appreciate the scent and the science behind it.)

"I heard there's bows and arrows," Knees says between sniffs, "and I'm ready to Hood up the Robin around here, *pa-schwing*!"

Corryn gives her page a cursory sniff, then folds it in half and shoves it in her pocket.

"You okay?" I ask her.

She shrugs.

And that's it. Just a shrug. So I try again. "What are you going to sign up for?"

"Radio."

A little bit of disappointment weighs on me. "Oh. I was probably going to take up photography."

She cracks the tiniest smile. "Take it up, huh?"

"Not as an avocation," I say, and that just makes her smile more. Squinting at her, I ask, "You're laughing at me, right?"

She shakes her head. "Nope. I'm deeply digging the Tezness."

Now, I'm not always the most adept at friendships, but Corryn is definitely my friend, and I know there's something wrong with her. And at the same time, with the exact equal amount of weight, I don't know how to ask her about it. I thought "You okay?" was sufficient, but we're operating on a new level here.

And since this level hasn't been covered in the guide-book or health class, I try again. "For real, you're okay?"

Slowly, very slowly, Corryn leans over. She gets right up close to me, so close I can see the pattern of her freckles. She purses her lips, then whispers against my ear, "This camp. Is still haunted. And nobody cares. But me."

I don't know if it's the proximity of the whisper or its content, but my face stings with a blush.

I pull away at the same time she does, and all I can say is, "Oh."

Because the camp *was* haunted. Past tense. We took care of it. We saved the world, and our cabinmates even know about it. They even kind of like us now because of it. (I think? Yeah, I think so.) There hasn't been a single screaming fire or incident of terrifying weirdness in the middle of the night for almost three weeks!

But Corryn won't let her guard down.

And I don't want to make her mad. So I let my "oh" stand, and Corryn's face smooths into that blank, slightly grimaced mask she's been wearing around lately. My heart sinks into the pit of my stomach. I let her down. And I don't want to. But I can't make her see that things are fine.

All I can do is hope that she comes around.

And soon, because camp isn't going to last forever.

6
Sweet Dreams Are Made of Knees

Corryn

We should have known this camp was suspicious. They paint everything blood red, for one. For two, we have only a couple weeks left, and they're just now giving us the rest of the promised activities. (Except library time. The poltergeist remodel on the library must not have been to code or something, because it's still not open.)

And for three, our Arts & Crafts activity today is Solar Oven. We're going to make s'mores with sunlight, in a short two or three hours. S'mores are good, but come on! You could blow up a marsh in the microwave in a short two or three seconds.

Ew stands next to me, folding the instructions into

a cootie catcher. "Okay, first, wrap the whole shoebox in tinfoil."

I whip out a sheet the length of my arm. Wrapping takes five whole seconds. It looks like an inside-out birthday present. A wrinkly, crinkly one, too. With that, we're ready for the next step. I pick up the baggies containing ingredients and flap them at Ew. "Time to go find some sun."

Leaving the A&C Building behind, we trudge up the paths to find a good spot of "concentrated sunlight." The instructions actually say that! I nudge Ew and say, "What if all we can find is fresh-squeezed sunlight?"

She grins. "I guess it depends if it has pulp or not."

A surge of affection broadens my smile. I've got some good ones, and sometimes Tez just doesn't get my sense of humor. It's nice to have somebody around who gets me without explanation. Especially because Tez is . . . Tez feels . . . far away, I guess. It's like when I drop a chain on my bike, Elliot. If I don't get it back on the sprocket exactly right, it just grinds and drops again.

I can't seem to get the chain back on my friendship with Tez. I wonder if I can talk to Ew about that stuff, too.

34

"You wanna hear something weird?" Ew says, inter-rupting my thoughts.

"Uh, yeah," I say. "I always wanna hear something weird."

She squinches her nose and glances toward the sky. Her lips move, but she doesn't talk yet. I can't tell if she's trying to find the words or if she changed her mind. With the wave of a tinfoil box, I say, "Spill."

With a sideward glance, she nods. "Okay. Okay. So like . . . you remember when I woke up speaking French?"

How could I forget? It was one of the creepiest things I'd ever seen, and I'd already seen an entire cabin full of thousands of bugs. Ew almost floated in the dark, her white nightgown fluttering at her sides like a ghost.

Hanging in the middle of our cabin, she mumbled in a language she didn't speak. Worse than that, her head snapped to one side. It looked like someone—*something*—had broken her neck. And when the spell was over, she fell to the floor like an abandoned toy.

Yep. Definitely got that one in the ol' noggin for-ever, so I say, "Oh yeah. Oui."

"Well," she says, interrupting herself to point out a

good patch of sunlight off to our left. We leave the path, high-stepping over brambles to get there. "I keep having dreams in French. And they're, like, really weird."

A sparkler made of ice runs up my spine. Is she getting messages from the other side? Is this how it begins again? Tensed all over, I try not to crush the shoebox. "Weird like how?"

"Winchelhauser is in all of them," she says, and hops over a log to reach the clearing. The sun beats down on her, brightening her blond hair but also darkening the shadows under her eyes. She waits for me to join her, then opens the baggies.

Crouching down, I lay the box in a couple different ways. If we're gonna get s'mores before this time next week, we're gonna have to get some good rays. Meanwhile, I'm trying to think of the right thing to say. Finally, I pick. "Are they scary?"

Ew kneels beside me, ready to construct our snacks. "No. They're just weird. Like, there was one where she was trying to explain to these four pale dudes why she hadn't given them any blood offerings."

At the risk of stealing somebody's catchphrase, ew! But out loud, I say, "Gross."

"Yeah, they . . . I mean, it's probably Knees' fault for

telling that story about the vampire devils, because the four guys? They looked kind of vampirey. Long teeth and—" She flutters her hands helplessly. "I don't know. They just felt like vampires in my dream."

My stomach clenches hard. So hard that I bet my breakfast just turned into a tiny cube, like cars do when you put them in a compactor. Tez and I haven't really talked to anybody about the vampire devils—about the fact that we thought they might be real. Sitting back on my butt, I sprawl my legs out. "And you're dreaming that, over and over?"

Ew shakes her head. "No. There was another dream where Winchelhauser was watching a cabin burn down, right? Like, a big one. And she was screaming as it fell down. And when it fell down, it disappeared into a pit of bones."

The ice sparkler is going full-speed up my spine now. My lips are dry; I smack them together to get them to loosen up. What if Ew isn't just dreaming stuff? What if her dreams are messages? Like she's a . . . radio or something?

But all Ew's dreams are about the Winch? What's the deal with that?

"I'm sorry," I say. Because I am. I don't want Ew to

have nightmares. I don't want this camp to be haunted either. But so far, Summer 1983 is all about me *not* getting what I want.

"S'okay. I'm not waking up in cold sweats or anything," Ew says. "Oh, oh! I had one where she was standing in the lake, and we all had to walk in to her. Except when we got to her, her face started peeling off. Her eyes turned yellow, and her tongue got all long like a sn—"

Before Ew can finish her sentence, we hear a rustling in the woods. Maybe it'll be Tez! Ew can tell him about all this. Because obviously, the camp isn't done with us! He needs to hear this stuff, and we need to start planning!

But no, actually, shoot. It's the Winch! I clap a hand over my mouth. Ew and I both duck.

The earthy smell of wet dirt rises around us, caught in the humidity and hanging like a stank bubble. I breathe through my mouth to keep from smelling too much grossitude, and Ew manages to make herself even smaller beside me.

"Did she hear us?" Ew whispers.

I shudder. "I don't think so. She hasn't looked this way."

The Winch, in fact, looks like a camp director on a mission. She tromps steadfastly through the underbrush, moving away from our clearing at a good clip. Then, all of a sudden, she stops.

I stop breathing. Ew hides her head.

The Winch shuffles around a certain way, and then . . . well, squats.

And she squats for a *long* time.

Ew. I guess she *was* on a mission.

It starts to get funny, because jeez Louise. How long is this gonna take? She needs some fiber, maybe. My face gets hot, and Ew's is pink, and we're both choking on giggles. Why is she even doing that out here? She's camp director. She has a whole apartment thingie! There's gotta be a potty in there.

Soon, and luckily before Ew and I burst into hysterical laughter, the Winch disappears into the foliage. The sound of her boots fades from a *cronch* to a *spspsp*, and once again we're alone.

Ew rises slowly. Squinting, she surveys our surroundings before saying, "She did just . . ."

Choking on laughter, I say, "Does a Winch wee in the woods?"

Cracking up, Ew shoves me and we both end up

sprawled on the ground, laughing like loons. Something weird is still going on in Camp Sweetwater, for sure. At least this time, it's the hilariously stupid kind of weird.

I know I have to be on my guard. But just for a minute, I let it down, enjoy the sunshine, and let my lungs loosen up with laughter. Ew is pretty cool. I'm glad I met her. Two friends, one summer.

Now I just have to find a way to protect them both.

7
Osmosis

Tez

Gavin waits for us on the cabin step, and as soon as he sees us, he starts barking.

"Turn right round; let's go!"

We glance at each other in confusion. After Arts & Crafts is our assigned swim time. We need to change—Knees, Nostrils, and Bowl Cut so they can swim, and me so I can sit on the shore and talk to Corryn. After what we've seen under the waves, it's hard to enjoy a casual dip.

"Our towels are in there," I say.

Gavin openly rolls his eyes at me. Coming toward us

like a very underfed linebacker, he says, "Don't reckon I asked, did I?"

I don't get to argue with him, because he sweeps us down the path with nudges, pokes, and threats. For the most part, Gavin has two speeds: sloth and cyclone. As he lumbers behind us now, he's sloth-*like* but somehow not *right*.

I don't know how to explain it, except his usual air of casual disinterest is gone. He's super *determined* for some reason. And that makes him especially creative when it comes to the threats.

"Quit your goggling, or I'll stuff you in a toaster," he says, punching a knobby finger at me.

Nostrils snickers. "Toast à la Chickenlips."

"Don't recall pulling your string," Gavin says, and it's Nostrils' turn for a jab.

Before we make it down to camp, he calls Bowl Cut a broken teakettle, Knees a three-kilo sack of hair, and Nostrils a folding chair. If his career as camp counselor doesn't work out, Gavin should try motivational speaking.

As the trees clear, I frown. Four vultures circle the lake—bobbing, weaving, but maintaining a patrol.

Theoretically, this makes no sense. Vultures eat carrion. They circle something that's dying; they *wait*. But there's nothing in the lake to wait for, except kids.

Wait a minute. There are too many kids in the lake.

Just like mealtimes, our swim times are usually separated by camp level. But I know for a fact that's not happening right now.

Right there, near the dock, Minefield tries to climb on Soft Shoes' shoulders. I can't tell if he wants her to or not, but it doesn't end well. They both fall into the water. My heart leaps a little, but they're okay. It's only a few inches deep near the dock.

They rise up, and something about them is different. They look sort of tired, and Minefield is never tired. Ever. Then they start wading listlessly with the rest of the Bantams. Their counselors cage them into a small area. It's like they're making kindergarten soup or something.

I shudder and murmur, "What is going on?"

Nostrils helpfully provides, "We're swimming, Chickenlips, keep up."

The senior camp kids, with their wispy mustaches and shellacked hair, walk aimlessly through the water.

43

A wall of their counselors lines the shore, shoulder to shoulder. It's like they're not allowed to get out. Same with the Bantam campers.

"In our clothes, though?" Bowl Cut asks, looking to me.

"Keep moving!" Gavin shouts. He pushes between Bowl Cut and me, cutting off my reply.

Even though the sky is an impossible, perfect blue, it feels ominous. It presses down, a lid on the weird cauldron that is the lake. The constant circling of the vultures churns it darkly. The water is just choppy enough to have waves, and those waves glitter like broken glass. The counselors keep us streaming into the water like lemmings.

Shuddering, I try to fall back in the crowd. Like I said, I've managed to avoid swimming since my test. I plan to keep it up. Usually, Corryn and I just sit on the shore and talk about stuff. With darting eyes, I search for her in the crowd. She's already at the water's edge, dressed in shorts, a T-shirt, and a scowl.

"Get in," Gavin barks. He puts out his arms, sweeping us inexorably forward.

Because he's pushing us toward Corryn, I keep moving. The waves look bright and clear today, like in pictures from Aruba or somewhere. That's *not* the color the lake usually is. The greeny-gray depths seem diamond clear now.

"I don't like this," I tell Corryn as soon as I reach her.

"Yeah, me either," she replies.

Gavin has moved to corral a couple of kids from Elm Camp. They're trying to sneak off toward the vending machine a big truck delivered this morning. Nobody knows what's in it or if we're allowed to buy anything from it (or how we would, since all of our cash is in the commissary, which isn't open yet).

I huddle with Corryn. "Did you see the vultures?"

"Hard to miss," Corryn says, stealing looks around. "And the campers guidebook says the diaper babies aren't *ever* supposed to swim with the big kids, but here they are."

For a moment, I'm distracted and smile. "You read the guidebook?"

"No," she says, sarcastically but not meanly. "I slept with it under my pillow and now it's in my brain."

I laugh. "Osmosis, then."

"Tez, I'm gonna osmosis you if you don't concentrate."

That's not really a sentence that makes sense, but that's Corryn. And she has a point. Still, there's a warm flutter in my belly because she clearly *has* read the guidebook, which she knows I think is important. Even though she never thought it was important before. The sensation tickles at the back of my neck, too.

"You wanna know what's heckin' weird? Scary Mary took a dip before she came to get us," Corryn says.

As if invoked by her name, Scary Mary appears at our sides. She's what my mom would call bedraggled.

Stringy, wet hair plasters against her head and shoulders, beads of water dripping everywhere. There's a grayness to her face that isn't usually there, and her lips seem sort of ashen, too. What isn't gray has a faint green cast to it: her hair and her hands.

She grabs both of us at once. A hot shot of pain pierces my shoulder. Scary Mary squeezes so hard, I'm afraid her nails might go right through the meat and into my bones.

I stare into her eyes. Every time we've seen someone in the grip of the camp's evil, their eyes have been black. Scary Mary's aren't. They're just gray and cold.

"Play snogface in the lake," she growls at us.

Corryn doesn't look panicked; instead, she's

determined. She actually digs her sneakered heels into the coarse sand. "I'm cold. I don't want to get wet."

A little yelpy *murp* escapes me when Scary Mary digs her fingers in even harder. "If I want to know what you want, I'll bloody well ask you. Get in the lake!"

"You can't make me!" Corryn shouts back.

Scary Mary tips her head to the side. It feels like she tips it a little farther than geometry and physics should allow. Even as a cold sweat of pain breaks out over me, I stare at Scary Mary. I can't escape the mental image of her with a snapped neck. My thoughts are sliced up in the blender of my brain and I freeze.

Sickly sweet, Scary Mary enunciates to Corryn, "Right you are, pet, I can't. You've got a little bull in you, haven't you?"

As she speaks, Scary Mary tightens her grip on my shoulder again. The soft cotton of my T-shirt actually pops. Tears spring to my eyes; the pain in my shoulder starts to feel like I'm being crushed with hot steel. I try to breathe through it, but all I manage to do is whimper. I can't cry. Please don't let me cry. Corryn's brave; I have to be brave, too.

But Corryn's posture softens when she sees me start to sink under Scary Mary's hand. Her eyes go wide. I see her mouth something, but I can't make it out. My vision is blurry, and it's all I can do to stay on my feet.

Corryn goes chest to chest with Scary Mary. "Let him go," she demands.

Something in my shoulder pops. Audibly, because I see Corryn wince. Scary Mary tips her head in the other direction, another impossible angle. "Get. In. The water," she replies.

I try to whisper *I'm okay* to Corryn, but I think what comes out is just muted gasps. Scary Mary's grip grinds into my bones. Blood blossoms on my T-shirt, spreading in circles around her fingers. My head goes woozy. Sounds ring in funny echoes, like we're underground. In a cave. Or a cellar.

Or a grave.

When Scary Mary smiles, her teeth are way too big for her mouth.

Are they *pointed*? I can't tell.

With another bone-cracking squeeze, Scary Mary simpers at Corryn. "Now, love, don't you want to be a darling and do as I say?"

I shake my head.

Corryn shakes her head, too.

Not at Scary Mary, at *me*. She looks a different kind

of green. Like, the color that comes on right before your lunch of bug juice, chicken strips, crinkly fries, and chocolate pudding makes an encore appearance.

With her jaw set, Corryn reaches down and wrenches off one of her shoes. Then the other. She throws them down hard at Scary Mary's feet. And then she takes one step backward . . . into the water.

"Happy now?" she asks.

"One more," Scary Mary says.

She does, and now the water is over her ankles, almost halfway to her knees. The waves lick at her skin, like they're . . . greeting her, somehow. The sun beats down, hot and relentless. Scary Mary says nothing; she just twists her grip on me and I can't help it. I yelp in pain. Immediately, Corryn takes a third step back.

Scary Mary straightens and drops me from her grip. "Well done, You!"

When I fall, my knees hit the sand and my face hits the waves. Although I shoot back up as fast as I can, my mouth is full of lake. My hair drains cold streams over my back and shoulders; the blood on my T-shirt washes away. I reach up to check my shoulder and . . . nothing. No wounds, nothing. Only the holes in my T-shirt remain.

Corryn scrambles to help me back to my feet.

"I owe you," I tell Corryn quietly.

"You owe me like fifty," she replies.

And then we spend the rest of this mandatory pseudoswim knee-deep but motionless in the water, making up stupid reasons why we owe each other. Number thirteen is "You owe me because of your face," and number thirty-two is ". . . because of your dumb Cheeto breath." We keep going, reason after reason.

We're the only ones talking, and I'm not surprised. Wading in this water is exhausting. It shouldn't be. We're just standing, after all. But there's a fog creeping in around the edges of my brain. Like the sensation you get just before you fall off to sleep.

Another moment, and the fog rolls over me.

8
I Hate Feelings

Corryn

This is the day that never ends. And not in a funny way that has a jaunty tune attached to it.

Gavin and Scary Mary frog-march us out of the water. They slosh up behind us and start prodding our backs with their knuckles. That part is pretty normal for them, but the weird part is they don't insult us. Or yell. Or threaten us. In fact, they're just silent, their eyes dull and glassy, their mouths gawping open almost as if to catch flies.

Instead of leading us back to the cabins, we get knuckle-knocked onto the path to the Rec Barn.

My head's kinda swimmy, but I know something isn't

right. "Hey. We need to dry off," I say, all casual-like.

In reply, Scary Mary lovingly pokes the back of my head and keeps pushing me forward. What is that about? I duck away from her and resurface between Ew and Tez.

"What the flip is going on?" I ask them under my breath. Everybody's weirdly quiet, so I don't want to draw attention.

"The schedule must be off," Tez says reasonably. That's a bad sign, because Tez isn't reasonable about anything that deviates from the schedule. That kid probably schedules taking a wee.

I nudge him gently and say, "Ya think?"

Ew digs her fingers into her damp hair. Combing through it, she makes it stick up in about sixty different directions. Then she answers for Tez. "It happens, I guess."

All around me, Oak Group, Cabin A, shuffles like zombies down the path. Knees and Nostrils? They don't karate chop *anything*. Not a single *hi* nor *ya*! Braids schlumps along next to Hairspray but doesn't hold her hand or whisper to her or anything.

As he walks, Bowl Cut's arms swing heavily, his

white T-shirt still clinging to his skin. He looks like a ginger chimp on his way to the vet *and nobody's laughing.*

This isn't right. None of this is right. My throat gets tight, and my eyes get hot. I'm not gonna cry or anything, but I *am* having some feelings. I hate feelings. My hands itch to punch something, which is a good way to get rid of the feelings. But what? The air? The lake? If the vampire devils would show themselves, I'd give them a one-two right in the biters!

Wait, *the vampire devils.* A realization sproings to life in my head.

"Hey!" I say, grabbing Ew's arm and shaking it. "Tell Tez about your lake dream!"

Ew blinks at me slowly. "What lake dream?"

"The one you had . . . about the lake," I say, also grabbing Tez's arm and shaking it. "The vampires talking to the Winch and the Winch standing in the lake and all the kids had to walk into the water. Like what just happened!"

Slowly, Tez blinks. "You . . . you dreamed that?"

Just as slowly, Ew shakes her head. "No. I don't know what she's talking about."

Now I want to shake them both hard, like I'm

snapping out a blanket for a picnic. Frustration and me, we go wayyy back, and I'm starting to wish I could crash into something to express it. "You told me about it right before swimming! When we were in the woods?"

"You were in the woods?" Tez asks, mildly surprised.

I boggle at him. "Yes! Right before swimming. We all were. Solar ovens, remember?"

Tez purses his lips and rolls his eyes upward like he always does when he's trying to remember something. Then he nods.

"I think . . . I remember now."

My heart leaps. Then it takes a header into my stomach, because Tez finishes that thought with, "Solar ovens are a bad idea. When we go back, we won't have s'mores. We'll have ant colonies."

At that, Ew laughs. No, she laugh. One laugh that sounds like *hur.* "Ant colonies."

"Tez," I almost yell. "Focus! Ew is having weird dreams in French! *The evil that lives here at Camp Sweetwater spoke French.* And we were in the woods together. We saw the Winch—" I cut myself off, hoping that Ew will fill in what we saw. It's not important, exactly, but it proves we were together and talking about stuff.

But Ew doesn't fill in anything.

When the silence goes on too long, Tez says, "Mrs. Winchelhauser works here."

"She might live here," Ew says.

"Possible."

"Or she could live somewhere else."

O-kay. Either I'm totally cuckoo banana splits crazy, or something really super strange is happening—*to them*. Ew and Tez are both smarter than this conversation, even on their worst days.

I'm the only one suspiciously aware, and that's as wrong as ketchup on Frosted Flakes. Ask my social studies teacher; awareness is *not* my strong suit.

I need more intel.

So I do what all good spies do. I zip my lips and open my earholes.

Quiet.

All I hear is quiet, and you know the one thing that summer camp isn't? QUIET! It's noisy *all the time*. The shoosh of hair spray, the grunt from a kung fu punch to the gut, the *schlorp* of a hall full of kids drinking the milk from the bottom of their cereal in the morning. And farts. So many, many farts.

Even at night, there are mumbles and arguments and whispers and the screen door of the cabin opening and closing quietly while Scary Mary goes out to visit Gavin and do . . . I don't know what they do, bite tree trunks or something.

Just then, Knees speaks up and says, "When do you think we get to pick our new activities? I heard there's bows and arrows, and I'm ready to Hood up the Robin around here, *pa-schwing*!"

See? Right there. That's proof that I'm not crazy. Everybody's acting like they fell off the turnip truck about fifteen minutes ago. We totally *picked* our activities. We *huffed* those dittos. We *made* those jokes.

Hours ago.

And these numbskulls don't even remember.

So the question is, why did they forget? And what else don't they remember?

9
Operation Floppy Disk

Tez

After a long day of rewarding camp activities, the ritual bonfire is the perfect finale.

And after six weeks of instruction, my cabinmates make the perfect tentpole-style fire. I distribute the wood, to ensure our fire burns long into the night—meaning we get to stay up later than anyone else. Once I explained that to Nostrils, Knees, and Bowl Cut, they were thrilled to name me fire captain.

(They didn't actually *name* me that. But that's clearly what I am.)

I think our fire tonight is the best one yet. Good

distribution of flames, excellent amount of crackle, enough floating embers for ambiance without risk of setting anything else on fire, and smoke in a perfect silver funnel toward the sky.

When I get home, I'm going to miss this. My cabin-mates are shadows, dancing around the fire. They whoop and holler and run when the girls chase them. Gavin and Scary Mary stay huddled under a tree, mostly ignoring us.

All through the night, other kids at other fires laugh and yelp and sing. There's not a cloud in the sky, but there's a slight breeze that carries our voices along. I'm going to miss hearing the senior camp doing their senior chants. I can almost pick out individual voices now.

I'm going to miss Corryn, too. So much. She's super tough, mostly fair, and an excellent bicyclist. When she's got a plan, her brown eyes sparkle, and Corryn almost always has a plan for something. Even if it's for sneaking through the breakfast line twice to get double the Danish. I'm not exaggerating when I say she's my best friend in the whole world.

Actually, I miss her right now. She sits on the stump next to me, but she's a million miles away. Propping both elbows on her knees, she rests her chin in her hands and stares into the blaze. Usually, I take care of contemplation in our duo, so I reach out and touch her shoulder. One finger only, right in the middle.

"Penny for your thoughts."

Slowly, she looks at me. "Dude, *Fort Knox* doesn't have enough pennies, so I know you don't."

I can't tell if I'm insulted, so I choose not to be. Turning toward her, my knees bump against the stump she's sitting on. I lean in and really focus on her. "Did you know a penny is ninety-nine point two percent zinc and point eight percent copper?"

She snorts. "No, Tez, I did not know that."

Admittedly, I'm new to having friends who aren't related to me. But even I can tell that once again, something's not right with Corryn. It seems bigger than her, somehow. Is it her paranoia—fear that we didn't vanquish the evil? Perhaps, so I prod. "What's wrong?"

Straightening up, Corryn slaps her knees and turns to me. "What did we have for breakfast today, Tez?"

Curious. She was there; we had the same thing. But since it seems important to her, I say, "Sugar Smacks, a cinnastick, and orange juice. Why?"

Now she squints at me. "What did we find out after lunch?"

59

Curiouser. "We found out a lot of things after lunch. We found out that . . ."

"Yeah?"

I scratch the side of my nose and try to think. According to the schedule, our afternoon goes lunch, Arts & Crafts, physical recreation, camp craft, free choice (we have to do something; we just get to pick what it is—I usually pick reading), then dinner. I roll my eyes up, trying to scratch an itch that's in my brain. "Ummm . . . we must have gone to Arts and Crafts. . . ."

"I *knew* it," Corryn exclaims. "You don't remember going swimming?"

I rear my head back. "We don't swim after lunch. It's dangerous!"

The more I lean back, the more Corryn leans in. "What about your shoulder?"

Automatically, I touch my shoulder. Ow. Peering into my shirt, I see three evenly spaced bruises. My stomach settles uneasily. "I don't know. I must have bumped into something."

When Corryn grabs my arm, it startles me. Her grip isn't tight, but her face is as serious as a grave. The campfire throws shadows up her face so that the furrow in her brows turns into a dark arch, and her mouth is twisted in a grimace. "Tez. What's the first thing in your head after lunch?"

Because she's so insistent, I rack my brains. I know the schedule. There's no reason for that to change. We must have followed it, but . . . the harder I think, the more blank it all is. We had lunch and then . . . I look up at Corryn. "Dinner. I remember going to dinner, because Nostrils caught that frog and named her Vicky."

"Ha!" Corryn says, pointing at me. "I knew it! Tez, something happened when they made us go swimming. Nobody remembers anything *except* me." Now she flaps her arms around, almost windmilling off her stump. "Ew had a dream about vampire devils and the lake, and now everybody that got wet got their minds wiped!"

I want to argue with that. We've been in and out of the lake all summer. (Sort of. It tried to kill Corryn on, like, week one, so mostly, we sit next to the water while everybody else plays chicken in it. But they all get out with their brains intact. Or at least as intact as they were when they went in.)

Still, I can't deny that my afternoon is a blurry haze.

"That doesn't seem right," I say.

With a scowl, Corryn stands up. "Why would I make that up, Tez?"

Because she doesn't want to think about what's happening at home? Because camp is boring without some big bad evil thing on the horizon? There are a lot of answers to that question, but she's so upset. And I don't want her to be. So I reach out to catch her hand. "You wouldn't."

Her gaze drops to our joined hands. She doesn't curl her fingers around mine. There's no grip at all; her palm is warm and sweaty but motionless. It's like holding a small meat loaf.

"No," she says with a sigh. "I wouldn't."

"Okay, so . . ." I dig around for a solution, then say, "We'll start writing things down. That way, if I forget, you can show me my journal. And if you forget, I can do the same. We'll even sign off on each other's entries. That way they're witnessed."

When she doesn't say something right away, I'm afraid I messed this up. Unknowingly, but still. Finally, though, she gives my hand a weak squeeze and nods. "Okay."

"Operation Floppy Disk is a go," I say enthusiastically, trying to get her to enthuse with me. I don't like seeing her so sad and distant. It must feel really lonely, and I hate that for her.

She screws her face up, pinning me in that look that says I've gone one geek step too far for her. She asks, with one skeptical eyebrow arched high, "What the heck is a floppy disk?"

"It doesn't matter," I say, and I grin because she rolls her eyes. That's more like it!

Then Corryn grabs my wrist and modifies my grip. Suddenly, we're in a thumb war. Which, by the way, I know I will not win. But she loves playing anyway, so here goes nothing. One, two, three, four, I declare a—

"Win!" Corryn shouts, pinning my thumb down in record time. I definitely didn't let her win because she needed it. Nope. I'm just a terrible thumb warrior. But if I were better . . . I think I might have thrown the match just to see that smile again.

That's what any best friend would do.

10
For My Eyes Only

Corryn

You know what the problem is with carrying a note-book around everywhere? Everybody wants to know why you're carrying a notebook everywhere. Even if you write, "FOR MY EYES ONLY" on it. Maybe especially so.

Okay, maybe that was a bad idea.

All the way down the hill to get breakfast, Braids keeps trying to peek. Meanwhile, Hairspray keeps stopping in the middle of the path to say something she thinks is deep. Then she turns around and waits for me to write it down.

Lemme put it to you this way: I've been in bathtubs deeper than Hairspray.

This gets in the way of me telling Ew what I'm really doing. Since yesterday's mind-wipe fiesta, she's been distant.

"Your brain," Hairspray announces, casting a look at me, "named itself."

Whoa. Hang on. That really *is* deep. Propping the notebook on my chest, I actually do write that down. Satisfied, Hairspray bounds into the Great Hall like she's the emcee of a daytime game show.

We slide into the good table with the guys. Tez and Knees are already there, and Tez is drawing a diagram of something for him.

"With the log cabin method, we build a long-lasting fire that's easy to feed," Tez says, then turns to me. With a quick slide, he lays his notebook in front of me. Of course, it's a fancy leather-bound field notebook, with leather ribbons to close it. It's the Tezest thing I've ever seen.

Still, I'm glad he brought it. Maybe he's starting to take my suspicions more seriously. Flopping open my notebook, I point at the heading that says BREAKFAST.

"Put your John Hancock right there."

Tez dutifully signs it, says, "Saved to floppy disk," whatever that means, then offers up his notebook for my signature, too. "Everything good this morning?"

I consider it, then nod. "So far."

"Good," Tez says, and pats my arm.

It's that arm pat that gives me a weird feeling. One that sends blood rage-rushing to my face. Is he . . . pacifying me with this notebook thing? Just playing along?

Does Tez Jones think I'm nuts?

He better not. He's too short in the first place, and I'll knock his block off in the second place.

Gavin stalks over to our table and thumps down a pitcher of red Kool-Aid. Well, *that's* new. We don't usually get served anything. But all around us, the counselors are passing out jugs and pitchers, two per table except the really big table in the middle, and they get four.

Nostrils slides in next to Braids and rubs his hands in glee. "Bug juice!"

Deeply suspicious, Hairspray eyes the pitcher. Her nose is severely crinkled. "Gross. What?"

Leaning over the table, Braids starts filling glasses. Some of the drink sloshes onto the table. It quivers, then slowly soaks into the wood. The stain it leaves behind is ominously pink. I glance at Tez, and he gestures at his notebook, as if to say, *I'm already writing this down.*

"Is it supposed to taste like bugs?" Nostrils says, hoisting a cup of his own, an evil grin (and red juice) on his lips.

"Is that a bug?" everyone says.

Almost everyone laughs. *Is that a bug* is one of those inside camp jokes that never gets old. In theory, I can laugh about it now, but the mother lode of bugs that tried to eat us on the first day of camp is still pretty fresh in my mind. Also, I'm just not in a laughing mood. Sue me.

"Why do they call it bug juice, anyway?" Hairspray asks.

"'Cause of all the bugs they blend up to make it," Knees says.

"Ew," says Ew.

"But for real, it's because it's the color of bug blood," Nostrils says. He takes another sip. If he believes that, it doesn't bother him.

I don't believe him. I mean, the juice is not unbloodish. It's a very rich red; it's definitely not unlike the color of a wound when, say, you shred your knee on a curb while trying to do a one-eighty bunny hop.

Knees says, "Bugs don't have blood."

"Yes they do!" Nostrils yells. "Ya ever squish a bug, what color is the squish? Red. I rest my case. In. Your. Face. *Squa-wish!*" He mimes squishing bugs in the air with his thumb and forefinger. Squish, squish, *squa-wish*.

Tez looks like steam might shoot out of his ears and/or elsewhere. I know this look. A lecture might be coming on. And by *might* I mean definitely. He sets his fork down gently, wipes the corners of his mouth with a napkin, and takes a deep, deep breath.

"I—I don't know where to start," he says. "Yes, bugs have blood, but it's not the same as ours. Only oxygenated hemoglobin is red. Most bugs don't have hemoglobin, and they don't breathe with lungs. They have hemocyanin and spiracles instead. Their blood can be blue or green or clear! If you squish a bug and the squish is red, that's *your* blood."

"Ew."

"Or its eyeballs. Fly eyeballs."

"EW!!"

Nostrils shrugs, says, "Whatever," then chugs and rips a window-rattling belch. Some of the red stuff is dripping off his lips. He's gross and Knees is gross and Bowl Cut is the most gross.

Basically, everybody in the boys' cabin is nasty and gross, except Tez, who's creepily tidy. Also, I guess his eyes aren't bad.

Anyway.

I SAID, *ANYWAY*.

This place is a total boy washout, to be honest. At home, the only guys I deal with are other BMXers, and they are *rad*.

Ugh. As I sit over a plate of limp bacon-like strips, contemplating bug blood and dumb boys, I feel sort of empty and sad. I miss a lot of things about home. I miss my bed. I miss Elliot, my bike. I miss drinks that don't need Tez to explain them. I miss the lack of vampire devils, and I miss good gum.

Oh, man. The gum was soooooo good. Sour apple, the shredded kind in the pouch that makes you feel like a baseball player . . .

But reality interrupts my thoughts. Again. Because you know what? I don't miss my dumb, divorcing parents who think I'm too dim to realize that they'll be split up by the time I go home.

For the second time, Gavin comes by our table. I

am definitely writing all this down, because this sudden table visitation is super weird. Pushing between Bowl Cut and Hairspray, Gavin suddenly raises his hand and swings.

The thwack of a heavy palm against the sticky wood table is punctuated by a couple of shrieks—and not just from the girls. Gavin rolls his eyes at all of us and then steps back. He leaves a purplish sheet of paper behind.

"Read it. Or don't. I ain't bothered."

As soon as he walks away, Knees snatches the flyer up. He immediately raises it to his face. "Yessssssss."

"Are you sniffing dittos again?" Braids asks. "You better stop. You're gonna wipe out your brain cells even more than before."

"No, not that," Knees says. "This paper has more to offer than the smell. It's the, uh, you know—"

"The words?" I offer. Did he forget the word for words? Maybe he really is running low on brain cells.

"Words." He nods.

He lets Bowl Cut take the flyer so he can read it next. It goes around the whole table, and we all look at it kinda funny. It's not typed. Somebody with spidery old-lady handwriting wrote it.

I'd guess it's from the desk of one camp director

Gladys Winchelhauser, but it's on tennis stationery—two crossed rackets at the top. So I'm guessing Örn, the tennis instructor, had something to do with it? The words—*yeah, that's what those things are called*—on the page are COLOR WAR. GET READY.

An "ooooh" comes from the assembled breakfast eaters. I don't really know what a color war is. And I don't like not knowing things, so I play it cool. Tez is also not used to not knowing things. He, on the other hand, has never played it cool a day in his life. Case in point?

"Uh, what's a color war?"

"You don't know what color war is?" Knees says with a cackle. "Everybody knows what color war is!"

"Uh, not everybody," I say. "Some of us have never been to camp before. Some of us were busy doing noncamp things over all the summers of our youths. Awesome things. Deeply awesome things too impressive to mention here." That's right. Eat that, dumb camp.

"Well, color war is the best," Knees says. "At my old camp—"

Tez cuts him off. "You've been to other camps?"

"Yeah, dude; you think this is my first rodeo?"

Instead of answering, Tez scribbles that down. Interesting. Nobody in the boys' cabin thinks it's weird that Tez is keeping a diary in front of everybody. Then, I guess diary keeping is a very Tez activity.

"My old camp had color war, too," interrupts Hairspray. "It was hard-core! We broke up into teams and savaged everybody. Capture the Flag, water balloons, booby traps, cabin raids—the whole dealio. It was epic!"

Knees agrees. "Total. All-out. Warfare. If you catch an enemy behind your lines, you get to hold them hostage. Make people pay to get them back. Or worse."

My boy, Tez, and his eternal curiosity save me from having to ask. "Worse how?"

Nostrils practically lunges across the table. "You throw 'em in the lake!"

Suddenly, our table is loud again, everybody talking over everybody. The sound of laughter fills the air, and it actually feels good again for a minute.

Hairspray eventually yells loud enough that we all have to listen. "ANYWAY, THE POINT IS, whoever has the most points when somebody captures the flag, wins. They're the bosses of the whole camp. They can make people do stuff, in tribute."

"Anything?"

"Like, you know, get someone to wear your bunk-mate's underpants as a ski mask."

"Ew."

"Well, they'd take them off first."

"Can you like, opt out?" Tez asks. "Like, if for example, maybe say you have a note from a doctor?"

"Or a strong feeling that the lake is trying to kill you and you don't ever want to get wet again?" I add.

"Nope," says Hairspray. "You have to do whatever the winners say. Eat gross stuff, roll in the dirt, climb a tree, run into the girls' bathroom . . ."

At that, Ew shudders. "For boys, you mean. Right? Because who cares if girls run into the girls' bathroom."

"Ob-viously," Hairspray says. "Duh."

Here's the thing. A color war at some other camp sounds like it might be fun. I could potentially be, like, super into it. And I know Tez's big ol' brain can be used for evil with some encouragement. (Fun evil, like color war strategy. Not like everybody's-going-to-die-at-this-cursed-camp evil.) Together, we would demolish everything in our path. At another camp.

But at this one? I have a real bad feeling that color war is gonna be more than hijinks and shenanigans. A *lot* more.

I gaze around at our bunkmates. Without me and Tez, they would already be vampire chow. And if *I* weren't here, I'd probably be a beach ball in my parents' game of summer vacation divorce.

So. That makes me glad(ish) to be part of Oak Camp. I have a partner—slightly unwilling, but he'll come around—and a mission.

Color war, huh?

Okay, Frenchie vampire devils. You want a war? You got a war.

Vas-y, alors! Bring it.

11
Scary Mary Scared

Tez

There's a dense mildewy stench in our cabin tonight. It's so thick, it almost has a color: brown-green, like the worst corduroys on the clearance rack.

Our windows are wide open, the chirp of crickets outside competing with the buzz of the box fan. It's pointed out the front door, theoretically to drag the smell outside. In reality, it makes no difference in the stench. It just feels like we tried to fix it.

Our cabin always has a slightly weird smell to it, but tonight, it's especially bad. Right after our latest barn dancing session, we *really* needed showers. (For the record, it was a steamy hour of polka; the waltz was canceled because none of the girls wanted to stand that close to us. Considering the guys had started spitting for distance out the wide-open windows, I can't blame them.)

Unfortunately, we didn't get to wash up before bed. Something happened to the plumbing, all over camp. We can use the pit toilets, but the sinks and showers are dead. All that came out when we turned the faucets were a few tepid drips. We brushed our teeth with the water left over in our canteens.

And how do I know the trouble was all over camp? People's shouts echoed over the lake as the news spread up the counselor grapevine.

By the time it got to us, we already figured out there would be no washing up tonight. That didn't stop Gavin from stalking into the shower house in his flip-flops. They slapped against the floor with each step, and Gavin kept whipping his towel off his shoulder. That made his pimply chicken-chest heave, and it made us snicker when Bowl Cut started humming "The Chicken Dance" song under his breath.

"Right, water's out!" Gavin shouted. "Bed now. If you're thirsty, hard luck, innit? Wait till breakfast. Off you go, gnats! Fly back to the cabin!"

Thus, our current stank situation in Oak Camp, Cabin Group A. We heard Scary Mary screeching at the girls that if the water was still out in the morning, they'd get a quick wash in the lake.

I can hear Corryn now. "What a coincidence," she'd say, trying to make me feel bad for not entirely agreeing with her. "More forced lake time."

She would have a point. But that's not the point. Coincidence does not equal causality. And that's what the plumbing thing is: a big coincidence. That's all.

Lying in my bunk, I stare at nothing and try to wrap my brain around the situation. I really don't feel like there's anything wrong. Corryn and I compared our journals all day today, and they were consistent.

She still insists that we went swimming and forgot yesterday afternoon.

I *don't* remember yesterday afternoon. But I don't know if I remember any afternoon in detail. Time is funny here at camp; it's Wednesday but it might be Friday. The days blur together sometimes.

From his bunk, Knees whines, "Man, I'm dying of thirst."

"Seems unlikely," I volunteer. "It takes the average human about three days to die of dehydration. But we can evaluate the statement. You're parched, obviously."

Knees snerks. "Ya think?"

I ignore him. It's part of my go-along-to-get-along plan for summer camp survival. I don't like it when they make fun of the way my brain works, but they probably don't like it when people make fun of their buck teeth, bald head, or size XS T-shirts, either. (Knees, Bowl Cut, Nostrils, for the record.) I start my dehydration checklist, asking, "Do you have a dry or sticky mouth?"

For once, Nostrils takes me seriously. I think. He says, "Yes. Is that bad?"

"It could be," I concede. "Do you have a fever?"

"I don't know. I'm sweaty."

"We'll say no, because the next question is cool, dry skin."

Bowl Cut pushes his feet into the mattress and lifts me up. "Why do you know all this?"

I know all this because I've spent a lot of time in many, many doctors' offices, and sometimes they have fascinating reading material. Pamphlets and fact sheets and advisory cards, and they're all free! Free and excellent reference material is the best!

In addition to dehydration, I feel confident that I can diagnose hypertension, ovarian cysts, and vasovagal syncope, as well as camp-related medical complaints such as trench foot, jock itch, and deer tick fever. In some cases, I can even make medication recommendations, although Mom says that I shouldn't. Not until we can afford malpractice insurance.

Nevertheless, I ignore Bowl Cut's question, because my medical history is between me, my parents, and my doctors. Oh, and Corryn. And Nurse Kortepeter here at camp. And the camp director, Mrs. Winchelhauser.

"Okay, what color is your urine?" I ask. Before the words are even completely off my lips, someone wings a pillow in my direction. With a soft yet solid whump, it hits me right in the face.

Nostrils rolls over in his bed. "Quit being a weirdo, Chickenlips."

"It was a genuine inquiry," I retort. I throw the pillow back at him. Instead of hitting Nostrils in the face, it hits the bunk rail and bounces toward the door. Its anemic splat is almost swallowed by the sound of the box fan.

Furious, Nostrils points toward it. "Go get it!"

"We're not supposed to be out of bed," I protest.

"No duh, egghead. But it's your fault that it's all the way over there."

Bowl Cut and Knees rustle in their bunks. One of them whispers, "Fight, fight, fight," while the other one snickers. In response, my heart pounds furiously and my face gets hot.

Not only do I *not* want to engage in fisticuffs with Nostrils, I'm not *supposed* to. One good shot in the sternum and I could die. For real. My Marfan syndrome can weaken the parts of my heart. Crash into my chest, and I don't just get the wind knocked out of me. I could get a tear in my aorta and bleed to death.

As you can imagine, one of the things I promised my parents when they agreed to let me come here was that I would be *careful*. A cabin fight is not careful.

But there's a solution at hand.

Sitting up, I yank my pillow out of its case (it's a special case for my allergies) and swing it. "Take mine!" I say, and throw it.

Much to my outrage, Nostrils uses his arm as a bat and knocks my pillow away. It tumbles across the dirty wood floor, coming to a rest right next to the other one. Nostrils points up at me and says, "I don't want your cootie pillow!"

"Ohhhhh," Knees says, laughter in his voice. "This is gettin' good."

"Ohhh yeahhhhhhh," Bowl Cut agrees.

I start to inform Nostrils that cooties aren't real, but the cabin door creaks. Kinda like Gavin is opening it but not coming inside yet. Or at least, I hope it's Gavin. I can't believe I'm praying for more Gavin in my life, but a place like Camp Sweetwater does that to you.

The sound is distinct, and everybody goes quiet when they hear it. But Gavin doesn't open the door the rest of the way. Or storm in with threats (because of the pillows all over the floor) or slink in with his own skunky scent to add to the mix. He's just standing there, and after a moment, we realize he's talking to someone.

Bowl Cut leans out of his bunk. He listens, then whispers, "What's he saying?"

From across the room, Knees says, "I can't hear."

This. This is now my chance to be proactive. A doer instead of a thinker. I slink from my bunk, flattening my feet against the floor. If I glide them, they make less noise. It takes forever to get to the pillows—and to a good listening spot—but I manage. There's just enough space under the built-in cubbies for me to squish into.

"What's he saying?" Nostrils whisper-yells.

Somebody kicks something—sounds like a wall.

Then Bowl Cut says, "Shut up, he's trying to listen."

A tiny defense and I accept it with gratitude. Carefully, I stretch toward the door. Fortunately, I stretch pretty well. I squint, too, for some reason. Maybe blocking out other senses helps me concentrate? Something to research at another time.

". . . can't stand the little blighters," Scary Mary says, no surprise. Then, surprise: "But they shouldn't be doing *that* to 'em, Gav."

Gavin, generally too lazy to care about anything except things that might affect him, says, "Right, but what are we gonna do about it?"

Do about what? What are they doing to us? This is why eavesdropping is bad! You miss all the pertinent information!

Wincing, I slide the tiniest bit closer to the door. My hip rests on our jumble of sweat-damp tennis shoes, and I have two thoughts: one, the shoe pile is definitely where part of the stench is coming from, and two, whatever "it" is, it must be bad if Scary Mary and Gavin are worried about *us*.

"I'm on the bakery run tomorrow," Scary Mary says. "Reckon I could tell the police?"

"They been out here once already."

"Saying something, innit?" Scary Mary retorts.

Then Gavin lets go of the door as he yelps. "Hey now, that's one of yours heading for the lake!"

"Get back here!" Scary Mary screams, a much more traditional form of Scary Mary, the one we all know and suffer. With a soft bang, our cabin door closes, and I hear Scary Mary and Gavin moving away.

"Something's happening!" I say, standing up.

All of us pile at the door in a split second, so fast, the fan gets knocked over. Through the screen, we watch Scary Mary and Gavin actually *run*. It's so weird, I almost feel like we're watching an arty film. Or maybe I'm dreaming. But I'm not dreaming—I wouldn't make up a detail like Bowl Cut huffing his hot breath behind my ear.

As Gavin and Scary Mary bolt, the girls spill out of their cabin. There's a lot of high-pitched screaming, and the night air carries it perfectly. It cuts through everything; it's like ice in the blood.

Since the girls are abandoning their cabin, we tumble out of ours. Everybody else runs toward the woods, but I have to fast walk.

"What's going on?" I ask Corryn, who loops back for me.

Grabbing my arm, Corryn walks with me—faster

than a stroll but definitely no quicker than an amble. Everybody else leaves us in the dust. The trees are dark and deep, but all we have to do is follow the yelling Brits. Their curses light up the night as we stumble after them.

"It's Braids," Corryn says. "She fell asleep first. And Hairspray thought it would be funny to put her hand in water to make her pee the bed."

"Hilarious," I say.

In the dark, I can see Corryn shrug. "Anyway, as soon as her hand went in the water, she *floated off the bunk.*"

Now the cold inside me grows. "She what now?"

"She turned so that she was upright," Corryn says, pointing out a downed log and helping me scramble over it. "And then she started *gliding* toward the lake. We all tried to stop her. But she was crazy strong. Like, Incredible Hulk strong. She busted right through us and out the door."

More shouts fill the air. Some of them are urgent, others just alarmed. Huge splashes mingle with English curses, and every sound drives my heart to beat faster. When Corryn and I break free of the tree line, we see Gavin *and* Scary Mary in the water. They're wrestling

Braids out of it, Scary Mary with her top half and Gavin with her bottom.

Her pajamas are wet; they cling to her like Saran Wrap. She fights, spitting like a bobcat and writhing between them wildly. It's not hard to see that our counselors are struggling—struggling to pick up one tiny eleven-year-old girl. From here, I can't see Braids' eyes, but I wonder if they're black. . . .

"This is bad," Corryn says.

"Agreed," I say. We can't do anything about this. All we can do is watch Scary Mary wrestle Braids to the ground and then sit on her.

Even weighed down, Braids fights, kicking her legs and clawing, too. The weird thing—if you were going to pick out only *one* weird thing in the middle of this—is that she's silent. Her mouth opens and closes; she bares her teeth . . . but she doesn't make a sound.

Turning around, Scary Mary yells at Gavin, "Get Winchelhauser!"

He's dumb enough to say, "You sure about that?"

Scary Mary's accent gets so thick and lush, I can't understand a word she's saying. But Gavin understands, and it appears to be very effective. After only a few seconds of verbal barrage, he sprints up the shore. He doesn't even stop to tell us off as he runs by.

"Back to the cabins now, or it's a hundred-bead penalty from both!"

This would probably be a super effective threat if the only people who could take beads from us weren't busy subduing a seemingly possessed camper and running like heck for help from the camp director. We feel Gavin's wake as he speeds past us.

Ew and Hairspray clutch each other on the shore, crying plaintively. Bowl Cut stands silent sentinel near Scary Mary, while Knees and Nostrils watch in flummoxed silence. And then there's Corryn and I, still back with the trees, watching this all play out.

Soon, Braids stops thrashing. Scary Mary doesn't move, but she slumps. In exhaustion or relief, I can't tell. And I can't tell because this is the first time this summer that Scary Mary has ever done anything decent. As the clouds part, moonlight filters down, and now it's obvious. Braids has passed out. And Scary Mary looks very, very tired. And afraid.

Taking another deep breath, she scrubs her hands over her face and looks up at the sky.

Now revealed by a full moon, the vultures circle ever higher. They're inky streaks against shadowy clouds, their patrol tight and specific. They're right over Scary Mary and Braids, and that's not okay.

Like I said before . . .

Vultures only eat the dead.

12

"Morning, Cuties!"

Corryn

There have been a lot of sleepless nights in this place.

And not the fun kind. Not the variety of staying up all night eating circus peanuts, laughing with your friends, chatting in the dark, giggling in the small hours, conspiring until the sun comes up.

No, it's been more the other kind these past few weeks. The kind where The Fear badgers you in your bed. Worry pokes you in the eye, whispers in your ear, and slaps you in the mouth.

Long nights of the soul, my dad would call them.

Except I don't think this place has a soul.

It has the opposite: a void where a soul should be. A

soul-stealing evil that won't rest until we're gone. And I'm talking gone-gone, not just out of here but *out* of here, shuffled off this mortal coil (another thing my dad always says): dead.

We begged Winchelhauser to let us stay at the infirmary with Braids, but she refused. "It's simply against protocol," she told us.

Oh, but having supernatural strength and floating around the woods *are* protocol? Getting summoned to a watery death in the middle of the night? Flipping protocol?

Nobody was asleep in our cabin—it wasn't just *me* having a long night of the soul. The other girls felt it too. The Fear. They sat together in one bed, huddled in their nightgowns.

Unlike me, who wears a T-shirt and shorts to bed like a normal person.

Not that I judge. It's just that, who thought it was a good idea to wear a dress to sleep in? Let's not kid ourselves: nightgowns are *gowns* for sleeping in! You don't see boys wearing night *suits* and night *ties*, do you?

Ew and Hairspray (hair flattened by lake water and sadness) are huddled on Ew's bed like puppies in a cuddle puddle. The cabin felt empty—not just because

Braids was in the infirmary either. Mary is gone, too. Who knows where? The last I saw, a frothingly angry Winchelhauser was marching her *and* Gavin toward her office.

Hairspray and Ew doze off first, and listening to them makes it hard for me to follow. My bunkmates both thrash the sheets and mutter nervous nos in the dark. Once or twice I hear Ew utter an annoyed little "ew" at something gross in her dream. That makes me smile, in spite of The Fear.

The sun is just starting to lighten the sky when I climb out of bed and do something I haven't done in a long time: I get down on my knees and pray.

We're not exactly regular churchgoers in the Quinn clan, so I don't remember the words to any prayers. My main frame of reference for praying is Hulk Hogan, the wrestler. He's always telling you to eat your vitamins and say your prayers. Seems to work for him: he's got really nice arms. (That could be the vitamins more than the prayers.)

Focus, Quinn! The only thing I can think to say to God or Zeus or "the divine unknown" (Dad again) is *please*.

I kneel on the floor next to my bed. I press my palms

together and close my eyes. *Please. Please let Jenny be okay.* (I don't refer to her as Braids because I don't want God to be confused.) *Please help us fight the evil in this camp. Please keep me safe. Please keep Tez safe. Bring Jenny and Scary—I mean, Jenny and Mary back to us. Please, please, please . . .*

The door to the cabin flies open with a high-pitched creak and a loud bang. Wow, I think, prayer really works! I should listen to Hulk Hogan more often! It must be Braids and Mary back from the infirmary!

Except that it isn't.

The form standing in the doorway is one I have never seen before. My brain scrambles in confusion. When you've only been looking at the same relatively small number of faces for a while, it takes your brain a minute even to remember that other people exist. Add to this the lack of sleep and . . . well, you could knock me over with a feather.

My brain honestly says, Oh, Princess Diana is here.

But obviously, the person standing in the doorway to our cabin is not Lady Di or any member of the British royal family. So who is it?

"Morning, cuties!" she says, in a voice far too chipper for this hour—or any hour. Ew and Hairspray don't stir from their slumber, and I'm too paralyzed by confusion to move either.

I'm stuck on my knees at the side of the bed, gawking at this strange, happy, strangely happy person in the cabin. Maybe it's because I really don't like being called a "cutie," but I have a bad feeling about this. The hairs on my arm stand up like they're ready for a fight. Settle down, arm hairs, this isn't about you.

"I said, *gooooood moooooooorning, cuties!*"

She's louder this time, bouncing around the cabin like Tinkerbell on Mountain Dew. Slung over her shoulder is a a spotless barrel bag with gold piping, which she tosses onto Mary's bed.

"Hey," I manage to say, my mouth dry and my mind stuck in neutral. "You don't sleep there."

She laughs and pats me on the head like I'm a dog. I should bite her hand. Treat me like a dog, you get the fangs, I always say. (I have never said that before.) I stand up as fast as I can. I don't want to meet a stranger on my knees. I give her what I hope she realizes is a very serious glare.

"Don't be a sillyhead," she says with a laugh. "I absolutely do sleep here, *now.*"

She sweeps her hands down her very neat counselor

uniform (the one Mary never bothered to wear), then over her Barbie doll hair.

Seriously, it's a red-blond pouf in front, and big ponytails on the sides that swirl around her face like soft-serve ice cream. Is it a bouffant? A flip? I don't know! I'm not a hair-fixer person!

Ew and Hairspray start to stir, rubbing the sleep out of their puffy eyes and joining me in beholding this strange early-morning visitor.

"Youuuu donnnn't sleeeeep there," Princess Barbie says. It's a bad imitation of me, and she mixes it up by giggling at me and my confusion. Slowly, she sits and smooths the sheet beneath her. "Not exactly the Ritz-Carlton, but it will do."

"I'm sorry, but who are you?" Ew asks, her voice small and groggy and far away.

"Oh, how rude of me!" she says, popping off the bed like a loaded spring and crossing the cabin to shake Ew's hand. "Cherry Cumberland, camp counselor." Then she giggles. "I know, that's a lot of Cs! And you're a lot of cuties! Even more Cs!"

Ew smiles, and Hairspray does, too. They're sitting up now, smiling. Why the heck are they smiling? Did they forget that Braids is down and Mary's missing?

What is this place doing to me? I *care* that Scary Mary's missing!

"Corryn is a C, too," Hairspray says, pointing to me.

"You're a C for . . . cootie . . . nest," I sputter. "Probably the biggest of all the cootie nests." Take that!

Wait, who am I attacking?

Ew adjusts her nightgown and comes to her senses, at least a little bit. "What happened to Mary?" she asks. "Is she okay?"

"Oh, Mary?" Cherry says with a quick dismissive flick of her hand. Like she's talking about some trivial thing from the ancient past, not the person who was barking orders at us/saving some of us from drowning like ten hours ago. "She's no longer with us."

There is a gasp in three-part harmony. The room gets very quiet.

"Oh, not *dead*, cuties!" Cherry says. "I don't know why people say 'no longer with us' to mean dead. All I mean is that she went back to England. When I tell you that someone is dead, I'll say 'dead.' Trust me on that."

Now there is a gape in three-part . . . whatever you call it when people do the same thing at the same time. Mirrory? Tez would know. But the point is, does she think she's going to have to inform us of a lot of deaths?

94

Is this, like, a thing she's expecting to do?

We continue to gape rather stupidly at her, and she skips back to her bag and begins unpacking. While folding and unfolding her pastel outfits, she turns to us.

"So we know Corryn already," she says. "Cutie Corryn, alliteration. And you must be Ew." She laughs, pointing to Ew. "And you're the one they call Hairspray, though your locks are looking a little . . . flat at the moment."

She puts her hands on her hips and does a little pout. "We'll fix that up, no problem." She pulls a sleek silver hair dryer out of her bag and points it at us like a gun. "Maybe we'll give you a makeover, too," she says to me with a wink.

"Maybe you *won't*," I say, and wink back. I have thoughts on what she can do with that hair dryer.

As the weak morning light starts to strengthen and shed some literal light on this gloomy situation, I get a better look at this so-called Cherry Cumberland.

She's not tall and it appears that her powder-blue Camp Sweetwater T-shirt is made out of origami paper. It's crisp. Like, it's possible that she ironed a polo shirt. Her collar pops to attention, so high it almost brushes her earlobes. Meanwhile, her white shorts are short (also

95

crisp) and her legs are very, very long. If daddy longlegs were preppies with two legs, Cherry would definitely be one.

Her ginger ponies wag like puppy tails as she bops her head from side to side. Her eyes are big and bright, and her voice is high pitched, like a cartoon character's—not a cool one.

"Oh, stop the attitudey, cutie," she says to me. "Or I'll have to shoot you."

What? Is she reaching for her bag? Is she really going to—

She aims a little pink squirt gun at me and mouths the word "boom."

My panic subsides, and I roll my eyes.

"I'm serious," she says. "Change the 'tude or I bring the boom."

"My 'tude is boom proof," I say, mimicking her high-pitched giggle voice.

"I warned you," she says, and pulls the trigger.

I snatch a pillow and hold it up like a shield. Water spatters on it, instead of me, but it looks like Cherry made her point. She tucks her damp, pink pistol into her pocket (alliteration) and goes back to unpacking.

Ew bugs her eyes at me as if to say, *What the heck?* I

agree with a nod. A subtle nod, so Cherry doesn't look my way again. When I scrabble for my journal from beneath my pillow, I can think of only one thing to write.

Day Whatever: There's a crazy woman in our midst. And she's named for a fruit.

Breakfast is rushing up on us, and we hurry to get dressed. Since we're doing it willingly, Cherry just chirps and sings compliments at us. Like, what? We're all wearing wrinkly shorts and wrinkly T-shirts because our cubbies are the size of bread boxes.

And the thing that kills me is that Hairspray is licking up all this fakery. I think the Aqua Net fumes are going to her head. And even worse? Every so often, Ew seems to forget herself and starts to giggle along. Apparently, I'm the only one who realizes that this whole sitch is W-E-I-R-D. The entry in the notebook for this morning is gonna be a novel.

Outside, I hear the telltale sounds of Nostrils and Knees karate kicking at things and/or each other, so I take a peek through the window.

Gathered between our cabins, the whole boy Oak Camp gang shuffles (and kicks) like the dorks they are.

Their presence is a good excuse to get out of here. After the night we had, Tez probably needs a hug, so I walk up to him and punch him in the arm.

"We discussed this," Tez says, rubbing the red spot I left behind.

"Oops, sorry," I say. "In all the weirdo-beardo baloney going on, I forgot."

He looks at me blankly. Then I add in one long burst, "What's happening? Mary's gone! Braids isn't back! We got a new counselor, and she's *way too happy.*"

Tez gestures toward the group of boys. They're all whooping it up with a new *boys'* counselor, who must be related to Cherry. Same deep tan, same manicured look—he even has the same ironed Camp Sweetwater T-shirt, the white shorts, all of it. He really is the spitting image of Cherry. And when I say "spitting" I mean I literally want to spit up my breakfast, not that I've had any.

"Is that Cherry's twin!?" I ask Tez, my eyes wide and my voice ticked. "Don't tell me you got a new preppy ultrahappy counselor, too?"

"Affirmative," Tez says. "You're looking at the new boys' counselor, one Charleston Calhoun Cumberland the Third. He told us to call him Chip."

"Holy smokes," I say. "I can't believe it."

"Neither can I," says Tez. He looks over at Chip and grins from ear to ear. "Isn't it the absolute greatest?

Oh no. My blood runs cold.

13

Charleston Calhoun Cumberland and the Oak Camp Lads

Tez

Finally!

Finally, finally, *finally!*

I've been waiting for this day since my parents put me on the bus to Camp Sweetwater, and it's finally arrived. Today is the day I have a counselor who wants to do normal camp things and doesn't dump us pointlessly in the woods! Chip is the second-best thing to happen to me here.

Making friends with Corryn is the best, of course, but she's super edgy right now. She keeps scrawling notes and shoving her notebook at me to initial. I know this was my idea, but it's already starting to get tedious. Data is only interesting when it reveals something.

I think it's imperative to state that, yes, something supernatural definitely happened to Braids last night. This means we're probably going to have to vanquish it. However, there's no reason why we can't frolic, jape, and romp concurrent to the vanquish. I mean, all I have wanted from this whole exercise is to have some normal kid fun. And with Chip leading our cabin, it looks like I'm finally going to get my chance!

As breakfast ends and we throw away our trash, Chip stands at attention by the bins. His nice clean uniform stands out with blindingly white socks and the whitest tennis shoes I've ever seen. Dare I say it? I dare: he looks snazzy. The way a camp counselor *should* look! Authoritative! Poised! Enthusiastic!

"Hey, hey, ho, ho, Oak Camp Lads, we've got to go!"

Chip makes the announcement in a firm but cheerful tone, clapping on each syllable. Hurrying to slide my tray into the rack, I bob my head at Chip with a smile. I love the way he calls us lads. It's more mature than *boys*, and *men* would be ridiculous. Lads feels exactly right.

"Activity train is leaving the station," Chip

announces when the rest of us get in line. It takes forever because someone (Nostrils) had to chug down the rest of his bug juice. Personally, I prefer orange juice. It provides a natural glucose high without the unpleasant crash later.

Chip leads us from the Great Hall and forms up next to Cherry. Her girls are in a line, too . . . and Corryn's T-shirt is damp. I don't know what that's about, but that's no doubt adding to her general level of discontent.

To be fair, I think I understand why Corryn is . . . shall we say, underwhelmed with Cherry. Corryn isn't bubbly. She isn't big smiles and enthusiasm or giggly and chirpy. Which means, Cherry is the anti Corryn. If they were magnets, they'd leap apart instead of snapping together. They're polar opposites. But I do truly think Corryn should appreciate having counselors who don't actively hate us at least!

Cherry claps her hands together three times, which I believe is supposed to call us to attention. I stand up straighter, but everybody else mills a bit.

They shuffle and murmur to each other. It's another really beautiful day—bright sky, warmth rising in the air, and the vultures are nowhere to be seen. Which is a relief. What happened with Braids last night was unsettling, made more so by the heavy flap of wings above our heads.

Perhaps, I tell myself, it was an isolated incident. . . .

Once again, Cherry claps to no avail. Then she and Chip, in perfect synchronicity, produce pink water guns and start shooting.

Their aim is *impeccable. Pew pew pew!* I remain dry, but everyone else gets a good squirt. The girls whine about it, but they line up and go quiet. My cabinmates, however, whine and *don't* go quiet.

"Come on, man," Bowl Cut says, kicking at the dirt.

Nostrils pulls his shirt out, flapping it madly to try to dry it. "Not cool. Not cool at all."

Knees just stares. He has the best stare. Somehow, it's baleful and accusing all at the same time. It's betrayal but also annoyance. It's a complicated flavor of an expression, and I admire its complexity.

Brightly, Chip says, "We could take away beads, but Cherry and I think that should be saved for *real* infractions. Besides, a little dose of fresh, clean H-two-O from Lake Sweetwater is usually the best medicine! So, are we ready to pay attention now?"

In a slow swivel, Corryn looks at me, as if to say, *Lake water?*

I acknowledge with a nod. This, along with Braids' unexpected dip last night adds to Corryn's theory that there's something *the matter* with the lake water. But also, what else would counselors fill their water guns with?

There's still no water running in the showers or the bathrooms. That's why they're giving us pitchers of bug juice now.

There's not a lot I can do about the lake water punishment except avoid it. And to avoid it, I do what I was doing in the first place: following directions. I turn my attention back to Chip. Somehow, I feel a new wave of irritation from Corryn. It's like a stick poking into the back of my head. But I do not look. It's time for instruction!

"All right," Cherry says, her pigtails bouncing. "Now that we have your attention! May I please have the gentlemen who selected camp radio as their activity join me over here?"

Then, in an identical tone, Chip says, "And if I may have all the archers and photographers over here?"

Trading glances, everyone hesitates. In fact, they hesitate just long enough for another volley from the water guns. Chip and Cherry have itchy trigger fingers, and now everybody around me is at least slightly damp. But my cabinmates do move faster and join the appropriate groups.

Unfortunately for me, Corryn is doing radio, so she stays with Cherry. Ew joins us while Bowl Cut defects to the other side. We line up again, but Knees gets another shot of water. He wasn't perfectly symmetrical with the rest of us. Geometry, it seems, is very important to Chip and Cherry.

"Let's go," Chip calls. He starts walking toward the northwest side of the camp. As he goes, he encourages us to chant. "Repeat after me, campers. I'm aLIVE, aWAKE, aLERT, and ready to, ready to GO!"

Behind us, Cherry leads her campers to the southwest. She got a whistle somewhere, and she tweets it in time with Chip's chant.

Stumbling through it the first time, our cadence sounds more like a sing-along by people chewing bubble gum. A lot of bubble gum.

Cherry's campers march away, their voices fading into the distance. In my line, after a couple of repetitions, we start to get it. I don't know why, but I love this.

It feels so . . . so *camp*-like. This is everything Camp Sweetwater was supposed to be.

Even though my heart is pounding faster than I like, I march at the head of our activity line. (No! Activity *train!*) My whole body tingles, in a good way. The sun is bright, and the air is sweet with morning mist. Every step feels like floating. This is good. This is so, so good!

Alive, awake, alert, and ready to go go go—oh.

As we curve around the Great Hall, I see that the kitchen doors are flung open. There are a couple of people in there in white aprons bustling back and forth. Huh.

I guess I had never thought about the fact that camp has cooks. And now that I think about it, probably other employees. Because the lawn near the Bantam Camp is mowed. And there are a lot of light bulbs that probably need to be changed regularly.

My brain grows another wrinkle with this new awareness. That really happens: the more you use your brain, the wrinklier it gets. Basking in new knowledge, I mentally salute all the people here keeping the camp running for us.

I take another peek toward the kitchen as we march

away. A man in white pants and a white apron hikes up the hill from the lake with two gallon jugs. They slosh as he walks, losing a splash of water on each step.

He hands them off to one of the lunch ladies in the kitchen. Ah! Makes sense. They must be boiling it so they can safely cook with it. Brilliant! They're using real camp knowledge to make sure we don't get dysentery or worse! I love it!

Except, as we turn the corner onto the tree-lined path, I swear I see the woman raise the gallon jug and dump it right in the bug juice dispensers. Someone I can't quite see (I can make out their arms!) dumps a canister of red powder in after it. Then she picks up a paddle, stained the same shade of red, and starts to stir the mix.

Unease trickles down my spine. Surely I'm mistaken. They had to have purified that water first. Those *must* be jugs that were already treated. Perhaps they used chlorine tabs instead of boiling—not ideal but functional!

I must be mistaken. Because if I'm not, they're risking poisoning us, the whole camp! Or if Corryn's right . . . they're dosing us. But it's just water, right? The evil's gone, isn't it?

The memory of Braids thrashing at the lake's edge fills my mind.

No. No! I'm not thinking about that today. I'm alive, I'm awake, I'm alert, and I'm going to have a good day at camp! And absolutely nothing will spoil it for me.

14

In Camp Murderface, Nobody Can Hear You Scream

Corryn

The radio station isn't exactly amazing.

When I'd listen to the Top 40 countdown at home, it always seemed so glamorous. Some super cool DJ with every song in the world at her fingertips, gold records on the wall, that kind of thing.

But this is camp radio, so this little room is less that and more card table and milk crates. It smells like the boys' cabin, only stale. Like, real stale.

What is probably the world's oldest microphone sits on the scarred and rickety table. What even is this building? It definitely wasn't built as a radio station. Maybe a garage? Bomb shelter? Corn shed?

It looks like a good room to hide in if you're avoiding a zombie apocalypse, which, now that I think of it, could come in handy.

It's down at the opposite end of camp from our cabins. It's alllllllll the way on the other side of the lake near the photo lab, the "technology" center, and a fourth building that remains a total mystery to me.

It's all clustered near the band shell, not that we've had a lot of bands in need of shelling. And hey, right there is the path that led us to the abandoned camp. The one where three girls disappeared all those years ago but left their ghostly traces in the dark wood around camp.

Bowl Cut and I shuffle around the tiny radio pod. It's just the two of us here, and that's all kinds of weird. Cherry dropped us off, then told us she'd be back in five. Also, she warned us not to touch anything.

I'm not touching! I've got my hands in my pockets, and I'm whistling to myself and definitely not touching the big juicy, beautiful soundboard covered in dust in front of me. Certainly not touching the enormous headphones and ancient microphone. It looks like it might be literally the first microphone in history. (But if it works . . .)

See, I know that radio stations play music but it's the DJs that make it rock. Bowl Cut can pick the tracks for all I care. Just as long as he lets me on the mic.

So my hands stay in my pockets, buuuuut maybe I bump some things until the mic drops closer to my face.

"Testing, one two three," I say into it.

Bowl Cut flips through the milk crates of moldering records. He hums a vaguely familiar, melancholy melody, eyes half-closed. The albums make a flap-flap-flap sound as he fingers through them. Then he pulls one out to study.

"We're gonna rock this town," I say. Bowl Cut does not respond, so I just pretend he did. "Seriously, we're gonna have the gnarliest radio show in history."

I don't touch the mic some more. I just look at it, and consider it, and imagine holding it with one hand. It kinda reminds me of the equipment you see in old movies. Like, it's a mic where a World War II pilot could yell, "Mayday," and get some coverage.

The more I look, the more I want to yell it, too. All the equipment kind of has a military surplus feel to it, and none of it seems to have been particularly well cared for. There are exposed wires galore, missing knobs, rusty everything.

I can't help but wonder if this stuff is even safe, and you know it's bad when I start to care about safety. But come on! There's a rat's nest of cables piled in the corner, which could be hiding an actual rat's nest for all I know! Chewy, bitey, wire-exposey rats!

"I like the idea of being a DJ, but I'd rather not get electrocuted if at all possible," I say.

Bowl Cut briefly looks up from the crate of records, shrugs, and goes back to soberly flipping through the offerings, as if there is a chance he'll find something cool like a Prince album mixed in with the mega old hits of the previous century.

"Captain and Tennille," Bowl Cut says, then flips on. "Wayne Newton. The Troggs?"

"At least we probably won't get zapped by Cherry in here," I say. "Gotta be dangerous to mix water guns and exposed electrical wires."

Still no response from old Bowlie, so I do my Cherry impression. "Drop the attitudities, cuties, or I'll spritz you in your boot-a-looties!"

At that, he looks up at me and slowly blinks his large watery eyes.

"You know there is another way to not get squirted," Bowl Cut says finally. "You could, you know, maybe just try to not be such a pain all the time."

Whoa, what the heck?

"It's like . . . maybe the problem is you?" he continues. "Just a thought?" He shrugs again. That shrug is starting to get on my shrugging nerves, but he's not done. Nope, he goes on to say, "I mean, you complained about Mary when she was here. Now we have Cherry, who is like the opposite of Mary, and you hate her, too? Maybe you have a problem with authority."

Um, *excuse me.* I totally do not have a problem with authority (do I?) but rather with the clearly disturbing trend of this camp hiring psychopaths to watch over us!

Just because I complained about Mary doesn't mean that I can't also have an issue with this evil airhead and her equally evil, equally airheady twin brother! What is wrong with Bowl Cut? With everyone? I am definitely writing this down in my notebook.

Just then, the door bangs open. Speak of the devil, I think. Never has the phrase felt more appropriate.

It's Cherry, bopping her pastel self into the room. I'm not sure where she was, but she apparently touched up her makeup in the process. Her lips are gleaming a darker red than they were earlier. She rolls in, gun-a-blazing.

Before we even have the chance to behave ourselves (or not), she's squirting her water gun like a chipper Yosemite Sam. I hold up a Starland Vocal Band album like a shield to deflect the blast. Bowl Cut doesn't even try to move. Instead, he opens his mouth and bites at the water like a dog drinking from a hose. Gross, Bowl Cut.

"Let's get ready to fill the airwaves of Sweetwater with sweet, sweet music!" Cherry says, holstering her gun. She picks up a drab green binder from the table and starts flipping through it.

She slaps the binder shut. "These instructions are boring," she says. "I'm sure we can figure it out with the power of positive attitudes!" She turns to the sound-board, studying it as she bops her head to music only she can hear.

Um . . . I don't love following instructions, but as I mentioned, this equipment looks a little complicated and/or dangerous. I feel pretty sure the power of positivity won't save us from the power of ungrounded electrical outlets.

I don't say anything, though. I'm really trying to keep myself from getting squirted and also trying to show Bowl Cut that I don't have a bad attitude!

"Are there, like, any modern records anywhere?" I

ask. Bowl Cut just stares. "Something by Kiss, maybe?"

"Those weirdos with the face paint? Oh, heavens no," Cherry says.

"They've started playing without the makeup," I say optimistically, though I know that this argument is not going to convince Cherry of anything, nor is it going to make cool records magically appear. Bowl Cut's just standing there with a floppy copy of Gordon Lightfoot's *Summertime Dream*. My *dad* has that record. He listens to it when he makes dinner for my mom. Or when he used to.

Anyway. It's the total *opposite* of rad.

"Um, what kind of music are we going to play?" I ask.

"Ever hear of John Philip Sousa?"

"John Philip Who-za?" I say. Hilarious.

Cherry hits a button that drops the needle on a record. She shrieks with delight and claps her hands together in a little golf clap. About forty million trumpets start blaring, *bwaa bwaaaa bwa bwa bwa bwa bwaaaaaa*. The song that starts playing is like a demented marching band. Horns, drums, a crashing cymbal. But it all sounds . . . off.

Is the record warped? Is her mind? Is the whole

world? Is it *supposed* to sound like this? Cherry smiles, puffing out her chest, doing a little four-step march, because this place is tiny!

"Perfect marching music," she chirps. Bowl Cut falls in step behind her. These doofuses are seriously doing this? Marching? In here? Together!

Bowl Cut stares. You know what? Fine. I don't have a problem with authority, so I join their little parade/conga line. *Bwa bwa bwa bwa bwaaaaaa!*

The room gets sweaty and hot so fast. But we keep going, marching maniacs in a knot. This is less like a parade and more like hyenas circling their prey.

After a few laps, Cherry returns to the record player and lifts the needle. It makes an earsplitting screech and then falls silent. All I hear is heavy panting. Maybe this was a warm-up? Because we're definitely warm. Dark circles of sweat form under Bowlie's pitters.

Anyway, I can see how our parade might be something to get the blood going before we rock Camp Sweetwater's socks. I'm feeling it. I'm alert, awake, and I want to blast some tunes.

"So, can I try the microphone?" I ask. "Test this whole thing out? I thought I'd be DJ CQ. Since, you know, it's my initials?"

"False," Cherry says.

"I mean, but it is?"

"I mean, but false because that will not be your radio name," she says. "I'm going to call you . . . Bubbles."

"What?" I protest. "Bubbles? Why?"

"You're such a grouchy puss! And no wonder! That awful counselor you had before didn't even give you a camp name! How can you get the Oak Camp spirit if you're not part of the clan?"

All summer, I've been bummed that I didn't get a nickname, but seriously, *Bubbles*? This does not feel like an upgrade.

I feel something. But it's not happiness. Or clannyness. Cherry does something with her face. Maybe you'd call it a smile, I sure wouldn't—not unless you call what a snake does before it devours a mouse smiling.

Before I can protest—and you can protest while still respecting authority, although I'm not sure why I should care what Bowl Cut thinks about me—Cherry whips out a tiny notepad and starts writing. She narrates her memo. "Camp Note: Corryn's name is 'Bubbles' from now on."

"Bubbles," Bowl Cut repeats with his stupid lakewater mouth.

Well, I've got news for her. I have a notebook, too, and I'm . . . Wait a minute! A zing of realization strikes me. The lake water! Bowl Cut just chugged some! Right from Cherry's handy-dandy water pistol, and he's been acting like a zombie ever since.

I mean, yeah, he's been quiet since he got the chrome-dome special but not like this. If *this* dude had schlumped off the bus on the first day, Gavin would have named him Pet Rock or something.

Swallowing down suspicion and frustration, I turn toward the soundboard again. "Okay, DJ *Bubbles* is ready to wake up central Ohio with some tunes."

With a sickly sweet tone, Cherry says, "Oh, cutie, slow down! We need to get a feel for this place before we can do anything. And besides, they're still working on the tower. The signal barely makes it to the other side of the lake. For now, we're just sort of . . . practicing."

My heart sinks. I feel like I ate rock cereal for breakfast. So, great. My parents sent me to a summer camp I didn't want to come to to keep me from finding out they're getting a divorce. I get here, and not only is this place a dump, but it is the nexus of some sort of primal evil, which Tez and I fought but apparently not hard enough.

And now the stupid radio station—the one thing that maybe I was actually kind of maybe looking forward to—isn't a radio station at all but some kind of practice closet with some dorky records thrown in it?

You know what? Fine. That's fine. I don't have time for this, anyway. I need to convince Tez that the evil's still here and has maybe returned in the form of two chipper counselors who we'll need to find a way to get rid of . . . somehow.

I make for the front door of the studio while Bowl Cut and Cherry start up their marching again. I throw a line over my shoulder before I go, about needing the bathroom. But I'm not coming back.

DJ CQ, signing off.

15

Best Camp Day Ever?

Tez

Hands on his hips, Chip repeats what I just told him.

"Birch is great to start the fire but to keep it going, maple. Avoid the damp ones, they smoke. And finally, watch out for black twigs; they're toxic."

Oh, MAN.

He heard me. More than heard, he *listened*, and he's *actually taking my advice*.

The night is clear and moonless, and there's just enough of a breeze in the trees to make them whisper. It's so rich, it almost sounds like conversation. What birds I hear over everyone else's talking and laughing are happy-sounding nocturnal species.

My skin tingles all over, and a pleasant shiver streaks down my spine when I hear the girls from Corryn's cabin approaching. And how do I know it's them and not the substandard campers in the rest of Oak? Because their voices fill the air with cadence to announce themselves!

Everywhere we go-oh-oh!
People want to know-oh!
Who we ah-are!
Where we're froh-om!
We're Oak Camp, A Group!
Mighty, mighty A Group!
Better than B Group!
Teeny, weeny B Group!
Destroyers of D Group!
Dummy dumb D Group!

I turn to watch Cherry march them right up to the clearing. They're each carrying an armful of wood, and I expect to see delight on Corryn's face. After all, she's leading the line. And her counselor is encouraging her to obliterate her enemies . . . I mean, fellow campers. *So* totally her thing!

What's shocking is how *not* delighted Corryn looks.

121

Her mouth is set; I don't even see her lips moving! She tips her head just forward enough that her bangs hide the slits of her eyes. Her pile of firewood is the smallest out of the bunch.

Corryn shuffles after Cherry, while the rest of her cabinmates make an attempt at marching. Putting my hands on my hips, I watch as they approach.

Much to my surprise, Corryn ignores Chip when he directs her to put her mixed wood into the pile of mixed wood. Instead, she just lets her arms fall open, and all the logs and twigs spill out everywhere. Then she slinks away from the woodpile and heads straight for me.

Before I can protest, she grabs me by the arm. As soon as we're directly across from our counselors, she huddles with me and hisses, "Can you believe these goons?"

Wary, I say, "Which goons?"

"Chip and Cherry!"

Neither of them turns our way, which is probably self-control on their part. Corryn shouted that pretty loudly. Embarrassed, I duck my head again and ask Corryn, "What's wrong with them? This has been the best day of camp ever. I wrote it all down in my field notebook!"

"Are you for *real*?" she asks in a way that strongly implies that I'm not. "Cherry wouldn't even let us touch the radio stuff. And after lunch, she made us march around the cabin three times because"—and here, Corryn imitates Cherry's voice—"'You're not smiling, cuties!' Uh, hello! Do you know what happens if you smile around here, Cherry? You get bugs in your teeth!"

"That might be a slight exaggeration," I say.

With a mighty *whup*, Corryn claps her hands down on my shoulders. She even shakes me a little. "Earth to Tezbot, snap out of it! What is your deal?"

I've told Corryn several times that I don't like to be punched or shaken. I thought it went without saying that I don't enjoy being mocked either. I take a step back, brushing her hands away. "I enjoyed my day. Chip knows tons about photography. And Ew is surprisingly voluble when it's just the two of us."

Corryn drags her hands through her hair. Her stare is just a little bit demented. "I don't know what that means—don't you dare tell me—but you sound like everybody else in our cabins. Like, how they don't want to talk about what's really happening."

"What's that?" I ask.

"Oh my gosh, the evil going on, and what we're

going to do about it?!" Corryn whisper-shrieks.

My cheeks sting as if slapped. "I haven't forgotten any of that. I can have a good day and still be concerned. What happened with Braids concerns me, absolutely."

"But the counselors don't? Cherry is a whole box of Froot Loops," Corryn says. "I think she's a part of the evil. And Chip's part of the same balanced breakfast of crazy!"

How dare she! I cast a quick sympathetic look toward Chip. Who is, I might add, at this very moment, holding out an arm to help Nostrils balance. And why? So Nostrils' high kicks can soar ever higher (and avoid people's faces).

Pointing toward this, I say, "He's *awesome*. He has a pocket sundial that's accurate to the quarter hour. He can identify the different kinds of moss we have in the woods here. And he's *interested in us*! After lunch, we had Personal Time with Chip."

Eyes flashing, Corryn says, "I don't like the sound of that."

"We just hung out in the cabin," I tell her. "And we went around in a circle. And shared something important to us! Chip even went first!"

"So, what's important to the Chipster?"

I lift my chin. Corryn is my best friend at camp and maybe my best friend ever, but there are some bonds you don't break for anyone. "It all stays in the sacred circle."

Under her breath, Corryn mutters something that sounds like a cuss, and she walks away from me. As she shakes her head, she continues to mumble. I think she's actively talking to herself. When she comes back, she doesn't grab me again, but she does stare me right in the face.

"He's trying to get you on his side. He's trying to find out your vulnerabilities! Lex Luthor is looking for your Kryptonite, dude!"

For one brief second, that silences me. That's exactly what a *competent* villain would do; she's right about that. Gavin and Scary Mary ruled with fear and got very little accomplished. I suppose it's possible, just a tiny bit possible, that Chip and Cherry are simply *better* bad guys—taking a different tack to achieve the same evil goals.

But no. I shake my head. That can't be what's happening, because it hasn't even been twenty-four hours yet, and Corryn *hates* Cherry. If they were supposed to ingratiate themselves with us to reveal our tender underbellies, Cherry's doing a terrible job of it.

Therefore, that can't be her purpose. Therefore, the problem with our counselors right now isn't them.

It's Corryn.

"You know what?" I say, my gaze trailing toward the pit. Chip and Cherry have constructed a *perfect* pup-tent formation with the birch. Everyone presses closer, waiting with bags of marshmallows and eyes as big as their entire orbital sockets. "How about we just enjoy a bonfire that's not going to scream at us from the beyond, and see what happens tomorrow?"

Absolutely incredulous, Corryn huffs and shakes her head. "You sound like Bowl Cut. Who was chugging lake water from Cherry's squirt gun the whole time we were in the radio station, by the way."

I don't have time to ask what she means before—

"Make way!" Chip shouts. "Make way for Bug Juice!" He carries into the circle one of those big yellow coolers with the spigot. It swings heavily in his hands as kids crowd around with the tin camp cups none of us have had the chance to use yet. Mine hangs from my belt, along with my tin mess kit.

A cheer goes up. At first, I'm confused. Hydration is surely important, but it's not usually *exciting*. Then the reason for the cheer appears. It's Braids. She tags along after Chip, smiling sheepishly and waving to familiar faces. She's back from the infirmary, apparently no worse for the wear. And she's the first person in line to fill her cup with bug juice.

After her, Knees sweeps in to get his drink. People are crowding—practically pushing—just to get their share.

A clear and sudden memory of the people in the kitchen rises up. The man carrying gallon jugs *from the lake*. The women stirring the water with red powder and a stained paddle. Had they treated the water? Or was it going into the tank straight from the source?

I wrote that down; Corryn signed it. And it was there to be signed because Corryn swears we had to swim and it made us forget everything. The equation is there. . . .

I put a hand on Corryn's shoulder, but she shrugs it off. I tell her, "I *do* think something's maybe happening with the water. I just . . . I don't think Chip and Cherry are doing anything but their jobs."

"Okay, Tez, whatever."

All the bouncing, bubbling excitement I felt a few minutes ago turns to a sizzling, acid fizz in my gut. I don't want to fight with Corryn. She's really wrong about this, but she's not wrong overall. So I want to give her a win. I remind her about the bug juice entry, and she flings out her arms.

"See?" she says, shouting again. People turn to look at us. The new fire licks up bright behind them—they're nothing but gold halos and shadows. Shadows holding cups full of tainted bug juice and sharp sticks for roasting marshmallows.

The thing is, for just a second, they look like a faceless army. A dark, impenetrable line ready to take orders and march out. And I have the feeling that it's not an army for good either.

Then at once, everyone moves again. There's no more shouting to watch, so they cluster around the fire. They laugh again and talk as embers swirl up to escape the canopy of trees. Without a care in the world, they raise their cups to their stained mouths.

If Corryn thinks we need to do something right now, then there's one thing I can think of. "Okay, the first thing we have to do—we have to get people to stop drinking that stuff. Can we agree on that?"

"Yeah," Corryn says shortly, already starting to walk away. "You bet."

My shoulders slump, and I drop my head.

So much for my best camp day ever.

16
Farewell, Flopsy

Corryn

As we walk back toward our cabin, the darkness is already nice and juicy and mysterious around us. I'm not afraid of the dark, not after what I've seen. There are enough things to be afraid of—dark hardly rates. Dark doesn't even make the list.

I turn the facts of this awful place around and around in my head. Mary and Gavin are gone. Chip and Cherry are here. They are soaking us in lake water, making us drink lake water. And the lake water is trying to kill us.

Or something in the lake is.

Tez is right. We have to put a stop to this.

Unfortunately getting a bunch of campers to stop drinking bug juice will be like trying to pull a starving dog off a bone. And I can't blame them—who among us doesn't enjoy a straight shot of sugar? Especially when there are few, if any, other options.

How long can a person live without liquids? I bet Tez knows. I bet I don't want to find out. It's only been a few hours, and I'm so dang thirsty.

Is it possible to pee dust?

We're walking back to our cabins, the smell of campfire smoke on the air and in our hair. There's no forced chanting, just friendly chatter. It is a pretty night. The stars are out in full summer numbers, twinkling out their cosmic messages.

There's Cassiopeia—she thinks she's so great. There's the moon—can't say I've ever been a fan. Always staring at you. Never can get away from it, following you all over the place. Get a grip, moon.

There's twinkling down here at earth level, too. We always called them lightning bugs, but some of the kids here call them fireflies. Nostrils is fond of saying the scientific term for them is blinkie beetles. This makes Tez have a hilarious breakdown.

Knees insists that, back where he comes from,

everyone calls them fire devils. I think he's just trying to get under our skin. Coupled with everything else, it might be working.

I feel a quick tap on my shoulder and turn to swat it. It's just one of the little girls from Bantam Camp. Her Camp Sweetwater shirt is so big that it hangs dress-like nearly to her knees. Her hair is a wild tangle, and her eyes are big with fear.

"Relax," I say. "I'm not going to hit ya." Her big eyes relax but only a little. Her lips are stained red with bug juice, and the bottom one is pouting out and shaking a little. Am I really that scary?

"I'm s'posed to give you this," she says, sounding a little like she might cry. In a shaking hand, she holds out a rectangle piece of paper. It's been expertly folded with an arrow drawn on the outside showing where to pull to open it. As if I don't know how to open a note. It also says, "To Corryn: FYEO"—everyone knows that means "for your eyes only."

Whoever gave the little Bantam shrimpster this note really didn't want her reading it. Put a right good scare in her, they did. Why did I randomly think that in a British accent? I miss Mary, I guess.

"Thanks, kid," I say. "I owe you one." She smiles just the smallest bug-juicy smile and sprints off to rejoin her group.

I hang back a bit, looking over my shoulders, trying to get some space to read this important missive with the privacy it apparently requires.

Tez is up with Counselor Chipstick laughing about something or other. I'm glad he's not here to peek at this. *I* don't even want to be here to peek at this. I have a pretty good idea what's inside.

There's only one reason people pass notes. I don't care who this is from, but the answer to the question "Do you like me? Circle one" is going to be a hard no. Is there a third option, which would be to burn the note in a pit of fire?

I pull the arrow-marked corner of the note, and the paper unfolds itself, accordion-style. FYEO is written on each folded corner of the paper. Seems like overkill, if you ask me.

When I finally get to the inner meat of this origami masterpiece, it's not a declaration of love. It's three words in all caps: I BELIEVE YOU. And then in smaller letters barely visible in the scant moonlight:

"MEET ME BEHIND THE BOATHOUSE. MID-NIGHT TONIGHT."

My heart dives into my Converse. There's only one thing behind the boathouse.

And that's the lake.

I've gotten really good at fake sleeping. If I've learned nothing else at camp (and oh, I have learned things), it's how to fake sleep.

I go through all the steps. I drag a comb through my hair to get the leaves and twigs out. I scrub off with a dry rag that I pretend to dip in the bucket of water Cherry brings up "from the cafeteria." According to Tez's own records, that water came fresh out of the lake. No thank you.

I suck on my toothbrush enough to get it wet, before brushing. No rinse. I'm not gonna have anything to drink until orange juice in the morning, even though I could really use just a sip . . . what if I don't swallow . . . ? No. No water.

I get into bed and close my eyes yet remain wide awake. I lie there trying to count the seconds off. I tally the minutes from lights-out to midnight. I can do it, I think, if I just concentrate hard enough. . . .

But no, it's impossible, and I find myself dozing. Get it together, Quinn, I think, and slap myself in the face. Ahh! Brisk!

"Did somebody just kill a mosquito?" Braids asks sleepily.

Hairspray says, "Is that a bug?"

Everybody giggles quietly, then trails back off to the land of Nod.

Luckily, thanks to Tez, I'm pretty good at telling time using the moon and the stars. I don't remember all the details. Something about Galileo was definitely involved, naturally. The kid can't go five minutes without mentioning Galileo. Galileo this and Galileo that. But I got the gist.

All you have to do is find the Big Dipper, find the North Star, go *back* to the Big Dipper, and pretend the two bottom stars are the hands of a clock. Except the clock goes backward. And you have to subtract something about March 6. . . . Yeah, maybe I don't remember all of this.

The more important question is, who is meeting me at midnight? Who? Who? I sound like an owl. If this whole note thing is a joke, I'm seriously going to murderface someone.

If some Elm Camp dingus shows up with her friends, they're all going face-first in the lake, and I won't even feel bad about it.

Eventually, the language of the stars says midnight. Probably. It feels midnightish. Well, actually a few minutes before, because I have to give myself time to get there. But it just sounds better that way. Like a vampire, I slowly rise, still dressed in my clothes.

It's a clear night, and though there isn't a cloud in the night sky, a shock of lightning breaks the darkness. There's a sound I didn't know I could make! I hope it doesn't wake anyone up. I press myself against the wall of the cabin, hoping to blend in among the shadows.

The ancient cabin door does its best at holding my secrets for me—this time, anyway. The creak is barely a whisper, and with a careful latch behind me, I'm in the outdoors. The stars tell me midnight is approaching; the moon lights my way. Sorry I was dissing you earlier, moon. You're okay, I guess.

It's a short walk from my cabin to the boathouse, but it's an unsettling one. I used to think it was ridiculous that you could "feel" like you're being watched. Watching is just your eyes picking up light. And light isn't something you can feel. Galileo was the first scientist even to try to measure the speed of light.

Gah, now I can't go five minutes without thinking about Galileo. Tez did this to me. I'm really going to have to punch him when I see him. Or something; he's getting pretty outspoken about friendly violence.

Anyway, I *used* to think it was impossible to feel like you're being watched.

But that's before I came to Camp Sweetwater.

I make it to the boathouse and it's as desolate as . . . well, as a boathouse at night. All I hear are little lake waves and the occasional hoot of a lonely owl. Yeah, owl, this is a real hecking hoot.

Then I hear a noise behind me that sounds a lot less like an owl and a lot more like a "psst." I whip my head around so fast, it's almost like *I'm* the nocturnal bird with the ability to turn her head 270 degrees.

What the what? Now I'm spouting random bird facts? I'm punching Tez twice when I see him.

"Who goes there?" I whisper, which I think you pretty much have to say in these situations. "Show yourself."

In response, the figure in the dark says one word. "Ew."

"*Ew?*" I ask incredulously. "*You* dragged me out here? Why couldn't we just talk in the cabin?"

"You know why," she says. "You-know-who." She gestures back toward our cabin with her head.

"But you were in the cabin five minutes ago," I say.

"Yeah," she says. "You left early."

"Well, not bad, considering I'm judging time by the stars!"

"It's called a watch. You should look into getting one . . . *Bubbles.*"

"You did not just call me that." I feel my hands ball into fists.

"Relax," she says. "We're not here to fight."

"What *are* we here for?" I ask. "And why so secretive? The kid with the note? So cloak-and-dagger. What's going on?"

But before she can answer, we hear a noise on the other side of the boathouse. It's a scratch. A scratch and then a snarl. "Hide, Bubbles!" Ew hisses. She did not just—before I can finish my thought, she grabs me by the hand. She pulls me down, and we dive behind a bush.

Out into the moonlight steps Cherry. What the

138

heck? No wonder it felt like I was being followed. Half the cabin joined me out here. But . . . it's Cherry and yet not Cherry.

Gone is her chipper smile, and instead she wears a hideous expression—eyes huge, lips pulled back to reveal large pointy fangs. And in her hands is a big brown rabbit.

Uh-oh.

She holds the poor creature by the scruff of its neck. It's alive, but it looks like it's given up. Its big feet swim in the air in quick spasms, but there's no fight in it. Not really. I can't look. But I can't look away.

Cherry's face swells, distorts. It changes shape, stretches like Silly Putty. She *unhinges her jaw*. Just like a snake. The entire top half of her head flips back like a box being torn open. She drops the rabbit into her fangy mouth and devours it. Three giant gulps, and Flopsy disappears forever.

Man! This is the grossest thing I have ever seen! And I've been in the boys' cabin. Then I remember the person hiding next to me. She is not exactly known for her iron stomach. She gets grossed out by pretty much anything. Don't say it, don't say it, don't say it, I think to myself. *Don't say it.*

She says it. Loud.

"Ew!"

She clamps her hand over her mouth after the "ew" escapes, but it's too late. Our cover is blown.

Cherry hears us, cocks her head like a dog on the hunt. She takes a step in the other direction—away from us—then slowly turns back. She rotates her head like a radar dish and locks eyes right on us. Red droplets slither from the corners of her lips.

She smiles.

We run.

17
Run!!!!!!!

Corryn

If there's a list of reasons to scream in the night, being chased by your shape-shifting, live-rabbit-gulping counselor through the dark is definitely near the top.

The woods are thick in the dark. Brambles everywhere snap at our ankles. Branches rear back to slap us across the face. Everything burns and hurts. *Go back*, the forest seems to scream, but we scream right back. *Not on your life, forest!*

"I saw her do it this morning," Ew shrieks. "I knew you had to see!"

She stumbles, and I haul her back to her feet. Unlike dummies in horror movies, we don't look back. We run.

Not to the safety of our cabin because it looks like *evil starts at home*! But back to the safety of numbers. If there are lots of us, I hope, then Cherry won't pounce on us.

Still running, I yell back, "You could have just told me!"

"I didn't think you'd believe me!"

"Note to Ew: I believe *everything* now!"

A fallen log jumps out and trips me. Seriously! I don't think it was there before. My chest hits the ground first. It knocks all the breath out of me. Cold, damp under-brush cushions my face. Briars bite on my bare arms and legs. I don't know where those stupid vultures are, but I bet I know where they're gonna be in about thirty seconds.

When I manage to breathe again, it's rotten. Moldy, mildewy. Full of decay and who knows what. Probably baby teeth and jars of spit, knowing this place.

Ew's tiny hands fall on my shoulders. She's scream-ing, "Get up! Get up! Get up!" like that'll help me find my feet.

I yell back at her, "I'm trying!"

Some kind of thorny vine wraps itself around my ankle. Every time Ew pulls me, sharp pinpricks pierce my calf. They dig in. They hurt so bad. Worse than catching a pop fly with my face. Worse than *road rash*. The thing has claws, and it doesn't want to let me go. I swear to dog, I feel them curl and cut deeper into the meat in my leg.

The forest rustles. Something's getting closer to us. Probably Cherry. Probably Cherry with her impossible jaw and razor teeth. What is wrong with this place? Why does it have this much evil in it? Counselors and vampire devils! Counselors who *are* vampire devils! They want us in the water. They want to control us. . . .

Stop thinking, Quinn! Thinking never gets us anywhere!

Even though I manage to stand, I'm stuck. This thornbush feels like a bear trap around my leg. When I try to move, it yanks me back. And for the record, it yanks me back by gouging my flesh! Since I can't run, I gotta be brave.

Grabbing Ew's arms, I say, "Just go!"

Her eyes are so big, I see the whites all around her irises. We're talking big old cartoon eyes going on here. She shakes her head. "I'm not leaving you."

I nod right back, and her wispy blond hair gets in my face. Spitting out a tendril of Ew-locks, I say, "Yes, you are! You can't get me loose, but you can get Tez! Or . . . or the Winch! Or something!"

That knocks some sense into her. She can't help me, but maybe somebody else can. Fear tightens her face. Uncertainty fills in the shadows. Her lower lip quavering, Ew promises, "I'll be right back, okay? It'll be all right."

I let go, even though my hands kinda want to hold on tighter. At least when she's here, she's warm. And breathing. And alive.

(aLIVE! aWAKE! aLERT!)

Dang it. I thought I made my peace with the Grim Reaper in the bone pit, but guess what? I *still* don't want to die at summer camp. I nod my head to encourage her. My stupid eyes are sweating, and I yell after her, "Live to tell my story!"

As she gets farther away, the forest gets quieter. I expected Cherry to come slithering up any time, but instead, all is silent. And dark. The only thing I hear is the blood pounding in my ears and my own heavy breath. I rasp my face against my T-shirt and try to sit down on the log that tripped me.

Big. Mistake.

As soon as my butt touches the bark, the bramble

around my leg tightens. I yelp in pain and rear back. Another vine drops—it winds itself around my throat. The thorns on this one are so little, they feel like needles when they dig in.

I grab at my throat. New vines snake up and catch my wrists. They pull tight; their thorns bite deep. They keep me from clutching my throat. My breath gets thinner. My head swims.

The vines stretch. My back pops like a glowstick. Pop-pop-pop.

The forest is going to swallow me whole. My vision goes dark and sort of sparkly. Can't see Cassiopeia anymore, nope. No more Mr. Moon Face above me. I'm all alone. Dying to death. In the woods. By myself. And Tez probably won't even avenge me.

Jerk.

Tez

I'm already wearing pants and waving my flashlight when the screams race closer to our cabins. I'm not the only one awake. Nostrils and Knees tumble out of the cabin behind me in their pajamas. And Bowl Cut makes his appearance in a T-shirt and underpants.

The girls across the way (nightgowns, primarily)

145

scream when they see him. So there's a *lot* of competing screaming going on when Ew tears into camp. She bursts into the small clearing between our cabins, her hair wild and her eyes wilder.

With swift steps that I can't even hear, Chip catches her in his arms. Because he's so much taller, he dips down to her level to talk to her.

"Hey, hey, hey," he says, like he's calming a horse. "What's going on, Tammi? Shh, shh, shh, it's okay."

Using her real name, more proof that Chip is a good bean. There's no reason for him even to *know* her name, but he does. And he's gentle with her. He holds her shoulders and sort of pats her at the same time. All his soothing sounds quiet as Ew finally regains her breath.

"It's Corryn," she starts.

My heart shears in my chest. We haven't been getting along, but she's still my best friend. Pushing forward, I ask, "What about her?"

"Hey buddy," Chip says without bite. "I've got this. Tammi?"

Waving her hands in little arcs, Ew pants out nonsense. "We were, and the woods, and Corryn fell, then the vine . . . !"

"You left her?" Wow, I didn't know my voice could go that high. I look toward the woods. I memorized a lot of the paths and landmarks, but what good is that if Ew can't tell me where Corryn is? I tighten the lens on my flashlight and start toward the tree line.

Somehow, Chip manages to hold on to Ew with one hand and grab me with the other. His palm is kind of clammy, but that's reasonable. This is a high-tension situation, and he's a responsible counselor.

"We're not losing two campers in the woods," Chip says.

"But she's out there alone and—"

Suddenly, something crashes through the underbrush, just out of sight. We all whip our heads around to look. My heart's pounding so fast, I feel sick to my stomach. Two more crashes, and then Corryn appears, Cherry's arm around her shoulders.

There are scratches and cuts all over Corryn's arms and legs. The hem of her T-shirt is torn, and she has this distant look in her eyes. Her gaze skims past me— past all of us, actually. Still, I leap toward her and grab her hands.

"What happened?" I ask. "Do you need medical attention?"

In strange, numb silence, Corryn just shakes her head. "I'm good."

Taking in her injuries up close, I see there are so many of them. It looks like she lost a fight with a rose-bush. The scariest part is, there's a ring of scratches all the way around her throat. Almost like something was trying to strangle her. "This doesn't look good."

"JUST KISS!" Nostrils yells like he's funny!

"SHUT UP!" Ew yells, which is genuinely surprising. (That she can yell, not the sentiment. Nostrils et al. get told to shut up fairly regularly by Corryn's cabinmates, and often I agree with them completely. Ew just usually doesn't have volume on her side.)

Cutting through the yelling, Cherry says in a raised voice, "That's enough, that's enough. We need to head back to our cabins, cuties. It's late, and there's nothing to see here."

There's nothing to see here tends to be grown-up for *We're hiding things from you for your own good.* I don't like that, and I don't like that Corryn's still standing there with a thousand-yard stare. If nothing else, she can't stand Cherry, but she came walking into camp with her arm around her?

I whisper, "Blink once if there's more to this story. Blink twice if you're okay."

As our cabinmates scrape and shuffle as slowly as possible, I hold my ground as long as I can. Then, just as Chip puts a hand on my shoulder to guide me back to my bunk and a world of peaceful slumber under his watchful eye, Corryn moves her head.

She squeezes her eyes closed and holds them there. Actual seconds pass before she opens them again.

"All right, Bubbles," Cherry says sweetly to Corryn, gathering her up again. "We're going to have to start locking the doors around here if you keep sleepwalking like this!"

I watch as long as I can. Until Chip gently chest-bumps me over the threshold of our cabin and pulls the door closed.

The second blink never comes.

18
Gordon Lightfoot and the Peaches of Doom

Corryn

I don't know what happened exactly, but I know I wasn't sleepwalking. I wasn't sleepwalking, and I was definitely *not* dreaming. I saw what I saw.

Cherry unhinged her jaw like a deranged snake and dropped a bunny rabbit in her maw. Little Bunny Foo Foo, hopping through the forest, scooping up the field mice, then disappearing down a counselor's gullet.

"Are you okay?" everyone keeps asking me, which is the stupidest question in the world. It's like asking—I don't know—maybe it's like asking a rabbit if it's okay right before the snake's jaws clamp shut. Or the counselor's. I wish the metaphor would stay metaphorical.

The image of blood dripping from Cherry's lips is burned into my brain. And since Bowl Cut is here in the radio station with me, I can add the visual of that dude in his underwear from last night also burned into my eyes. Some things you can live a whole life without having seen, and it really would be totally fine.

When he asks me if I'm okay, I don't even dignify it with a response. I just stare at him with my arms crossed over my chest. How about as an answer, you just look at my whole—I don't know—like everything?

There's a ring around my neck like I'm wearing a necklace of scars. The forest was trying to kill me! And possibly the scariest part (besides all of it) is that I don't know how close it got to succeeding. I just like . . . blacked out. I was getting pulled into the ground. Down, down, down. And then I wasn't. I was sitting up with my palms pressed into the earth, burning all over like I was taking a bath in a pit of fire ants.

Cherry stood over me, head back to normal (for her). She was smiling so sweetly I could almost believe that I imagined the whole thing, that it was a hallucination or a dream. Almost.

The thing was, I was soaking wet, and she had a canteen in her hand.

She dosed me with the lake water, and yeah, I have a blank in my memory. Still, I know what I saw before that happened.

That was last night, and now we're here in the radio station, just me and Bowl Cut. He found his pants, so that's a big plus. He's still weird, though—newly obsessed with the music of Gordon Lightfoot.

All he wants to do is spin "The Wreck of the Edmund Fitzgerald" over and over again. It's this slow, folky moan of a song about some ship that sank in Lake Superior. Or Lake Gitche Gumee. I don't know, there's a lot of lakes in it. But the part Bowlie likes to sing at the top of his lungs? The part where ol' Gordo sings that the lake never gives up its dead.

It's starting to feel like a warning.

"You know the radio tower is busted," I tell Bowl Cut over the repeated strains of Monsieur Lightfoot's sappy crooning. "The cast of that broadcast isn't exactly broad."

"Huh?" Bowl Cut says.

"I mean, the only people who can hear this so-called radio show are me and you. What's the point, exactly? What's the difference between what we're doing here and just sitting in a room listening to records?"

"I don't know." Bowl Cut shrugs. "I just like it."

The song reaches its mournful final chords, and Bowl Cut delicately lifts up the arm of the record player to start it all over again. I can't take it! I smack his hand away, and the needle skids across the grooves of the record, making a terrible scratch and clatter.

"Hey!" Bowl Cut shouts. "Be careful with that!" He grabs the record and hugs it in a way that makes me think of Gollum and his stupid ring.

I ignore Bowl Cut and his precious. I flip the input switch on the board from Aux to Mic. "I'm DJ Bubbles, and I'm on the mic!" I shout, half-crazed. Maybe more than half. What does it matter, though? No one can hear us anyway.

"You're listening to Camp Murderface Radio," I bellow, doing my best impression of "The Hedgehog," the morning zoo radio guy from 95.1 FM back home. "Traffic is looking clear out there, weather is warm and sunny, but oh yeah, there's something in the water that's trying to kill everyone, and your counselor is some sort of literal bloodthirsty monster. Now over to my main man, Bowl Cut, with sports." I hand him the microphone, but he flips the switch to Off.

"Did Cherry really try to kill you?" he says in a low voice.

Since Bowl Cut is listening, I lean against the soundboard. "I mean, I think she did. She definitely mowed down that rabbit—that was *not* natural."

"Maybe," Bowl Cut says, cuddling ol' Gordo's album to his chest, "we should call a meeti—"

An absolutely violent knock on the door interrupts him. Bowl Cut goes even paler than his usual translucent redhead pale, especially when the pounding comes again. It sounds like someone is trying to break the house down, Big Bad Wolf style. I whip open the door, and there is the smiling form of one camp director Gladys Winchelhauser. She stares at us—more at me—with an unsettling smile.

"Let's take a walk, dear," she says.

Gulp. I've never wanted to do anything less.

She continues, "And keep playing music, Graham. I do so love a song with a story."

Then she lays a hand on my shoulder. Even through my shirt I can feel how cold and wet it is. Like a soggy piece of bread fished from the bottom of the sink. I turn back toward Bowl Cut to mouth "help," but his back is turned to me, and he's dropping the needle on the record again. Once again, Camp Sweetwater is awash with lyrics about lakes full of dead sailors.

As the Winch leads me down the path toward her office, my mind races. Is it possible that she heard my on-air rant? Is the broadcast radius of camp radio bigger than Cherry implied? Or did she just happen to be sitting, like, right outside with her boom box tuned to our frequency?

I decide I'm going to keep quiet before I apologize or anything. I don't want to be like the guilty-conscience camper in Elm who admitted to having a copy of *Truly Tasteless Jokes Volume Nine* when he got called to the Winch's office for a pair of lost swim trunks.

Don't be stupid, I tell myself. Be cool.

So I'm cool as an absolute cucumber as we pass some of the senior campers headed out to the rifle range. I blink and twist my head around—wait, I thought their counselor was a shaggy, scruffy guy with a bucket hat practically nailed to his head.

Instead, there's a prepster with them. He even has a nonstandard sweater hanging over his shoulders. His is pink-and-green argyle. Yes, argyle. I know I would have made alllll kinds of fun of him if I had seen him before.

But I haven't. So that means—

Wait. Have *all* the counselors been replaced?

I'm cool as a cucumber when we enter Winchel-hauser's office. Which is ironic, since the inside of the office is not cool but *hot*. Literally. What the heck! It's like she has a heater blazing in the corner.

That's not all. The whole place is so different from the last time we were here, when Tez and I stole—I mean *borrowed* a map.

This must be where all the camp budget for renovation is going. Just a few weeks ago, it had the personality of a parking deck, filled with dusty boxes and air that felt like the inside of a cough. Now it's got, like, the softest chair I've ever sat in. So, *so* soft . . .

"Do you like the new furnishings, dear?" Winchel-hauser says with a grin. "I've done a lot of work to get this feeling hospitable. The humidifier was a must. It keeps my plants oh-so-happy."

The small office is indeed like a little greenhouse, with happy ferns on pretty much every surface. The humidifier must be turned up to ultrahigh because there are fat drops of water on all the leaves. The air is thick and moist, and it's hot but yet somehow . . . totally wonderful.

The Winch, gotta hand it to her. How did she turn this place around? This chair hugs my butt the way a squashy chair should. I love it. And the beaded curtains separating the rooms are kind of awesome.

Besides the deep green of the plants, pretty much everything else is peach—it must be Winchelhauser's favorite color.

The walls are peachish pink; there is even a piece of needlepoint art on her desk of a fat, ripe peach. Everything Is Peachy, it says. I take a deep breath and try to imagine a world where that is true. I let the hot air fill my lungs. I let the hot air give me a snuggle.

"Now about last night, dear," Winchelhauser says.

Oh yeah. We're not just here for a high-humidity hang. My hand rises to my neck to probe the cuts from last night. But they don't hurt so much now. Do they? They don't. I smile at the Winch.

"What were we talking about?" I ask her.

"What you *think* you saw . . ." She folds her hands gently together and places them on her desk. "Is not what you saw."

Hey, I was first in line for *Star Wars*. I know about Jedi mind tricks. I'm not an idiot. And she's not Obi-Wan. Still, there is something soothing in her voice.

Something sparkling in her eyes. Something . . .

No! Snap out of it, Quinn! I say to myself.

"Listen," I say to the Winch. "I know what I saw." I lean over on the table and meet Winchelhauser's smile with a patented Corryn scowl. "Cherry murder-chowed a rabbit!"

"Isn't that interesting?" Winchelhauser purrs. Her voice is warm. Everything is warm. Maybe she does believe me. And maybe it's not that big of a deal. Maybe it's . . .

"Maybe it's fine," she says, like she's reading my mind. "It's fine. It's fine. What's done is done, dear."

My eyes feel sleepy, my lashes wet with dewy drops.

And then I'm at the door, Winch leading me by the elbow back out into the bright afternoon. "Have a good day, dear," she says. "I hope you're looking forward to color war as much as I am. Are you prepared?"

"Not yet, but I'm gonna be," I say. "You betcha."

My feet take slow, gliding steps down the path. I'm not more than a few feet away from the office when I hear Tez calling out to me.

"Corryn, Corryn!" he's shouting in his high-pitched chirp. "Wait up!"

I do, and he runs (well, Tez's version of running,

speedwalking like a mall granny, which is adorable) to meet me.

"What were you doing with Mrs. Winchelhauser?" he asks. He winks—maybe it's just that the sun is in his eyes—and it cracks me up.

I wink back. I even say it. "Wink." Ha! I start giggling, then full-on crack up. I even snort once, which only makes me laugh even harder.

Tez gives me a concerned look. A. Very. Concerned. Look. His lips are pursed so tightly there should be a roll of Certs in there. This is a joke about how my mom always has mints in her purse and is not funny to anyone.

So, I'll describe it better. He looks like a scientist peering down the nose of a microscope. The eye. Does a microscope have eyes? Potatoes have eyes. My dad has a record about eyes without a face. . . . Where was I going with that? Oh! Tez is peering at me in a most intense way.

"Do you feel all right?" he asks.

I do not feel all right. I feel weirdly weird but maybe, I guess, not in an unpleasant way. "Why does everyone keep asking me that, man?"

"Because we're concerned about your well-being?"

"No concerno necessary-o! I'm good!"

Suspiciously, Tez says, "Let me see your notebook."

Huh. I pat my back pocket and discover I have a notebook. It's grimy and tattered, but there it is. Just a lil guy, spiral-bound, the size of a notecard. I offer it to Tez and say, "I feel like a nap. Write that down for me. N-A-P."

Flipping through scribbled-on pages, Tez knits his brows. "There's nothing in here since lunch."

Dreamily, I wave my hand. "It's all good."

That doesn't seem like the answer Tezzy wants, but that's the answer Tezzy gets. Pulling the tiny stub pencil out of the spirals, he writes something down. That's not how this is supposed to work, is it? Maybe it is. Oh, wait! I told him to write down my nap, ha ha ha! I forgot!

He returns my notebook slowly. "I was coming to see if the mail was in yet. We haven't had any for a couple days."

"We haven't?" That's weird. Not that I would notice. I get like a letter a week. But Tez gets stuff *every day.* Then slowly, my brain realizes this might be bad. Tez hasn't gotten anything from his folks in *days*? "Dude, are you out of Botan Rice Candy? That would be tragical." It would be so very tragical. They're wrapped in plastic that you can *eat*. It *melts*. Tez says it's not actually plastic, but I don't believe him.

"No, but I'm out of my dried plums," he says. "And so you know, I asked my parents to send some extra stuff for you. But that was several missives ago. Something is going on."

"Relax, Tez," I say. "You worry too much. Everything's fine. It's cool. It's Copacabana."

"*Copacetic*," Tez corrects, sputtering like an angry engine. "And *you're* the one who keeps saying everything is a box of Froot Loops right now!"

"That doesn't sound like me," I say. "But the only thing I'd say about fruit at the moment is a very wise thing I heard somewhere."

"Oh yeah?" he says. "What's that?"

"'Everything is peachy,'" I say. I put my arm around his shoulders and say it again. "Totally, totally peachy."

19
Bedtime Rocks

Tez

One of my favorite times of day now is bedtime.

Settled into our bunks, lights-out, fan going, we have this great in-between kind of space, between awake and asleep. It used to be full of farts and British-accented threats. But now it's full of—

"Schist is my favorite rock," Nostrils says. "We did a whole project on metamorphic rocks last year, and this one is . . . Sometimes it has scales; sometimes it has layers. And you can peel it apart into teeny, tiny sheets of . . . schist, I guess. Some of 'em are so thin, you can see through them!"

From his bunk, where Chip lies in a pair of excellent

button-down pajamas, he says, "That's downright interesting, Nostrils. Isn't it interesting, lads? Because when I think of rocks, I think of mighty granite, but here we have a friend with a different favorite."

I can't believe the conversation we're having. I can't believe how amazing it is. I can't believe that Nostrils and Knees and Bowl Cut all have thoughts about stuff unrelated to karate and flatulence!

My excitement bubbles in my stomach, like a good dose of Pop Rocks and Coke. It's so hard to keep my mouth shut, because I know stuff about this stuff! I realize I need to let other people hold the floor. But I know something really, really relevant!

"That's the mica in it," I say. It just slips out! "That's what makes it peel like that."

"Huh," Nostrils says. He stretches, reaching out and trying to touch the ceiling and the wall at the same time. His gangly limbs wobble, and his skinny body teeters precariously on the edge of his bunk. "I didn't know that."

Knees kicks up from the bunk below and firmly plants his feet on the bottom of my mattress. I know this, because I can feel him pushing me up. Sometimes he likes to bounce me as hard as he can, to see if I'll fall off. (Data point: if he bounces me the right way, I will. Otherwise, I end up trapped against the wall.) Tonight, though, he just gently walks up and down, unintentionally giving me a massage. "My uncle has a steam room with lava rocks."

Bowl Cut asks, "It's made out of them?"

"Nah," Knees says, continuing to knead my back through the mattress. "They go in a box in the corner, and they get real hot. Then you pour water on them, to make the steam."

"Now that's something I've never heard of," exclaims Chip. "Have any of the rest of you heard of that?"

We all murmur our nos, and I want to bring up the Oracle of Delphi—a seer whose entire "gift" for determining the future was later determined to be hallucinations brought on by gases leaking out through volcanic rock. But I'm starting to learn how to talk to other people—cramming in the things that interest me occasionally backfires. So I keep the petrochemical fortune-telling gas to myself. Instead, I ask, "Isn't it neat how you don't know something, and then once you know it, you can't unknow it?"

Bowl Cut raises a pale hand in the dark. "Wrong. You can forget something."

"No, I know people can forget," I concede. "But I mean, like, right now. Can you actually remember that you didn't know about lava rocks in steam rooms before?"

And because it's our special sharing time before bed, nobody throws a pillow at me. Or laughs. Or tells me to stuff my own head up my butt. Instead, Knees actually says, "Whoa. You're right."

"It's kinda like what Bubbles was writing in her note-book," Nostrils says, wholly unaware that he's about to tell on himself. "She wrote down, 'The brain named itself.' Blew. My. Mind."

"That's cool," I say. "Don't call her Bubbles, though."

"Sorry, Chickenlips. Didn't mean to insult your *girl-friend.*"

The cabin fills with provocative *oooooooh*s in response to that. My face flashes hot, but that's okay. It's dark and nobody can see it. However, this is starting to shift from special sharing time to . . . whatever it was back when Gavin was here. Killer kids hopped up on bug juice mentally and physically attacking each other before los-ing consciousness?

Just then, Chip interjects, "Now, I don't like the sound of that."

My face grows even hotter. Usually, when grown-ups defend me, things just get worse. But it's a testament to the power and awesomeness of Chip that what happens instead is practically a miracle.

"Oh. Sorry," Knees says, and bounces me once.

Nostrils finally sits up and flattens one hand on the ceiling. "Sorry."

"Yeah, sorry," Bowl Cut says.

It's possible my face might burn off. This is why I'm *sure* Chip is one of the good guys. Even when it doesn't matter, even when he could ignore it, he says and does the right thing. The honorable thing. He's turning this cabin full of semiferal boys into thinking, refined *lads*.

No matter what happens, I just know Chip will be on our side.

Corryn

There's been an invasion, and I don't know if I like it.

The second that Cherry turned off the lights for the night, Ew slipped out of her bunk and into mine. It's not like she's crowding me out. She's not big or anything; I could probably fit her in my pocket.

It's just weird because Braids and Hairspray are the night-talkers. I'm a night-sleeper, unless something messed up is happening and I'm faking it. Or I'm meeting someone at the boathouse at midnight. Or . . .

I guess I'm *not* a night-sleeper. I'm not usually not a night-talker either, but here I am, Ew scrunched up on my pillow, whispering.

"Okay," she says, her warm breath in my face. "Everybody except Nostrils has stopped drinking the bug juice. So that's good."

I tell her, "I don't think Nostrils could get dumber, anyway, so drink up, buddy."

She covers her mouth and giggles. "Totally."

"I feel like the trick to the water is, if you're not paying attention, it washes everything away. But if you are, you can make yourself remember."

Ew wriggles around, clutching Dobert, her stuffed dog. "For real? You think so?"

With a nod, I dig under my pillow and pull out *le notebook*. Tapping the tattered yellow cover, I say, "A hundred percent, because I've been writing stuff down. And look. . . ." I flip forward and show her my notes. "I didn't expect Cherry to douse me in the woods, and I don't remember what happened. But I knew they were forcing us into the water for swim time, and I remember."

Everything on Ew's face goes round: her eyes, her mouth—even her eyebrows turn into raised half circles. "Omigod, you're *right*."

She takes the notebook, riffling through the pages. It's too dark in here to really read it. But she can probably make out some of it. I use a lot of capital letters when I get heated up. And underlines. And exclamation points. I don't know why teachers tell me not to do that. We have that stuff for a reason! To yell on paper like we yell out loud!

"This is a really good idea," Ew says when she gets to the last page. She looks up at me. "Thanks for showing me."

I take the notebook back, cramming it into my pillowcase again. "Yeah, no problem."

"Can I ask you something?"

Joking, I toss out my dad's favorite reply. "Besides that?"

She rolls her eyes but snorts a little laugh. "Yeah."

I'm feeling a little sparkly and happy. Ew is really, maybe, my friend. And she's pretty rad. A tiny pea-sized ache appears in my chest. We have only a week and a half of camp left. Then we're all going home (if we survive). I wonder if she'll write me letters. Let's be fair, I wonder if I'll write her back. The dumbest thought ever starts spinning around in my head: I'm gonna miss this place (if I survive).

"Go 'head," I say. "Ask me anything."

Ew rearranges her arms around Dobert, her chin resting on his fuzzy brown head. Black bead eyes stare at me, unblinking. But that's okay. He's got a smile pasted on, and it's not even creepy.

"Did you guys ever think about talking to us?" she asks. Her voice is serious; she looks kinda vulnerable. "Telling us about the ghosts?"

Oh, wow. Rubbing my temple, I try to think. But I already know the answer. It was me and Tez against the evil, all the way. Stuff happened to other people, like Bowlie's midnight shave and Ew spewing French in the dark. But I don't think we ever considered going to them for help or, like, backup.

Grimacing, I admit, "No. We were the only ones seeing stuff in the fire. So we thought . . . you know, we were the only ones who could do something about it."

"That makes sense," Ew says quietly. She squishes Dobert with her face, quiet for a moment. Then she says, "But I'm having crazy dreams now. And I saw"—she drops her whisper to a bare flutter of sounds—"*you-know-who* do the snake thing first."

We both glance toward the front of the cabin. Cherry's bunk is separated from ours by the cubbies. All we can make out is a lump under a sleeping bag bathed in moonlight. We can't do anything about the monster in the room . . . except this.

"Yeah, you did," I concede. "And you believed me about the water first."

"I *totally* did," Ew says. "So maybe we should be . . . partners?"

It feels wrong to be making big decisions without Tez. But Tez's head isn't even in the game. He's trying to pick and choose what he believes in so he can keep having the Best Time Ever™ at camp. But the evil is rising.

Studying Ew's face, I ask, "Do you want a notepad, too?"

She breaks into a smile. "Totally."

"I've got an extra one in my stuff," I tell her. "I'll give it to you in the morning. In the meantime . . ."

I pull my notepad out again. Opening it to the first blank page, I slip the pencil nub out of the spirals. Out loud, I say as I write, "After lights-out. Bringing Ew into Operation Floppy Disk."

"What the heck is a floppy disk?" Ew asks.

I shrug and hand her the pencil. "No idea. Tez named the mission. Initial here. And here."

She does. Then she makes me hug Dobert before she climbs back into her bunk. Sprawling on my back, I stare at the bars above me. There's not a whole lot to smile about right now. Still, I've got a big ol' grin plastered to my face.

It turns out, I *am* a night-talker . . . when I have a friend to night-talk with.

20
Contrast in Nature

Tez

The next day, Ew and I are supposed to be taking pictures of contrast in nature.

Instead, we're taking pictures of contrast in nature—a good distance away from the designated photography area. We already have an excuse for this malfeasance: we saw a subject, and the muse compelled us to follow.

Actually, Ew says she'll let me do the talking, and if caught, that's what I plan to say.

As I kneel on the forest floor to take a picture through the canopy above, I say, "So what happened with Corryn wasn't just getting trapped in the woods.

And you've seen Cherry do this before . . . eat a wild animal whole."

"Twice," Ew says. Then her expression goes fuzzy, and she nods her head. "Yes, twice. Once by myself, and once when I took Corryn."

"But you don't know when the first time was?" I ask, snapping a picture. This shot will be so contrastful, and possibly worthy of a *National Geographic* cover. A bird flew through just as I touched the trigger. I'm positive I caught it in perfect relief against the sunlight. And in just a few short days, I'll know for sure!

Ew winds the film in her camera. Then holds the Nikon up haphazardly. The shutter clicks, three times, and then she drops the camera to her side again. "It had to be the first day they were here. Around the same time the bug juice showed up everywhere. And did you know? Since they brought up the coolers from the kitchen, we always have a 'bedtime tipple.' I don't even know what a tipple is. Cherry just gives us Dixie Cups full of bug juice."

"A small drink," I say. Lying back a bit, I refocus my camera. "My grandma acts like she's being naughty when she has *a little tipple* at Thanksgiving."

"Of what?"

"Eggnog," I say with a shrug. "Dad always jokes that he cuts off her tipple before she topples."

"Weird."

Because of the way Ew says it, it doesn't offend me. It almost comes across like a scientific observation. And I've made some observations of my own. For Ew, unfamiliar things that aren't gross are *weird*. Weird things that are unsettling are *creepy*. Things that displease her in general, *ugh*. And of course, things that disgust her in any way, *ew*.

Since she meant it genially, I agree. "Very weird."

"Okay, let me ask you this!" she demands, draping the camera around her neck and sitting down on a stump. "You haven't seen Chip do anything creepy, have you?"

The camera slips from my hands and falls on my face. It cracks against my cheekbone, and my eyeballs briefly spangle with pain. Also, I blush, because that's very embarrassing, but Ew doesn't seem to notice.

Still sprawled in the middle of my mossy clover patch, I say, "Not a thing. He's been great. The only thing he does that Cherry does is use that stupid water gun. And even that he doesn't do very often. I think he really likes us."

Verrrrry slowly, Ew takes a nibble of her thumb and looks up at me. "Isssssss iiiiiiiiit possible that he makes you forget the bad stuff?"

Confidently, I shake my head. "Of course not. I'm very aware. Perhaps hyperaware. If he made us forget, I'd remember."

In a tone that seems to say she's unconvinced, Ew shrugs and says, "Ooo-kay."

"And," I say, pulling the field notebook from between my underpants and my hip, "I've been keeping meticulous records. See?"

Ew makes no move to look at my entries. Instead, she looks at me like I grew a giant spider on my head. It's not my fault I don't have pockets. These shorts were made for athletics, not for cargo storage.

Twigs and leaves crunch beneath me as I sit up. The middle of my back feels particularly damp. Wet, almost. Too much exposure to podzol and moss, obviously. I wait for Ew to say something—anything—but it doesn't happen. So, cradling the camera in my lap, I speak.

"I do believe you guys about Cherry. The Corryn that came back from the woods was not the usual Corryn. And she was acting really dopey when I saw her before lunch yesterday."

"That's when the Winch steamed her brains," Ew says. "I have a notebook now, too."

Surprised, I move my camera to look at her. "You do?"

"Operation Floppy Disk," she says, invoking the code name I created.

I swallow. Corryn *told her*? I mean, it's not bad that she did. The more minds on the operation, the better the results, I'd say. But realizing she brought Ew in on our operation, without even talking to me . . . well, it makes me feel kind of . . . I don't even know.

"Awesome," I say. "The more data, the better."

"I guess," Ew says. She raises her camera and points it at me. I'm not much of a subject, but I do hold very still for her. Shutter speeds have improved considerably since the early Brownie cameras, but a moving target can still be tricky to capture. After the click, I stand up and start to brush myself off.

Ew makes a strangled sound and stands. Pointing at me, she burbles more weird noises. Then stalks over to grab my arm, my *bad* arm. The one that Corryn claims Scary Mary pierced at the lake. I still don't remember how I got those bruises, but it doesn't matter now.

Ew pulls my arm super hard, I think to turn me

around, but it doesn't matter. There's a terrible, audible pop. Pain explodes in my shoulder, fiery and blinding. My stomach turns from it, and tears spring to my eyes.

Son of a biscuit, Marfan strikes again!

When people say they're double-jointed, they're misinformed. No one has two joints. It's one, held very loosely by incompetent musculature and tendons. Basically, a single stretchy joint.

Because of my Marfan, I can be stretchy, too—when I manipulate *my own* frame. However, when a four-foot-tall girl from Indianapolis just *yanks*, the ball of the bone pops right out of the socket.

I suck in a breath, but my body won't exhale it. Sweat trickles down my skin and my stomach swirls threateningly.

Getting a shoulder dislocated hurts like fireworks going off in my skin. It's going to hurt like fireworks and arson when Miss Kortepeter yanks it back into place. And then it's gonna hurt like arson and bees for a couple weeks after.

My throat tightens and sours. Thoughts strobe through my head. The painkillers I've avoided so far this summer? They're going to be front and center now. I hate that. They make me itchy and tired, and this is *not* what I want. I won't be able to climb or lift or—

"Tez, *look*," Ew demands like I'm ignoring her. No, Ew. I am very much not ignoring you. In fact, right now, the only things that exist for me are your face all screwed up in horror and the Roman candle blowing up in my shoulder.

Finally, Ew manages to make me twist so I can look behind myself.

My shirt. Is covered. In blood.

Now I try to twist myself, forward, backward—did she rip my arm *off*? Yanking on my shirt with my only good hand—my other arm dangles uselessly, flapping like those yellow dish gloves they use in the cafeteria at school—I pull it over my head.

Ew barks at me to turn around—very authoritatively, so I do. Her hot hands roam all over my bare back. She searches for wounds, and I try to flap my T-shirt around to get a better look. Maybe I lay on an unusual fungus; sometimes their sap turns red or blue when exposed to the air. This might not be blood at all!

"You're not hurt," Ew says, coming around to my front again. "Wait, what happened to your arm?"

I shake my head. Corryn already knows, and that's enough. "Nothing. It's okay. Help me with this."

Leaning over, Ew drags her reddened hands on the ground like that might wipe them clean. Then she grabs one side of the shirt. Together, we unfurl it. And there, in deep, vivid scarlet, a message appears—in blood. The color . . . the tangy, coppery scent . . . are unmistakable.

"Ew, creepy," Ew says, under her breath.

Nodding, I say, "Extremely."

Because written in blood, on the back of my shirt, is a single word. It's not like a Rorschach test, where Ew and I look at a splatter and just happen to come up with the same image. No.

These letters are tall and neat, and little beads of red drip from them. The message is short but not sweet. My shirt says:

SOON

21
The Winch Clinch

Corryn

"Last one in is a rotten egg," Chip and Cherry chirp in unison.

I've never been one to care about being an egg, rotten or otherwise, but coming from them, it sounds like a threat.

Backing up the threat is the fact that they're pointing their pink squirt guns at us, and you know those trigger fingers are itchy. When I close my eyes, I see Cherry chomping down on that rabbit all over again. Rotten eggs, huh? Maybe they'll actually turn us into scrambled eggs. Maybe they'll eat us with ketchup and a side of bunny bacon.

What's worse, though? Getting squirted with a little lake water, or getting submerged in the evil thing? Because, yes, it's mandatory swimming time in the lake. Tez and I could cheese off when Gavin and Mary were in charge. But these supercharged counselors are not taking no for an answer.

At least some of the Oak Camp crew is peacefully resisting with me. Once more, we're at the beach, and once more we're trying not to get doused.

Tez and Ew circle on the dry land with me and Bowlie. Tez, partially because his arm is in a sling and partially because I think he's humoring me. Ew, because she believes me. Bowl Cut, because he *really likes* hanging out with Ew.

Knees and Nostrils join in. They don't know that the lake may be a source of supernatural evil, but they're always up for some counselor disobedience just on general principle. Eventually, Hairspray and Braids join us, too, because they'd rather die than get left out.

And there's a weirdly lot of counselors around . . . like, more than usual, and I don't recognize most of them. Hairy-Guy-Bucket-Hat is gone. So is Tall-Girl-Feather-Earrings, and the Whoa-Whoa-Whoa Chick. She's one of the Bantam Camp counselors, so basically a living goalie. *Whoa, whoa, whoa, let's all sit down. Whoa, whoa, whoa, put down those rocks. Whoa, whoa, whoa, wipe your hands!*

All of them—gone. Replaced with country-club strangers, identical down to the pleated shorts.

Now we lounge under a tree, far enough away from the lake to be free of the splash zone. Chip and Cherry are distracted, helping some other preppy clowns keep Elm Camp in the water. Here, in our peaceful hideout, some of us are making annoying wind instruments out of thick blades of grass. Nostrils is particularly good at it—it sounds like an amplified trumpet or maybe an unhinged elephant.

"Why is being a rotten egg so bad, anyway?" Bowl Cut asks between the bleats.

Tez of course takes the question literally. "Haven't you ever smelled one?"

"Ew, why would you do that?" Ew asks.

"Somebody had to smell the first one to find out they were stank," Nostrils says.

"You're stank," Ew replies.

"No duh, so are you."

Knees defends her by telling Nostrils, "All her stank is on your face!"

Nostrils says, "Your face is stank, 24/7."

Annnnnnd now I am listening to the dumbest conversation of all time.

"We're not going in the lake," I say. "No matter what."

"Why not?" Knees says. "It's hot, lake's cold. Simple geometry."

"That would be physics," Tez says.

"Well, *you* have donkey butt stank. How's that for physics?" Knees retorts.

I take back what I said earlier about the dumbest conversation of all time. It seems there are always new lows in stupidity to be reached.

"Ew," says Ew.

"He's not wrong, exactly, no offense," Hairspray says. "I mean, we're all kinda . . . ripe. When are they going to get the showers fixed? Maybe we should get in the lake, just a little bit. . . ."

"NO!" I shout. "Last time: there is something evil in the lake. It messes with your mind. It makes people forget things."

"I wish I could forget this whole conversation," Braids says, shaking her head.

Hairspray rolls her eyes so far back, they're nothing

but whites for a second. "Lakes can't be evil, Bubbles. They're just water!"

Standing up, I point at her furiously. "That's what you think!"

My shouting might have been a little too shouty because it catches the attention of Chip the Drip. He comes strutting over like a cowboy with his squirt gun drawn.

Blech. I can't believe this guy is Tez's new fave.

"What's going on, friends?" he asks with a big smile. He's doing an accent that I guess he thinks is funny, some kind of Wild West movie drawl. "I can't help but notice you're looking a little dry. Why don't you take advantage of this fine natural air conditioner and take a dip?" He's smiling but his finger is tapping his gun.

"No," I say. I could say more, but that about sums it up.

"Excuse me, camper?" Chip says. He takes a few more steps in my direction, close enough that his shadow is cast on my outstretched legs. Ugh. I don't even like his *shadow* touching me. I stand up and cross my arms over my chest so he knows I mean business.

"Which part did you not understand?" I ask. "The N or the O?" He doesn't respond, but if I have to guess,

I'd say it's the *O*. "Listen," I say. "Tez hurt his arm. He can't get his sling wet. *I'm* his friend and I'm keeping him company and we're not swimming and you can't make us."

"Aw, Tez, we can figure out a way to get you wet and keep that chicken wing dry," Chip says.

"I know you can," Tez says. "I'm just exercising an abundance of caution." Then Tez turns and whispers to me. "Counselor, a sidebar, please." I don't know what he's talking about. "Come here," he says, through gritted teeth, frantically gesturing for me to come close.

I join him at "sidebar," which is one foot away, where everybody can still hear us anyway.

"I don't want anyone to know about you-know," he says, clutching his sling and doing something like a wink.

His very blue-and-white, very noticeable sling is kind of very noticeable already. Come on! It's not a secret that his arm is hurt. I didn't say anything about his *condition*. I'm not revealing classified information here, am I?

"Dude, if it's between hurting your pride and hurting your actual self . . . Killing your rep and actually getting killed . . ."

"Listen," he says. "Ew already saw my arm pop out, and now I'm wearing this thing! I'm back on painkillers that gork me out! I don't want anyone to think I'm—"

"Who cares what Ew thinks?" I interrupt. Does he care about what Ew thinks? He better not. He better not be liking her more than he likes me. "And the painkillers are the perfect reason not to go in! I'm pretty sure it says it right there on the medicine bottle that you shouldn't swim."

"It says I shouldn't operate heavy machinery."

"Same thing!"

"Is it, though? The point is, *I don't want anyone to know I'm diff*—"

Our argument—I mean, friendly discussion—is interrupted by a solid figure jogging in our direction.

Heads turn, and we see no other than the town's top lawman, the head cheese of Fan du Lac Police Department himself, Chief Wolpaw. Tez and I have had the opportunity to make his acquaintance early on, because that's just the kind of summer this has been.

He jogs toward the lake, panting heavily. He puts his hands on his hips and surveys the scene, squinting at the splashing lake-goers like he's a birder trying to find a rare cormorant.

(Tez has informed me that cormorants are birds, and people who look for birds are known as birders. This is news to me, as I had always assumed they were more accurately known as dorks.)

Chief Wolpaw looks like he got here in a hurry— he's not wearing his full police chief uniform but rather shorts and a sweaty blue T-shirt. He does have his policeman's hat on and his mirrored sunglasses. He also has, it's impossible not to notice, his gun in a holster on his hip.

He takes off his hat, and I notice a wide stripe of gray hair in the middle of his black locks. Stressful job, I guess. He really does seem to be looking for something, or *someone*, because he takes off his sunglasses and strides purposefully in our direction.

To my surprise, he stops in his tracks and points right at me. He starts waving frantically like a guy with a handkerchief saying goodbye to someone on a train in an old movie. His strides are quick and long, and in just a couple of seconds, he's a few yards from me. "Miss Quinn, Miss Quinn," he's saying with a sense of purpose in his booming voice.

"Me?" I mouth. I'm not getting arrested for not going in the lake, am I?

Wait: am I?

Out of nowhere, Gladys Winchelhauser steps in between us. She must have been swimming because she's still in her suit. And this bathing suit. Wow. I don't know where she got it, but I'm thinking she should take it back. It's thick and green, with shoulder straps as wide as mag tires and a weird skirt thing that goes almost to her knees. Also, it's made out of something that doesn't shine when it's wet. I'm pretty sure it's helping her marinate in evil.

Her walk slows, her wide hips rock, and she runs a bright green beach towel through her sopping hair as she approaches. "Why, if it isn't the chief of police, right here in our humble little summer camp," she says. "Looking all handsome out of uniform. To what do we owe this absolutest of pleasures?"

Oh lordy. She is flirting. Say it with me: grooooooooosssssssssss.

"Oh hello, Gladys," he says. He cleans his sunglasses on his T-shirt, exposing his virulently violently hairy midsection. "I just wanted to have a word with Miss Quinn here, if I may—"

"Are you sure you don't want to hop in the lake with us, show off that world-class backstroke?" she says. She's flapping her eyelashes at him; I hope there's just something stuck in her eye.

Chief Wolpaw smiles. "That's been a while."

"And yet," the Winch says. She better not have just checked out his backside in those shorts, or Tez won't be the only person who's barfed on the dock this summer. My stomach rolls when Winchelhauser continues, "I remember."

"It's nice to be remembered," he says, his mustache twitching indecently.

"Oh, don't be modest, you big goose. You had the best stroke in the county." She snaps her wet towel playfully in his direction. A fine spray of mist snaps off the towel and gets him right in the face. He wipes the water off, and she giggles. "And oh look, now you're already wet."

He blinks a few times and then smiles. "Hold my belt?" he says to her.

"With pleasure."

And so now this is happening: the chief of police is taking off his shoes and socks and shirt. He walks to the water's edge and executes a not-exactly-graceful dive into the lake.

The Winch might have been somewhat exaggerating

his prowess as a swimmer. She's watching him like he's a beautiful sea creature, though, smiling appreciatively at each awkward splash.

Then she turns to me and smiles a toothy smile. "Well, would you look at that?" she says. "My old friend, the chief of police, doing whatever little thing I tell him." She slithers off toward the lake.

I look over at Tez. His jaw is basically at the bottom of the lake, it's dropped so far. "What. Is. Going. On?" he asks, which sums it up pretty well.

Bowl Cut walks over to us, shaking his head. "You ever notice how she does that a lot?" he says.

"What?" I ask.

"Keeps people from saying stuff they want to say."

Score one point for Bowl Cut. On this, he's not wrong.

Camp Director Gladys Winchelhauser's swimsuit might thankfully leave too much to the imagination, but this much is clear: she definitely has something to hide.

22
On Top of Confidence Tower

Tez

Though the first weeks of summer held on to a spring-time chill, summer has now fully arrived. Humidity leaves us sticky with sweat, and the air in our cabin tastes like funk and swamp water. No AC at summer camp: we are roughing it!

Our fan points out the front door, because Nostrils says it can be deadly to have a fan blow on your skin. Knees sides with him, and Bowl Cut refuses to take a position. Everybody ignores the fact that heat rises. Even if the fan manages to suck air out of our cabin, it's draining the *cool* air.

And that's why we lie on the wood floor. It's covered

in bits and dust and probably bug stuff. But we can breathe down here, and Chip lets us take off our shirts, which also helps. I know Corryn thinks Chip's evil like Cherry, but he really does nothing but help.

With a deep breath, I try to blow on my own chest to encourage evaporation. The coolness is momentary, but it's scientifically delicious. Lazily, I ask, "Did the mail get here yet?

"All right, lads," Chip says, taking the damp washcloth from his forehead. "Sharing time. Camp's almost over. How do we feel about that?"

Wait. I asked a question. Did Chip just *ignore* me? Around me, my cabinmates show a tiny display of interest, mostly by groaning a vaguely positive sound.

But I'm not finished, so I say, "Wait, though! What about the—"

Bright as ever, Chip cuts me off. "Thoughts?"

This isn't normal. Chip is all about information. Giving it, sharing it, and he never tries to shut us up. But now he's pretending he doesn't hear me? Is it just the question about the mail he's avoiding, or is it me? Time to launch an experiment.

"I have feelings," I say. Then I quickly add, "About color war."

Everyone but Chip groans. Knees makes a vague motion in my direction. I think he's trying to hit me with his shirt, but it would take too much energy to do it right. He can keep flapping, for all I care. It might generate a breeze.

Without a hint of annoyance, Chip says, "Well, let's hear 'em!"

So, there you have it. Questions about color war? Okay. Questions about the mail? *Verboten.* Interesting. Let me see if I can gather some alternate information.

"First," I say, ignoring more groans, "where will we hide our flag? I have some radical thoughts on that."

Bowl Cut slightly raises his head. "On top of the confidence tower."

Great place, although it may be indefensible. Once you climb to the top of the three-story timber structure, there's nowhere to hide. Or run.

"I was thinking in Winchelhauser's office." Knees gives his own idea a thumbs-up.

"My thought," I say, "was to dig out a hollow and plant it beneath the earth."

With a gentle laugh, Chip says, "I do believe there are some rules you have to follow. It has to be outside and it has to be visible. And you're gonna want to assign some soldiers to protect it."

I refold my T-shirt into a pillow and roll on my side. My back peels off the floor, like plastic wrap off the top of a potluck dish. "Protect it how?"

When Chip laughs, it's an indulgent sound. "Any way you can, CL. Within reason, of course. No dropping boulders on other campers!"

My breath loosens up when he calls me that. When he found out I don't like my nickname, he started calling me CL.

See? Chip is a good guy and a good counselor.

"Now, what else is on your mind?" he asks patiently.

To be honest, a lot of things are on my mind. Just like a lot of things are sticking to my skin. Moment by moment, I'm more aware of the things on the floor that are now on my body. They itch, all over; my skin crawls.

We haven't showered in days. I feel grimy, like my gears are grinding, and suddenly, I can't stop thinking about it.

I ask, "Is it true that, during color war, people can tie you up and throw you in the lake?"

"Whoa, whoa, whoa, that's a little much," Chip says. He swings his legs over the side of his bunk and sits up. His face is pink with warmth, and his blondish hair is turning brownish around the edges from his sweat. "Throw you in the lake, yes. But tie you up first? Where did you hear that? That's just silly."

Nostrils rolls over on his belly. Then he pushes his hands underneath himself and snakes up. "Dude, you're making this way harder than it has to be. It's just gonna be a dumb field day with capture the flag at the end. Three-legged races and stuff like that."

"Thank you, Nostrils," Chip says with a bob of his head. "Does that make you feel better, CL?"

"I guess," I say. Color war doesn't concern me. I understand its concepts just fine. It's more a conflict inside me. I'm torn. I really am. It feels like I'm at a fork in the road. One way branches off with Corryn—and now also Ew, I guess—and the prospect of more evil to come. The other way branches off with Chip, and it leads to good times and everything I wanted camp to be.

Maybe there *is* still something to fight at Camp Murderface. Who says it has to be *my* fight?

Chip jumps to his feet. "All right, lightning round," he says.

Waving his hands expansively, he comes to stand over us. His pink cheeks turn scarlet, and he shakes his head so hard, his bangs unfeather themselves. "Ready?"

All of us on the floor murmur affirmatively. I like lightning round. Chip names a feeling, and if we're feeling it, we raise our hands. It's supposed to help us get closer to each other. To become a team.

We all watch Chip. He rubs his hands together and rolls his hazely green eyes toward the ceiling. His lips move, as if he's testing out words before saying them. After just a moment, he lights up and spreads his arms wide in triumph. "Worried!"

I raise my hand. I'm the only one.

"Nervous!"

Again, just me.

"Excited!"

Three hands go up. Mine stays on my chest. I feel more anticipatory. And accuracy is important.

Chip claps his hands and shouts, "Tired!"

Four hands. That's an easy one.

"Hungry."

Six hands go up, because Nostrils and Knees raise both of theirs.

Winding through us, Chip says, "Thirsty!"

Eight hands up, before they all drop. My mouth is dry and spongy. I ask, "When do you think the water's going to be fixed?"

Chip ignores the question. "Powerful!"

Only Bowl Cut raises his hand. Mine stays on my chest, feeling my heartbeat, and I'm marveling. Chip just ignored one of my questions again. If he shouts out *uneasy*, I'll raise my hand *and* my foot.

Coming to stand over me, Chip looks down at me with a smile. It takes him a second to choose another feeling. But when he does, I get a weird, wiggling sensation in my stomach. It's like worry turned into a worm and now it's burrowing through my insides.

"Suspicious."

My dry mouth goes drier. He's looking right at me. Even if anyone else raised their hands—and they don't—he wouldn't see them. It's just me and Chip. The worm in my gut burrows faster. Two paths. Right in front of me. It's like Chip read my mind and he's waiting for me to choose. Him or Corryn. Fun times at camp or a war against the supernatural.

I do not raise my hand.

23
Eggs Over Squeezy

Corryn

"Listen, cuties. I have to step out of la cabine for just a moment. Try not to get into too much trouble while I'm gone!"

Cherry turns on her heel and does a jaunty cheerleader step, almost kicking herself in the rear end. And she's out the door. We wait for a second to make sure she's out of earshot and then let out a collective groan.

"Ooh la la, la cabeeeen," Hairspray says, giggling.

"You said one too many *la*s," says Ew. "It's ooh la la, not ooh la la la."

Braids agrees, shaking her head ruefully. "Too many las."

"No," I say. "That was right. Two las for ooh la la and one la for la cabine. The last la just means 'the.' This is stupid. Why are we having a Frenching lesson? Who am I, Madame Anderson?"

Everyone laughs at the word "Frenching," which I should have seen coming.

"Ew," says Ew.

"What else are we going to do all night?" Braids asks. "We're stuck in here like a bunch of sweaty pigs in a pen."

"That more accurately describes the boys' cabin," Ew says.

"It's not exactly *in*accurate here," Hairspray says, gesturing broadly at the mess among us.

Everyone starts straightening up. I mean, *I* don't, but I feel the collective stink eye, so I decide to participate. With my foot, I scoop a dirty shirt off the floor that has, I think, been there since day one. I kick it up into the air and almost but don't quite catch it. Ugh, who cares? It's hot and it's late and we're bored. The air feels too close.

"You know what else we could do?" I say in a whisper. "We could follow you-know-who." I gesture toward the cabine door with my head.

"Seriously?" Ew asks. "You're not worried about you-know-what?"

"Well, duh," I say. "That's why I want to follow her!"

"I'm up for it," Hairspray says. "What's the worst that could happen?"

"You do *not* want the answer to that," Ew says, and okay, she's right. There are definite gaps in the old memory reel. But there's strength in numbers, right? And we have two operatives recording at all times now. I gave Ew the Day-Glo-pink notepad, and she hasn't let it leave her side. Operation Floppy Woppy, full speed ahead.

And you know what? Something rotten is still totally, like, afoot around here, and if Tez is going to go all goo-goo-faced over Chipper Chip and pretend that everything's fine, then I guess it's up to me and the B Team to figure it out before we all get eaten.

"What if she comes back while we're not here?" Ew asks.

"Let's not go and pretend we did," Braids suggests. "Can't we just play truth or dare?"

"Sure," Hairspray says. "We can play truth or dare if *you* promise to tell us the *truth* about what happened to you that night with the lake."

Direct. I like it.

"No problem," Braids says with a shrug. "I'll just choose dare."

"Fine. I *dare* you to tell us what happened that night with the lake," Hairspray says. (Whoa. Did Hairspray just discover a heretofore unknown loophole in truth or dare? Proper. Also, did Tez subliminally teach me what "heretofore" means and how to use it? Dude, maybe I'm better off without him. He's turning me into a dweebo.)

"Staying alive is daring enough, and I don't want to know the truth," Ew says.

"I dare you to stay out of the lake," Braids says. "I dare you to stay alive."

"I dare you to . . . I dare you to ask the Winch where she got her super smoky camp bathing suit," Hairspray says. I laugh.

"Oh, that's easy," I say. "I have the same one. I just forgot it at home. My parents are sending it. Should be here any day."

"I realllllllly do hope the mail gets here soon," Hairspray says. She looks really sad. Like, sadder than when she was considering dying at the bottom of the lake. Her hair is limp, and she squints at me in dismay.

"What are you waiting on?" I ask. "Jonesing for Doritos that bad?"

She looks down at her feet, purses her lips. "I lost a contact lens," she says finally.

"So what?" Braids says. "Big whoop."

"I—I'm kind of blind without them?" Hairspray says. "I've been just going with one for the past day and a half. It's giving me a headache."

"That does sound bad," I say. "Are they sending you your glasses?"

"Are they sending you an eye patch?" Ew teases.

"Yeah," Braids says, swinging her arms like a pirate. "Arrrrr they?"

"Shut up!" Hairspray says. "And no—they're sending me a new contact. Glasses, I have."

"Oh," I say with a shrug. "Why don't you just wear those, then?"

"Because they're nerd-city," Hairspray says.

"Who cares?" I say. "This isn't a fashion show at the mall. Knees has been wearing the same socks for the whole summer, and they were gross to begin with."

And with that, Hairspray reaches into the bottom of the barrel bag at the foot of her bed. She roots around in there for a moment and then retrieves a pink eyeglasses case. Immediately, she shoves it back into the bag. "No, I can't!" she squeals.

"Seriously," I say. "How bad can they be? Gotta be better than walking around like a cyclops. Take out that other lens, and let's see the magic."

"Magic isn't exactly what I'd call it. Nope."

"I don't think so!" Braids hops up, swipes Hairspray's bag, and retrieves the case with a cackle. Hairspray tries to tackle her, but she misses.

Braids tosses the case to Ew like a football. Ew catches it and flips it to me like a game of hot potato.

"Nooooo!" Spray yells, and dives for me. I hold the case behind my back so she can't get to it. I pass it quickly back and forth from hand to hand then pretend to toss it back to Ew. Braids doesn't fall for it. Funny, that move always works on my neighbor's golden retriever.

But I don't give in. I just sit on the glasses. They're in a hard case, so they're safe. Hail the almighty power of the butt!

"Fine," she says finally. "Just give them to me, and I'll put them on. I don't want them to get broken, or I'll be totally blind."

"You promise?" I say.

"Yes," she sniffs. I hand over the case, and she slowly opens it. She takes out the glasses and puts them on, and oh my Winch.

They are *huge*. Somehow, they manage to be tall and wide and thick all at the same time. It makes her look like Scooter from the Muppets. But much, much worse.

"Ohh, hey, that's . . ."

"Not too . . . uh . . ."

"Really . . . nice. Just . . . nice."

"I told you!" Hairspray yowls, and pulls them off her face. "They're awful!"

"Listen, you're gonna need both eyes!" Ew says. "Especially if we're going to see where Cherry goes when she thinks we're being perfect cabine cuties."

"For real?" I ask. I thought they just . . . weren't interested.

I guess I was wrong!

"I love the taste of danger in the morning," Braids says, then dares anybody to point out that it's not morning right now.

Hairspray jumps up and starts for the door. "Heck yeah! Let's get to doing some Nancy Drew-ing! The time is right for some late-night clue-ing!"

A smile pulls at the corners of my mouth. I make a note to consider upgrading this bunk to the A Team.

* * *

So the four of us—me, Braids, Hairspray, and Ew—head out into the forest. Poor Hairspray. Her mighty hairdo has been flattened by time, grime, and lack of Aqua Net. And now her contact lens fiasco means she's wearing what really do have to be the world's worst glasses.

It's like we have a whole new camper in our midst. And not a happy one. I decide it's up to me to keep her spirits up—though let's be honest: we're all a little scared. How dumb are we, sneaking around after a proven bunny killer like Cherry? Pretty stupid, but we're doing it anyway! And that means keeping up morale!

"Hey, Hairspray," I say, half whispering, "what's worse than finding a worm in your apple?"

"Ew," says, well, you know.

Gamely, Hairspray asks, "What?"

"Finding *half* a worm."

There are more *ew*s and some *gross*es and one "barf me out" for good measure. But voilà, Hairspray's not thinking about her glasses anymore, is she? I'm a tactical genius.

"What are we even looking for out here?" Braids asks as we begin to skulk out into the night, like prowling prowlers on the prowl.

"We'll know it when we see it," I say. Specifically, I suspect we'll see more proof that Cherry is evil and she's out doing evil things. And this time, we're going to document it. Oh hey! That reminds me!

"Ew!" I shout-whisper. "Bring your camera!"

"Nine steps ahead of you, Quinn-ski," she says, pointing with both thumbs to the camera hanging around her neck. It's technically just one step, but whatever.

"I'm not the best at shooting in low light," she says. "The flash on this thing is kind of—" She adjusts something on the camera and the flash goes off, a bright blast of white light. It was pointed right at Hairspray, and she does not appreciate it.

"Oh my gosh, please tell me you did not just take my picture!"

"I didn't!" Ew promises. "It's just the flash on this thing. It goes off at random. . . ." And then the flash lights up again, this time pointed right at Braids.

"Oh, my eyes!" Braids whines, and for some reason, this strikes us as really funny. Probably because she says "eyes" like "ay-eeeees." We snorf-laugh and guffaw all over the place.

"Be quiet," Ew says. "This is supposed to be a covert mission."

"You're the one lightin' up the sky like it's the Fourth of Ju-ly," Hairspray says. She says it in a funny accent for some reason, and so we're giggling even harder.

"Oh, my *eyes!*" Braids says again, and we're officially over the edge, lost in the giggleweeds.

"We are really bad at sneaking around, you guys," I say. "Try to keep it down." We all take a much-needed deep breath and try to plan out a route.

"Okay, which direction should we go in?" Hairspray asks.

"Which way did she slither off to last time?" I ask.

"I think east?" Ew says without much confidence.

"I don't know which way is east," Hairspray says.

"Camp has failed you," Braids says. "You have failed camp."

"I didn't come here to learn directions," Hairspray says.

"Why did you come here?"

"It's because it's always been a dream of mine to die in a scenic forest setting," she says. We crack up again. I'm really seeing Spray in a whole new light this evening.

"I'll tell you what I came here to do," I say. "I came here to drink bug juice and murderface vampire devils. And I'm all out of bug juice."

This time, Ew only has to look at me. We have this psychic connection now. I can tell just by staring at her that, in her mind, she just said, Ew.

And now we're off.

We march through the woods, on our way toward the lake but trying to avoid the main pathways. I'm a little nervous about getting stuck in the forest but feel like there is no way all four of us will get taken. Right? The ants go marching two by two. Hurrah.

After a few minutes of walking in relative quiet (broken by the occasional "oh, my eyes!"), Ew's flash randomly goes off again and this time isn't pointed at anyone's face. It's pointed off into the shrubbery, where it surprises all of us by reflecting off . . . something. Something big and bright and round and white and what the?

"Did you see that?" Hairspray asks.

"Oh, my eyes," Braids says.

"I'm serious," Hairspray says. "Something is over there."

"And that's why I'm over here," Ew says.

"Is it . . . alive?" I ask. "Did anyone bring a flash-light?"

"Just a flash," Ew says.

"Well, flash it over here," I say.

She does, and I crouch closer to . . . whatever this is. Ew keeps clicking the flash so I'm just getting strobes of it—it's like searching for a contact lens at a disco. It's very disconcerting and kind of giving me a headache. But it's enough to get the picture.

"It looks like . . . ," Braids says.

"A nest," we all say at once. It definitely seems to be some sort of a nest—with twigs and eggs in it and everything. But what kind of eggs? A nest of what?

"Big deal," Hairspray says. "They're eggs. From birds. Egg birds."

"On the ground?" I say.

"Bird nests can be on the ground," she says. "That's where some egg birds, like, prefer it."

"Aren't they usually in, you know, trees?" Braids says. She has a point. "And not so . . . huge?" The eggs really are big. Like the size of an actual football—or a Chihuahua.

"Birds can be big. Like, what's his name, Big Bird," Hairspray says.

"Hate to break it to you, but this ain't *Sesame Street*," I say.

"Uh, guys? There's something else that lays eggs besides birds," Braids says.

"What's that?" Ew asks.

Braids gulps. "Snakes."

Something about the word sends a giant chill through my entire body. Cherry turns snakey and . . . Oh, wait a minute. The snakes. Me and Ew keep seeing them, all over the place. But except for my counselor, I'm not *afraid* of the things. I even wore Bart Richter's boa constrictor around my shoulders once.

"Ew! Are they moving?" Ew hides behind her fingers.

Now that my eyes have adjusted to the dark, I can see the nest more clearly.

"Yes," I say. But they're not rolling, like you'd expect an egg to. They're more like pulsating. Throbbing. Beating like a human heart. Or the heart of something else. "And . . . listen closely. Do you hear that?"

The eggs are nastily pulsing and . . . unless I'm mistaken . . . *humming.* We all listen closely, the muted sound of the unmoving air, the quiet, quiet night underscored by a gentle, eggy thrum.

It sounds like a whisper. *Az. Azz. Ast.*

They swell. There's a crackling, cracking noise. One of the eggs swells more; a faint green glow surrounds it. Underneath the thin bready skin, something thrashes.

Holding out an arm, like my mom does when she hits the brakes too hard, I back my team up. Yeah, that's right. My team.

"Look out. I think that one's gonna pop," I say.

And then, with a blast, it does.

24
Whatever's Out There Wants In

Tez

Something terrifying is happening.

All five of us sit up at once—even Chip is alarmed. A high-pitched sound rips through the night. It doesn't stop. It just gets louder. Nostrils reaches for the flashlight he keeps under his pillow. It's one of the big chunky ones—perfect for flooding our cabin with light, and if need be, for cracking somebody, or something, on the head.

Chip stands up, pointing at the four of us. "Now, you all stay right where you are."

He creeps toward the door—oh, the insufficient door! Sure, the wood-slat one is closed over the screen, but they're both just locked with hooks! Even a swift kick from me would (probably) render them useless.

I roll to my feet, trying to straighten out my shoulder so my arm isn't completely unusable. Bowl Cut must feel vulnerable, too, because he snakes a pair of dirty shorts out of his laundry to pull over his tighty-whities.

Knees is the only one who seems calm. Then I realize, that's probably only because he's crammed back into the corner of a top bunk and he has a tennis racket as a shield.

"What *is* that?" Nostrils whispers.

Chip waves a hand at us, which is counselor for *shhhh*.

Closer, the screaming comes. It's not one voice, I realize. It's more. Almost harmonizing in evil. The sound tears through the trees and echoes into the darkness. It's impossible to tell which way it's coming from. Only that it's getting closer . . . and closer. . . .

CRACK!

Something throws itself against our door! The screen rattles helplessly. We all jump. Another chorus of screams rises up. It pierces through us. It's like ice needles in our ears. The door rattles again. Whatever's out there wants in here, badly. I should have listened more closely when Corryn told me about Cherry at the

213

boathouse. I should have done a lot of—

CRASH!

The screaming coalesces into one voice. It's ragged, high-pitched. The sound makes my skin crawl. Whatever's out there wants in here. Even though Chip is pressed against the door, I'm not sure he can stop it. I'm not sure anything can!

Lightning flashes outside.

There's a whine, a keening sound like a—

Wait.

It whines. It whines like a Canon Speedlite 133D! I jump to my feet and throw myself toward Chip. Catching his shoulder, I say, "It's the girls! It's Ew and Corryn!"

Through the door, we hear Braids say, "Oh, my eyes."

Then Corryn says, "Just knock on it, dummies!"

Relief bursts through the cabin like a water balloon exploding on the ground. We don't know *why* the screaming, but now, at least, we know the *who*. And it's mostly stopped, so Knees cautiously slides to the edge of his bunk, while Nostrils points his flashlight at the door.

Chip starts to smile. "A good old cabin raid. Now

that's the kind of camp spirit and fun I'm looking for!"

And with that, he unlatches the hooks and opens our doors.

Three girls from Oak Camp stand there, bunched together. And there's a newcomer, too, with straggly blond hair and giant pink owl glasses. I was just thinking about how weird it is that no one around here wears glasses.

"How now?" Chip says jauntily to the girls. "What can I do for you?"

They mutter among themselves, then Corryn says, "We need Tez."

Me? I look back at my cabinmates. They all wear identical dubious expressions. Nostrils can raise one eyebrow so far, it disappears beneath his bangs. Impressive.

"Actually," Ew says, her hands on her hips, "we need everybody."

With a knowing smile, Chip nods. "I see. Well. I tell you what. I'm going to take a little dipsy doodle down to the latrines. I estimate I'll be gone for five minutes. I sure hope when I get back that there aren't any girls in this cabin."

"There won't be," Corryn promises. She yanks the

door open like she owns the place and waits for Chip to walk out. She stares at his back as he goes, her eyes narrowed. I'm not sure what she's expecting to see, but when Chip estimates he'll be gone, he usually comes right in on the wire.

Ew, Braids, and the new girl spill into the cabin. They're all talking at the same time. And, at the same time, Nostrils, Knees, and Bowl Cut are trying to figure out where they should be, now that there are girls all over our cabin. They fill up the space like shaving cream. A little dab of Ew goes a long way.

"We followed Cherry," Ew finally says, her voice rising from the pack.

I turn, and Corryn walks in to stand beside me. She says, "And we found something."

"Why are you following Cherry?" Nostrils asks, obviously a little behind on everything since he still chugs bug juice like it's going out of style.

Nostrils gives the new girl a once-over. In the weirdest voice I've ever heard, he says, "And where did *you* come from, mama?"

"Ew!" shouts Ew. And Braids. And the new girl, who suddenly sounds very familiar.

"Hairspray?" I ask tentatively.

"What?"

The new girl whips around, glaring at me, well, owlishly. Her glasses are so round. And so pink. There's even a little gradient of pink at the top and bottom of the lenses. I can't make out the metallic charm on one side, but I think it's safe to say, it's likely to be a unicorn or a butterfly. I don't know why she's wearing them *now*, but I can see why she doesn't wear them usually. They're the opposite of the cool-girl-with-big-hair aura she puts out.

Holding up my hands, I say, "Nothing. I like your spectacles."

Knees snorts. "Spectacles," he repeats.

"Why did we even come here?" Braids demands, frustrated.

"Ugh," Hairspray adds, and sits right down on Nostrils' bunk. He turns a funny shade of gray—probably in the light, it's green, but you really can't tell that with only one flashlight illuminating the cabin.

Ew walks to the back of the cabin and turns to face us all. Clinging to the camera around her neck, she says, "We have a *big* problem. We found a nest."

Hanging on her every word, Bowl Cut almost falls out of his bunk leaning toward her. The motion startles

Ew, and the whole cabin bursts with blinding light. Everybody's talking again, all at the same time.

Screwing my eyes closed, I turn away from Ew in case there's another case of accidental flash-itis and say, "Okay, okay, everybody be quiet! You followed Cherry and found a nest and *what*?"

"You have to come look," Corryn says. "It was full of mega gross-out eggs, like the gnarliest you've ever seen. They were big and fat and squishy, and they—"

"HUMMED!" Ew fills in.

"And moved! Like they were . . . breathing or something!"

"And then one exploded!"

Knees leans in, captivated. "What came out?"

Corryn shakes her head. "Something gooey. We didn't stick around to find out!"

Horrified, I try to dig through my limited egg-related knowledge, but I come up short. "Were they wet?"

Suddenly, Braids twists to look at me, so fast, I'm afraid her head might go all the way around. "Boy, what is wrong with you?"

Corryn defends me. "He's doing his encyclopedia thing. Just go with it. Not wet, Tez. At least, they didn't look wet."

"They looked *pulsey*," Ew says.

I'm still not sure what that means, but if it's a nest and they're not wet, it narrows things down a little. Dry, pulsey, hummy, explodey . . . Okay, I'm ignoring the humming part, because it makes no sense. Also, the exploding part. File those under Camp Sweetwater Anomalies, Part 482.

I ask, "Were they leathery?"

"Nobody *touched* them," Hairspray says. She's instantly unmistakable when she talks. It's like a mean girl got trapped in a book girl's body. Which, considering where we are, probably isn't out of the question. "And when one *exploded* on us, we ran."

"The eggs pulsed," I say. "So they were soft."

Corryn storms into the middle of the cabin. She waves her arms like she has to clear the air. "Look, it was a big bundle of nasty, and stuff moved in them, and they hummed. I heard them humming. Those eggs weren't right!"

Raising a hand, Bowl Cut asks, bewildered, "Why didn't you stick around to find out what came out?"

"Uh, because we didn't want to get murderfaced by egg monsters! The goo smelled like armpit farts!"

The boys look at each other briefly. All of their faces

read, "Armpit farts have a smell?" But I recognize the look on Corryn's face—she means business, and she's gonna kill one of my bunkmates if we don't stay on target.

Cautiously, I step closer to Corryn, notebook in hand. "Do you think they're related to the Mechants? The French dudes who cursed the lake?"

Corryn slumps. "I don't know, Tez. The eggs weren't wearing little berets!"

My chest is tight, full of anxiety and pollen and dust and frustration. Things seemed so much clearer last time. We had the ghosts to guide us; they helped us figure out what we needed to do. Now, we're here on our own, yelling about undulating ova of unknown origin!

Finally, Bowl Cut scoots closer to the edge of the bed. I feel like he's actually moving closer to Ew, but I can't prove that. Clearing his throat, he says, "Okay, look. Something hinky is probably going on around here."

"It's *definitely* going on," Ew interrupts.

"You followed Cherry, but you found weird eggs. So probably, those are *her* eggs and she almost caught you looking at the nest."

"Hold on here," Nostrils says, waving the flashlight

under his face. "Why are we just accepting this, huh? Cherry's *laying eggs in the woods*? Come on! This is all crazy. This is, like, movie stuff."

Bowl Cut shrugs. "Do you have a better explanation . . . ?"

"The Winch!" Corryn shouts, and turns to Ew. "Please tell me you remember. Tell me you remember the Winch wee in the woods."

The cabin goes quiet, all eyes on Ew. I think it's fair to say we're all confused at this moment. Knees continues to clutch his racket, and Hairspray is trying to make that face of shunning she does. It just doesn't work as well with super flat hair and pink, sparkly spectacles.

Slowly, Ew nods her head. "I . . . yeah, I think I do. But we thought she was—"

"Doing a one," Corryn says. "Peeing in the woods. I know. Gross. But what if she was . . . you know, cluck cluck, *ba-gawk*?"

Braids briefly closes her eyes, like she's praying for patience. "Chip's coming back any time now, but we need to have a meeting. Nature hike, tomorrow."

Nostrils spreads his hands out. "For WHAT?"

Just then, Bowl Cut does something that breaks everybody in the cabin. I know my mouth drops. I feel like I can smell the smoke coming out of Knees' brain. Hairspray and Braids turn into horrified statues, and Corryn bugs her eyes out. None of us can believe it.

Bowl Cut reaches over and holds Ew's hand!

Then, while we're all stunned, he says, "Braids is right. Meeting tomorrow. Because if we keep acting like there's nothing wrong, it'll be too late to save ourselves." He looks to Ew with a slightly gooey expression. "Or anyone else."

I glance at Corryn and gulp.

25
Dead, Silence

Corryn

The next day, our cabin group plays get lost in the woods on purpose.

We're *supposed* to be appreciating nature and taking notes so we can make a book of camp memories. Instead, we take advantage of Cherry's weird disappearances, and Dipster Chipster's willingness to let us off leash. He hasn't been here long enough to know the woods like we do.

So we get ourselves good and away from everybody else, in a clearing not far from the archery ranges. Yep, that's right, we infiltrate the senior side of the lake. All the better to blow you off, Chippy!

The seating options are thin, so there's a lot of aimless shuffling going on. Nostrils throws a fierce kick and takes off a chunk of tree. It goes flying and whacks Hairspray. Good thing she's wearing glasses the size of greenhouses. He could have taken an eye out.

"Oh my god," Hairspray says, turning so Braids can de-bark her, "You guys are such *children*."

"We're all the same age," Knees points out.

I clear my throat, which just makes Knees clear his, so he can hock a loogey into the woods. A chorus of disgust rises from Hairspray, Ew, and Braids. Since they got such a good reaction, Nostrils and Knees go directly into loogey-hock mode. It's like a phlegm-off as the sound of throats grinding fills the woods. I could probably out-hork them all, but we're not out here to play games!

I stand and raise my voice to cut through the gargling. "Knock it off, you knuckleheads! This is important!"

Tez smiles and gives me a thumbs-up. I can't explain it, but it feels good that we're on the same page again. Sort of. I'm still not sure how much he's just going along and how much he believes. But the important part is that he's here and we're making plans.

The gargling trails off, but that's mostly because Ew

and Braids have turned their attention back to Hair-spray and the nugget of bark lodged in her slumped, unsprayed tangle of hair.

Braids huffs, "Look, *Bubbles*, this *is* important."

"I'll tell you what," I say. "If you find a dancing chupacabra in there, you get the floor. Let me know if it happens."

Tez says, "Okay, since Bowl Cut called this meeting, I think he should start. We should go over the evidence we have and determine the inferences we can make. . . ."

Rising to his feet, Bowl Cut looks at each and every one of us. "Here's my deal. I keep having dreams about the lake. Like, there's something in it that wants us."

"He didn't tell anybody, because he thought it was just weirdness," Ew says, looking toward Bowl Cut, her big green eyes taking him in, in all his pasty, bald glory. "But he told me. And I've been having dreams, too. I told Corryn all about them."

I puff up, pointing at her. "She did!"

"But I forgot them after they started making us swim. And Bubbles can't remember what happened in the woods after it tried to eat her," Ew says, pointing back at me.

Real slow, like he's drawing his firing irons in the

Old West, Tez half raises his hand and says, "Corryn and I have been keeping journals. Because there's a gap in my memory, too."

"And I started keeping one, too," Ew says.

Is it my imagination, or did Tez just flinch? No time for that. We have limited time for this meeting, so we need to get cracking. I lay it out as plain as I can!

"They took away the showers so we *have* to get in the lake, and they took away our water at mealtimes so we *have* to drink the bug juice—"

Nostrils interrupts. "I don't have to drink it. I love to drink it."

"Would you love to drink it," Tez asks, "if I told you I saw them mixing it up with water straight out of the lake?"

"The lake where the diaper babies pee!" I exclaim.

Knees mutters as he looks at the sky, "Not *just* the diaper babies."

Gag me. Seriously, just gag me with a spoon. My stomach lurches, but I hold it in.

"So, this is what we got. Eeeeeverybody saw the ghosts we freed, yeah? Since then, we have all new counselors, and we have written proof that the water is making people forget things or just be"—I give Nostrils the stink eye—"dumber than usual."

Ew interjects, "And we have two people having bad dreams about the lake wanting us. And two people who have had run-ins with Cherry, or whatever she turns into when we're out in the woods. And what happened to you in the lake, Braids?"

She's a stone wall. "Nothing."

"Uh-huh," I say. "Just like *nothing* happened to me when the forest tried to eat me, and when the Winch dosed me with steam heat action!"

There are murmurs all around. Yes! They're getting it! I add, "Again—all the old counselors are gone. Just, poof. Where did they go?"

"*And* Mrs. Winchelhauser is suddenly everywhere," Tez adds.

Yes! The kid is getting back into the game. Thank Pete Rose; I was starting to lose hope!

He goes on, "Plus, she stopped Chief Wolpaw from talking to us."

"Which makes me wonder, *why did he want to talk to us, anyway?*" I ask out loud. "He was looking for me, and she just dunked him in the lake instead. This place is teeming with evil, you guys!"

Me, Ew, Bowlie, and Tez, are kind of faced off with

Nostrils, Knees, Hairspray, and Braids. They all look skeptical, in their own ways. Braids crosses her arms over her chest, while Hairspray lifts her chin. Nostrils narrows his eyes at us, while Knees . . . Well, Knees is doing mini karate chops.

"It's gonna take more than us," I say, gesturing at the believers. "Whatever's coming is . . . it's big. Bigger than the bone pit. Bigger than the spirits of the ghost girls."

"And it's gotta be stopped," Ew says.

Bowl Cut nods. "By us."

Tez is quiet for a moment. Then he says, "Mrs. Winchelhauser is the one who wrote out the stuff for color war. I think—if something's going to happen—it's going to be then. It's gonna be the whole camp."

Come on, you guys. Come on! I look from face to face. My brain wills them to get with the program. I kinda wanna punch some sense into them, but I don't think that will work here. They have to come around on their own. They have to see it. They have to *believe*.

Just then, something moves. Out in the shadows. Fast. Like a rabbit. But too tall. Too pale.

Everyone around me is still blabbering, and not about the things they should be blabbering about.

Tez, at least, notices me looking away. He stands next to me and peers into the tangle of trees around us—just in time to notice the overpowering *nothing*.

The forest itself, normally so full of noise, is suddenly quiet—no birdsong, no animal rustling, no laughs and shouts from other campers playing Get Lost in the Woods. It's just silence.

Dead silence.

"What did you see?" Tez asks quietly.

"I—I'm not sure," I say.

We both stare hard into empty space. Ew and Bowl Cut come to stand next to us, and they look into the trees as well. The problem is, there's nothing there.

Now that I think about it, I can't even say that I *saw* something. It was more like a sense. A feeling vivid enough that it created a flash of sight and sound.

Another streak hisses through the woods behind us.

Ew whips around. She drops Bowl Cut's hand and takes a step toward the woods. "Was it that?"

"Yeah," I say. My chest tightens, my guts squirming like Jell-O in a plastic bag. The silence presses in. Like the rest of the world just doesn't exist anymore. Like we're all alone with whatever that was.

Like we're in serious danger.

The rest of our cabinmates go quiet. Hairspray and Braids sort of clutch each other. Nostrils and Knees sit back to back, their eyes wide. In the middle of our circle, Bowl Cut puts his hand on Ew's shoulder. They're the ones who suffered the most. They're the ones who already believe.

The trees tremble; the thing—this pale streak that sounds like a razor sizzling through paper—cuts closer.

"What was that?" Braids asks.

Hairspray whispers, "This is stupid. I want to go back."

Branches break. Closer now. A cold wind streaks into the clearing. The sun is bright today, but it suddenly feels like winter. The cold steals our breath. Aches in our bones. Our breath frosts in the air, and I wave my hands.

This isn't like the last time something like this happened—the time in a bonfire Tez and I had visions of campers swallowed alive by monstrous forces beyond our control.

This doesn't feel like a vision.

It feels like a threat.

The streaks come faster. Now there's two—three! They're a blur. There's a whisper in the . . . I want to say wind, but it's *inside* me. The voice echoes along my tendons and my veins. It pumps through my heart and pounds in my ears.

Come.

In slow motion, Knees and Nostrils rise to their feet. Braids stands and helps Hairspray up. They shiver, their lips faintly blue. At once, they all turn west. Toward camp. Toward the lake. There's this frosty, glazed look in their eyes. And even though Ew and Bowl Cut seem to turn, they fight it. Their eyes turn to us.

"It's happening again," Ew says.

Come.

An invisible touch pulls at me. It's like a chain in my chest being hauled by impossibly strong arms. I resist, but it hurts. My breath dies in my throat; I can't pull it in. Push it out. I can't speak or turn or anything. All I can do is fight back, until another voice rings out—

"Well, there y'all are! I was looking everywhere!"

The cold shatters. The impossible pull toward the lake falls away. Nostrils hits the ground, confused by the way gravity suddenly betrays him.

We all turn toward the owner of that particular voice: the one, the only, Dipstick Chipstick. Whose face is already red from having to march out here to find us. I hope he popped a squat and wiped with some poison ivy.

"I bet your books are going to spill over with memories," he says, panting. "But you have wandered way out of bounds. We need to get back. Pronto. Soup's on!"

I feel Tez slump in relief. I shoot him a look. Chip seems to have somehow, maybe rescued us. But we know *something* just happened. And I'll eat my hat if Chip's not a part of it.

We march back to the Great Hall. One by one, the unbelievers slip closer to us and say, "I'm in."

Excellent. We have a team. Soon, we'll have a plan.

The evil in this camp is going *down*.

26
A Tall Frosty Glass of Elmer's

Corryn

"And with that, you will find that making tissue-paper stained glass is fun and easy!" says Winnie the art counselor. "Do you have any questions?"

Knees slowly raises his hand and squeaks out, "Whyyyyyyyyyyyyy?" His voice sounds like someone squeezing a balloon at the neck and letting the air squeal out. Winnie gives him a nasty look.

She's one of the nice counselors here, usually smiling and wearing brightly colored, tie-dyed everything. It's always a relief to see her. She's a nice, regular person among all the identical Revenge of the Preppies robots.

Of course, Winnie might be one of the nice ones,

but! Art teachers do not like being asked why. Perhaps because there is no good answer.

I am really not in the mood for making stained glass out of tissue paper myself. I'm not even in the mood to make real stained-glass windows! There's really no way out of it, though. It's not like you can fake a sprained ankle to get out of art.

Örn, the tennis counselor, thinks I've sprained both my ankles, I've had tennis elbow, tennis knee, all the tennis parts. I guess I could claim to have sprained my glue hand. But no, Winnie's too smart. She would probably not fall for that. So here I sit.

"I wanna get out of here and go look at them eggs," I tell Tez. "I was dreaming of omelets all night."

"Seriously," Tez says. "You think I want to sit here making a replica of Saint Vitus with those Unidentified Egglike Objects humming it up in the woods?"

I have no idea what Saint Vitus is, but U.E.O. makes me laugh. Guffaw, actually. Tez looks very proud of himself. He sits up a little taller.

"You usually love arts and crafts," I say. "You're a lean, mean lanyard machine."

"True, but this craft in particular sucks," he says. He turns to me and shows me his hand. He's covered in glue, fingertips to wrists. Glue-soaked strips of tissue paper stick to his palm. There is somehow none on the construction paper that is supposed to be the future home of the stained-glass glory of Saint Vitus or whatever.

"Winnie is going to be so disappointed," I say. "No beads for you."

"Mine is still better than Knees', though," Tez says, and he's not wrong.

I look over at Knees' "art project" and see that it's literally a pool of glue on the picnic table. That's it. Just glue. A big old pond of Elmer's. He looks very proud of himself. Maybe he'll drink it. Lord knows it's hot, and we're all thirsty.

Winnie raises an eyebrow, almost says something but doesn't, then moves on down the picnic table to survey the rest of the mushy tissue-paper piles. Actually, one or two of them look pretty nice. Hairspray's is looking pretty much like a real church masterpiece. Some people, man.

"I just realized something!" Nostrils yells out. "Connect-the-dots books were scamming us. I pay you and still do all the work! Connect your own dots! Am I right?"

"That kid has taken one too many hits from the water guns," Braids says, shaking her head.

Ew slides a little closer to me. "But he has a point about connecting the dots. Something big and bad is going to happen. Therefore, dot to dot, what's the picture, you know? What are we facing? And what are we gonna do about it?"

"Good question," I say.

Bowl Cut, who has the right idea, cuts out blocks of tissue paper and just lets them drop onto the glue. The no-touch method. I admit, I wish I'd thought of it. He reaches for another color and says, "We have to get other people in on this."

Peeling glue off her fingertips, Hairspray says, "Like who?"

Tez makes a quavery sound, then says, "I spend a lot of time with the Bantam campers."

What the what? I give Tez a look. "They're diaper babies. They still believe in the monster under the bed."

"Which is a good thing," Tez says defensively, "since there actually are monsters at Camp Murderface. Under the bed and elsewhere."

Knees interrupts. "Me and Nostrils do archery with

some of the Elm Camp kids. We could probably get them in on it."

Holding up her hands, Ew raises her voice slightly. "We have to figure out what 'it' is before we get people in on it."

"She's right," I say, "And it's probably not gonna be easy, because the whole point of color war is to beat the other camps. They're naturally going to be suspicious of us. They're going to think we're trying to outflank them before it even starts."

Bowl Cut cuts another stack of confetti. "I think first, we arm ourselves. Whatever's coming, we need to be ready."

Finally looking up from her extremely perfect stained-glass picture, Hairspray says, "Nostrils and Knees can get some bows and arrows. And me and Braids found a stash we can probably use."

I frown. "A stash of what?"

With a shrug, Hairspray says, "Fireworks. Stuff like that. They're in the rifle range storage."

"Uh," Nostrils says, aggrieved, "and this is the first we're hearing of it?"

Knees clutches his chest. "You kept news of *explosives*

from us? Wounded. Seriously."

Dismissing both of them, Braids says, "We needed to know they'd still be there when we came back. So, yeah. Radio silence."

Tez straightens and claps his hands on the table. "All right, you four are in charge of pilfering weapons, including fireworks. And if you see anything else that might be useful, grab that, too. There's a hollow under our cabin you can put them in."

"I think you should tell Bantam Camp," Bowl Cut says. "I have a sister their age. Trust me, they can do serious damage when they're let loose."

Ew raises her hand briefly, then goes ahead and talks. "If we're going to be working together, we should have a name."

I roll my eyes. "How about the Knuckleheads?"

Tez practically vibrates before he throws in his suggestion. That's how you know it's gonna be extra dweeby. "How about the Locards? He was a famous detective in France that—"

"Nope," I say. "This whole place is cursed because of the Mechants, who came here and messed with the native people. France is evil."

"You can't say an entire country is evil," Hairspray says, carefully smearing a layer of glue on the back of her hand. "Your weird French guys are evil. But France is awesome. They have croissants there."

Bowl Cut begs to differ. "They have croissants at the grocery store, too. That doesn't make it France."

This discussion is going off the rails. I slap my hand down, which is a mistake, because now I have more paper glued to my skin than I do on my project. "We're the Murderfaces. Got it?"

"I mean, duh," Braids says, backing me up. "What else would we be?"

Now that we have a name, my juices are flowing. More than a name. We have a group. A whole posse of people on *our* side. It's, like, miraculous.

Bowl Cut says, "Okay, these two girls in Elm Camp got in trouble for using their radio time to talk about some guy named Matt Dillon—"

Hairspray collapses into Braids. "Sooooo cute."

"He's no Tom Cruise," Knees says.

A frustrated Bowl Cut presses on. "Cherry said the tower is busted. But if that's so, how would anyone know about the Matt Dillon incident? We need to find out if that's true. And if it's not, figure out how to use the tower to our advantage. Does anybody here know anything about radio towers?"

There's a long silence when people look at Tez, waiting for him to say something. Weirdly enough, he doesn't. But Braids raises her hand. "My dad is into CBs and ham radios."

Suddenly, Knees stands to attention. "I'm into building stuff."

"Okay," I say. "You guys are gonna be on radio tower duty. Me and Tez are gonna sneak into town, and we'll get what we can from the library. The second thing we need to do is—"

"Wait," Bowl Cut says. "Why are you going to sneak?"

You know what? I'm about to tell them Tez and I can handle this on our own, because they're clearly not as smart as I thought.

No. Wait. I gotta lead. Patiently. So, P A T I E N T L Y, I say, "Because we are not allowed to leave camp?"

Bowl Cut sort of shake-nods his head. "Yuh-huh. There are sign-ups at the Great Hall. Volunteers to help with the grocery pickup. You ride into town with the counselors and help them get all the milk and food and stuff."

"Since *when*?" Corryn demands.

"Since always." Bowl Cut shrugs. "It's right next to the other volunteer sheets: Trash Pickup Team, Kitchen Helpers, Latrine Cleaners—"

This time, Hairspray and Braids both say, "Ew!"

Ew agrees. "Seriously."

I, on the other hand, am kinda mad. All of the work me and Tez put into stowing away in the back of the van a couple of weeks ago, and we could have just added our names to a *list*. "Thought that handbook you memorized told you *everything* about camp, Tez."

When that kid shrugs, he looks like a raw turkey. I'm just saying.

Taking a deep breath, I collect myself. "All right. We'll *volunteer* to go into town. We'll get some books about the radio station so we can boost its signal."

Rubbing a hand over the downy ginger stubble on his head, Bowl Cut says, "And maybe you can try to talk to the furry policeman, too. He wanted to tell you something. You could find out what."

"Wow, Bowlie. Good thought," Tez tells him.

Okay, then. We're officially a squad. The A Team. A lean, mean mission machine, and we're gonna make this camp safe for all of camper kind!

And you know what? I love it when a plan comes together!

27
Patient Pants

Tez

It's shamefully easy to sign up for grocery duty.

Corryn signed us up after dinner last night. And now, while everybody else goes to breakfast, we walk down to the parking lot together. No sneaking, no lying, nothing. It's the easiest thing in the world, and I can't believe I didn't know about it last time.

I feel the urge to apologize to Corryn, but she's in her own world. Rubbing her hands together, she mutters about snakes and vampire devils. I keep my eyes on my feet and keep moving. What else can I do?

Örn Odinson, our tennis instructor, waits for us at

the bottom of the hill. His tennis whites are blinding, the full morning sun lighting him up like a menorah on day eight. He's so tan, he's leathery. When he shuffles back and forth, you can actually hear his legs rasping together.

"It's about time," he says, tapping on his watch. "I have to be back for class by nine!"

I tap my own watch. "It's seven forty-three. We're here early."

Örn makes a grunting sound—the same one he makes when he serves, actually. He paces away from us, which is fine by me. Last time we left camp, Örn's eyes went black, and he tried to crush Corryn's hand as he delivered a message of doom. Slightly annoyed Örn is entirely preferable to possessed-by-evil Örn.

"He's starting to look like beef jerky," Corryn observes, accurately.

I agree, and then I turn when I hear footsteps behind us. It's Chip! He didn't mention being on this trip when we were getting ready this morning. Cool!

Oh, wait. Corryn's not going to like this. Excitement to nausea in 3.5 seconds.

"Good morning, lady and lads!"

Corryn groans. "Great." Then mutters, "I'll good morning *you*."

"It's about time!" Örn shouts at him. He jumps in the van like the asphalt turned to lava. The rest of us pile in, Chip taking the passenger seat. Corryn and I settle in the way back. Örn starts up the big old shuttle van, and she chugs and coughs to life. We roll down the long driveway, turning onto the main road to Fan du Lac, the little town just outside of camp.

"Well, it sure is nice to have some familiar faces this morning," Chip says, craning around to look at us. "I love seeing the spirit of service flowing through you!"

Corryn opens her mouth.

"Don't," I warn her, before something sarcastic comes out. "We're on a mission. Focus on the mission."

Plastering on a grimace, Corryn says out loud, "It sure has been a long time since I was in a car! Isn't it weird the way we get used to things? 'Course, this van smells like old farts!"

Chip is amused. "You're always welcome to roll down a window, Bubbles!"

But she can't. The van windows are these little weird contraptions where you can only pop them open like an inch. But Corryn's stubborn. She opens the window a crack and sticks her nose out.

It turns out that Örn, even though he was in a hurry just moments ago, drives *very* slowly. I rarely pay attention to things like that. I like to read in cars—it makes the time fly—but even I can tell that Örn is navigating the road to Fan du Lac like, as they say, a grandma.

"Come on, man. Gas is the one on the right!" Corryn says, pulling her nose out the window to make sure Örn hears her. In response, he turns up the radio.

Slumping beside me, Corryn crosses her arms over her chest. "It's like they have no idea we're trying to save the camp from utter destruction."

"Shhh," I say. "You'll blow our cover. Or something. You'll definitely reveal something that's secret."

"Van," she says. "Van van van."

"Are you going somewhere with this?" I ask.

"Van. Such a weird word, you know? Say it: van, van, van."

"Van," I say. The more we say it, the less it makes sense, I admit.

"It's like Von only not," she says. "I've always liked a good Von. You know what? I'm going to make my last name Von Quinn. Hello, I'm Corryn Von Quinn."

"You can't just add a Von," I tell her. "It's reserved for German noblemen."

"*You're* a German nobleman!"

"Thank you," I say. "I'll take that as a compliment. Also, Van is Dut—"

"Is that ein bug?" Corryn asks me in a fake German accent. Then she pokes me in the ribs, right in the ticklish spot. I laugh and squirm, and this only encourages her. She rains more pokes down on me as she says, "Ein bug, ein bug, ein bug."

Örn whips his head around and yells, "Would you two nerds shut your heads? I love this song!"

"I think there's a better way to ask for—" Chip starts, but Örn cuts him off by turning the radio up even louder. I never took Örn for a big pop radio guy, but there you go. He's really rocking out to something about a jitterbug and dancing all night.

Slumping in our seat, just slightly below eye level for Örn, Corryn and I start giggling again. By the time the song comes to an end, we are in town. Örn finds a spot in the lot just outside the grocery store and slams the van into park.

"Get out," he growls.

"Yessir," I say with a half-hearted salute. We have arrived.

"Okay," Örn says. "I got this shopping list, so do you want to divide it up or stick together or . . . ?"

"I have to scoot off for a quick errand for Mrs. Winchelhauser," Chip says.

"Come on, man," Örn says. He throws his hands up in disgust. "That's what you said last time! I ended up carrying all the stuff myself!"

"To be fair, you decided to shop before I got back from—" Chip says, then cuts himself off. It's strange, the way his eyes dart to me and Corryn. He continues, "My *personal* errand. Now, if you'll just put on your patient pants . . ."

"Yeah!" Corryn chimes in. "Slap on some patient pants, man!"

Örn looks like he wants to murder her. Almost like she's the ball, he's the racket, and he's down thirty-love. I tense up because we need to draw as little attention to ourselves as possible.

"Uh, what she means to say, Örn, sir," I say, "is that we, too, have to scoot off for a quick errand. In fact, we could accompany Chip and—"

"No, that's fine," Chip says. "I need to fly solo on this mission, sport." He places his hand on my shoulder. It's warm and solid and completely genial. A smile leaps to my face. And I smile on, despite Corryn's sour expression. Chip is one of the good guys. She'll see.

"Are you sure?" I ask, just to be sure.

There aren't words for the expression on Corryn's face now. It's twisted up so tight, it looks like her features are spiraling in a kaleidoscope.

Very precisely, Chip says, "I know you want to nip off to the library, and I'm turning a blind eye. Let me take care of my business, and I'll let you take care of yours."

Örn looks like he's about to grow a racket in one hand, just so he can smash it on the ground. *"What about the groceries?"*

"Patient-pants," Chip says, and he stares at Örn real hard. And something in that look makes Örn back down. Not just back down but retreat! I turn my attention to Chip, but he's just standing there, pleasant as can be.

Retying the arms of the sweater around his shoulders, Chip smiles at me and Corryn. "All right, CL, Bubbles . . . enjoy your trip to the library. And don't be late. We have to get back to camp in time for swim fun!"

I feel Corryn radiating with anger beside me. Why can't she see that Chip's just as trapped at Camp Sweetwater as we are? In a way, with this mission, we're saving him, too.

28
Legitimate Research Purposes

Corryn

We walk into the library and find it buzzing with half the kids of Fan du Lac.

Little kids run around with plastic Slinkies and handfuls of Play-Doh; kids our age huddle in the stacks with Pixy Stix. They down the sugar with sneaky sips, their eyes darting with suspicion.

I grab Tez back at the last second, and a rubber bouncy ball flies past the place where Tez's head was. "You can thank me later for saving your life," I tell him as we make our way past the summer reading club prizes gone mad.

We found the history of Camp Sweetwater here,

and thankfully, there is no Grody the Party Clown in here the way there was last time. Let's just say I still have nightmares. And it wasn't because of the mystery of the Sweetwater Three.

Mr. Ferdle the librarian is at the desk—he's a nice guy. He's shagged out a little bit since the last time we were here. His goofy chin beard is bushy, and he traded his dress shirt and tie for a bright blue T-shirt that says, "1983 Summer Reading Stars." Also, there are a bunch of shooting stars on it. Bold.

"Hello," Mr. Ferdle says with curiosity. Does he recognize us? Probably not; we were only here once. His smile doesn't falter. "How may I help you today?"

"Hi, yes," Tez says. "Do you have books on radio repair?"

"Oh, wow, a couple of fellow ham heads," Ferdle says.

"Who are you calling lunch meat heads?" I growl.

"No, no, not the food. Ham radio?" he says. "You know, the kind of radio you can build and broadcast from home."

"Oh yeah. No, that's not what we're doing," I say. "It's not from home. It's from camp."

Tez looks like he's just about to explode. What is his deal? Oh . . . whoopsie. Was I not supposed to mention camp? Well, the truth is out now. We're a couple of campers off the grocery path, noodling around in the library. And hey, if anybody asks, we have Chipster Dorkwad III's permission to be here.

"Soooo," Mr. Ferdle says. "You guys are from Sweetwater, huh?

"Yes," Tez says, and spills his guts. "We're the weekly errand helpers. Our tennis instructor is getting groceries, our counselor is running an errand, and here we are, getting books to help improve the radio at camp. This time, we're here for legitimate purposes."

"But you weren't before?"

Even though Tez is usually as smooth as chunky peanut butter, he shakes his head and doesn't stutter or blush or anything. "No. But we're really excited to be back at the library. The one in camp is still closed."

Mr. Ferdle takes that all in. There's so much truth going around right now, even I'm almost dizzy. Has Tez been practicing his lines? Is he actively developing the necessary sneakitude to pull off a heist? The tiny lump of my heart grows three sizes.

This conversation, however, is getting frustrating. Because Mr. Ferdle says, "So you two are doing the radio from camp?"

Wow, he's a really swift one, this librarian.

"YES," I say loudly, maybe too loud for a library, but it's not getting through his thick librarian skull. Are they usually this slow? I hope Tez doesn't become a librarian. I'll have to get a turtle translator to keep up.

For a second, Mr. Ferdle scratches his chin beard, then breaks into a big smile. He points at us with a double finger-gun salute. "Murderface Radio," he says.

Wait, what? I think.

"Wait, what?" Tez says.

"I listen to you!" Ferdle chirps.

"No way," I say.

"Way!"

"The camp radio doesn't broadcast past the lake," I tell him. "They were reeeeaally clear about that. It's because something is messed up with the radio tower. That's why we were hoping to find some books. . . ."

"Well, I don't know why they told you that, but it's just not true. I listen to it all the time. Love me some Lightfoot! And Katie and Violet in the morning aren't too bad either. They play a lot of Chicago."

"This is blowing my mind," I say.

Mr. Ferdle smiles. "Oh yeah, lots of folks in town listen to it. Why, just the other day I was talking to a big fan, a real big fan. Do you happen to know Chief Wolpaw?"

"The chief of police listens to me on the radio? This is crazy."

"Wait, are you DJ CQ?" Mr. Ferdle asks. "Your voice sounds familiar! 'This is Murderface Radio,' too funny. You guys have got some imagination!"

I am stunned into silence. I literally cannot think of a word. What are words? My brain is spinning like a squeaky hamster wheel filled with ghosts. Thankfully, Tez is quicker.

"You . . . know the chief?" he says. "Can you get him a message from us?"

"Sure," Mr. Ferdle says.

"Tell him this," Tez says. "Watch the Winch."

Ferdle furrows his brow. He gives Tez a very suspicious look. Kids probably mess with him, sometimes. Librarians have got to be skeptical. I get it. But Tez gives him a very serious look in return that says, *This ain't no joke, library man.*

"'Watch the Winch'?"

"Yes. Watch the Winch."

Mr. Ferdle hesitates. He strokes his chin beard once, furrowing his salt-and-pepper brows.

I don't like it when grown-ups get super thinky, and I say, "I mean, if it's a problem, you don't have to."

"It's not that. It's just"—he lowers his voice—"is everything . . . *okay* out there?"

The question knocks me back on my heels. Holy bejeezus. I forgot that, sometimes, real adults aren't out to get us. They aren't *all* our enemies. Should we tell him? Maybe yes. Then again, maybe no. One or the other. Pick one, Quinn!

"It's just . . . disconcerting that we found those remains this summer," Tez says smoothly, picking one for both of us. And wow, he really is getting good at semi-lying, for real. "And since we can't call for help if something happens, we thought . . . why not send a message on the radio?"

"Huh," Ferdle says, and strokes his chin again.

"And Mrs. Winchelhauser is a friend of his," Tez finishes. "So, we thought if he was worried about her, he'd, you know, come to help. If we needed it. Which we probably won't."

Ferdle hesitates again, then finally, slowly says,

"Okay, if it makes you feel better, I can tell him." Then he repeats, "Watch the Winch," back to Tez again, and they shake hands for some dumb reason. "I'll tell him to keep an ear out."

And even though I don't know what exactly Tez just accomplished, it's obvious he accomplished . . . something.

I just hope that something helps when the evil finally shows itself.

29
Mail Crime, Federal Jail Time

Tez

So the radio station *does* transmit beyond camp borders!

Chief Wolpaw can hear it! Which is probably why he came to camp to talk to Corryn! *And then*, Mrs. Winchelhauser used the lake power to stop him from talking to us! Evidence! Hard evidence that we're being cut off from the outside!

Hypothesis: likely!

As we step onto the sidewalk and into the morning light, I tell Corryn, "So, I have a thought. Before, it just seemed like maybe the mail was slow, or our parents got less interested in writing. But what if I was wrong?"

"I'm all ears," Corryn says with a faint grin. "Tell me about the time you were wrong, Tez."

I smile and say, "If Mrs. Winchelhauser wants us cut off from the outside world, she might have cut off the mail *on purpose*. I mean, I didn't write home about the bone pit, but I did allude to finding remains."

Corryn gapes at me. "You didn't!"

"I did," I say. "And other kids probably wrote about the police coming. That's a good way to get a lot of parents worried, right there. And yet, not a single parent has come to check things out or to take a kid back home. This is a sign that we're in big trouble."

"I would say the Snake Lady was the big sign that we were in trouble," Corryn says. "But all right. Let's say you're right. What can we do about it?"

With a flourish, I point down the street. The post office's blue-and-white sign is visible from here. Corryn acknowledges with a nod, and we head that way.

Waiting between two parking spaces, we check for traffic, then cross the street. I feel like I catch a glimpse of Corryn petting one of the parked cars, but I'm not sure. It seems like a weird thing to mention, but then she says, apropos of nothing, "Mustang. Beautiful, beautiful Mustang."

"Pinto," I reply, a little proud. "Another car named after a horse."

Corryn smiles and messes with my hair. "You're so weird, Tez."

As we walk, we pass a little diner. My stomach growls at the scent of bacon wafting on the air. We haven't had breakfast yet, and the picture window gives us an amazing view of temptation.

Corryn groans and bumps into me. "They have water *on every table*. I never thought I would miss water before. It's always been a big glass of cold nothing, but now it's something."

As I stand there, my mouth waters. It waters for *water*. It turns out, there is such a thing as too much juice. We're getting distracted, and we realize it at the same time. We drag ourselves away, and I say, "I know exactly what you mean."

"Oh, and look. Challah French toast, too," she adds. "That's *always* something. My dad makes that for special breakfasts, like for birthdays or the Fourth of July. . . ."

Pressing a hand against my rumbling stomach, I shoot her a plaintive look. "Please stop. You're killllllling me."

"With big fat pats of butter," Corryn says, taunting

me. "And maple syrup and powdered sugar and—"

"Stop!" I almost shout.

Corryn laughs and leans in to whisper, "And strawberries and whipped cream—"

"No," I say, hauling her into an alcove by a hair salon. "Stop, and look."

I nod meaningfully down the street, where Chip is pulling a wagon—a canvas-sided wagon that says US Postal Service on it—out of the building! There's a hunka hunka mail in there, as Corryn might say, if I hadn't just basically shushed her.

With a narrowing of her eyes, Corryn points out, "He ain't pulling that wagon back to the van, man."

A pit opens in my stomach. Tampering with the mail is a federal crime. "There's probably a good explanation for this."

"You just said the Winch might be stopping the mail. And good ol' Chapstick just told us he was doing an errand for *her*."

She's right. If Chip were just collecting it to bring back to camp, he'd be headed right for us. Instead, he whistles as he turns away from us and keeps on walking. His gait is jaunty. I almost expect him to jump up and click his heels.

Instead, he turns down a side street. The mail wagon rattles as he bumps it over the pavement. A box on top wobbles—it almost falls. My heart stutters a bit.

Even though we're a quarter of a block away, I know that's my *care* package! I know because my little sister, Hi, always decorates the outside of the box with stickers and drawings. That box is covered with futhark runes, which means she's studying Vikings these days—and with Lisa Frank unicorns, which means Nana sent her some money to spend.

"That's *mine*," I whisper at Corryn.

Reassuringly, Corryn whispers back, "We'll get it. Don't worry."

As soon as Chip and the wagon are completely out of sight, Corryn and I follow. Corryn's always a couple of steps ahead of me. But she looks back to make sure I'm still with her, and then at the corner, she stops. When I catch up, we both look slowly around the building.

Chip's out of sight, but the wagon is visible for a moment. It disappears behind the building. What the heck is he doing? Is he just wasting time so he doesn't have to help Örn?

That doesn't seem like him. He's all about teamwork

and camp family and being an exclamation point instead of a period. (It made sense when he said it. I still feel the general sentiment, although I'm also feeling some other stuff right now.)

Like confusion. And sadness. And anger. Every time I think there's something good at camp for me, it turns out to be a lie! Or a trick! Or . . . it's just not good. And that's not fair. My face is hot, and I stalk down the sidewalk toward a truth I probably don't want to know.

"Doesn't he *know* that tampering with the mail is a federal crime?" I ask Corryn.

She's pressed herself flat against the building and is walking against it—as if we're on a ledge.

Sometimes, I think the fact that we're dealing with really weird stuff on a daily, semidaily, even hourly basis isn't quite exciting enough for Corryn. I bet she wishes she had a bandolier and some grenades, and a white T-shirt covered in soot right about now. She looks at me significantly and says, "We're about to find out."

Very, very, *very* slowly, we peek around the corner.

Chip stands in the middle of, well, an alley, basically. There's room for a mail truck back here and a small dented dumpster. He stands next to the dumpster but seems careful not to touch it. Leaning down, he picks up a carton full of letters. The letters slide slickly against each other.

For a moment, it seems like Chip is just admiring them. Then he tosses the whole carton into the trash.

There's a tiny wasp nest in my throat. It grows and grows, buzzing and stinging. That's what it feels like when I'm trying not to burst into furious tears. My hands clench so tight, my nails dig into my palms. And I barely have any nails.

Another carton catches Chip's eye. He pulls it out, and in it are larger envelopes and small boxes. Probably little treats from home for people. Maybe money for the canteen that hasn't even opened. One of the boxes, pristine and shiny white, Chip raises to his ear. He shakes it—do I hear a jingle? Or am I imagining it? —then he tosses it over his shoulder like an old banana peel.

Into the dumpster that carton goes, then another full of letters. Finally, he reaches for the carton with my care package on top. He lifts that box, turning it to read the recipient. Maybe he'll realize what he's doing is wrong when he sees my name there.

He knows how much I've been missing letters and packages from home. I've told him as much during quiet time.

"Well, gosh darn it," Chip says as he reads my name. My heart soars. Then he gives the box a single shake—and it bursts into flames.

Corryn nearly falls into me. She realizes she's going to smoosh my slinged arm and manages to catch herself on the building. She's still kind of all over me, so I feel her breath when she hisses, "Now they're slinging *fire?*"

The flames lick up the side of my care package slowly. It darkens the stickers. The crayon decorations melt and run down the sides. And the whole time, Chip holds the blaze in his hands like it's a warm bowl of soup or something. Shadows and light play on his face, and for the first time, I really see what Corryn's been telling me all along.

Chip's *enjoying* this.

Chip *signed up* for this.

And the worst part. The one that makes it feel like the wasp nest in my throat is growing to fill up my whole chest:

Chip doesn't care about me, or anyone at camp, at all.

My body is fighting itself. Half of it wants to cry, and the other half wants to do anything except cry. The stuffy nose makes me sound like a dork, but I tell Corryn with all the fury and rage in my heart, "I want. To punch. His lights out!"

Softly, she says, "I know. But you can't fight that fight today, buddy. Come on."

No. I stay fixed in place. I have to see what happens. And what happens is, Chip tosses my burning box into the dumpster. A couple of shiny things spill out when he does. And then a *huge* gust of fire billows out of the trash. Blackened bits of paper blow out. Feathery, glowing embers float aloft on the wave of heat coming from the conflagration.

Chip doesn't laugh like the bad guys in movies do. He just gazes at his handiwork with a smile. The same sweet, excited, interested smile he gives me when I tell him about wolves in Ohio or that the atomic weight of oxygen is 15.99903.

I'm burning up inside, just like that mail. Corryn tugs me away from the scene. She says comforting-ish stuff, but I don't really hear it. All I can hear is blood pounding in my ears, and fury raging in my heart.

Chip's some kind of monster, obviously. But worse than that, he's a fraud and a liar.

And I'm the fool who fell for it.

30
I Told You So Radio

Corryn

As soon as the wheels of the van touch camp property, Tez and I pop open the door and book it. I *think* the van was stopped, but who can be sure? We just wanted *out* of there.

Örn might have yelled out the window at us about how we were supposed to be helping to carry the groceries and how that was the whole point of blah blah blah. Who cares? I'm done with Örn. Over it. And I am definitely done with Chip. DONE.

Beside me, Tez almost limps. He clutches his slinged arm to his stomach, his face a sickly shade of tannish-green. After Chip toodled out of the back alley, we rushed in. We tried to save something, anything, from the load of camp mail. Mostly, we failed. Chip incinerated it pretty good. Then the clerk yelled at us for wasting her time when we tried to report it.

Outside, Tez stood in betrayed silence as he turned over a slightly melted bag of sour plums—all that remained of his care package. He stuffed those inside his sling without a word. There were tears in his eyes— kid is taking this hard. I don't blame him. I really don't. He really built Chip up, so the fall was a hard-core, full-body, road-rash collapse.

"I'm not hungry anymore," Tez says.

My stomach barks furiously, but I'm not in charge here. "Okay, we'll skip breakfast."

"And I'm definitely not in the mood for aerobics."

What? Oh yeah, I forgot that's our first activity today: aerobics in the Rec Barn.

"*We are so totally attending aerobics!*" I shout, so as not to arouse suspicion. "*Because we both just really love aerobics!*"

We cut through the lawn by the parking lot to blend into camp life. "I sensed that about you," he says. "I know you want to get physicalllllll."

"Ugh. I hate that song," I say. At least he doesn't sing

269

the part about hearing your body talk. Which, what even does that mean? I can only imagine like a belly button with the power of speech. "Hellooooo!" from somewhere under your shirt. Gross.

"I have to conclude at this point," he whispers, "that every single one of the instructors and counselors and stuff at this camp are *not* on our side. If Chip can be evil, *anyone* can be, right?"

"Yeah," I say. "Too bad *no one* saw that coming."

Tez gives me a look I can only identify as *puppy who accidentally pooped in a bad place*. Miserably, he replies, "You were right about him. I deserve that."

"What? I didn't say anything," I say, holding my hands up to show that I am very innocent.

We're outside the Rec Barn, and the music within is audible, pumping through the thin walls. It is indeed the dumb song Tez was singing earlier. Way to be predictable, Winnie. I'm guessing aerobics has already started, and I'm guessing it's just as dumb as I thought it would be.

Tez balls his one hand into a fist and punches at the air. His other arm, in the sling, flaps like a mad chicken wing. "Gah, how stupid can I be? This goon flatters me and—and I fall for it hook, line, and sinker. I liked him so much, and he seemed like he liked me for real, and I couldn't see what was going on right in front of my stupid face. . . . I thought I was smart, but I guess not!"

"No, hey," I say. "You're plenty smart. Probably too much smart. But you're also human."

"That's the nicest thing anyone has ever said to me," he says.

I can't tell if he's kidding, so I continue. "It's okay. You're not perfect. *One* time you got *one* thing wrong. I know this might be a new experience for you, but it happens to all of us. Like, a lot."

Tez looks up at me, eyes shining. "That sounds a lot like 'I told you so,'" he says.

"No," I tell him. "If I was going to say, 'I told you so,' I'd just say it."

"Listen," he says. "I understand that you're trying to be nice. I also understand that the effort may cause you to sprain something inside your head. So, just get it out. Just go ahead and say it as many times as you want for . . ." He checks his watch. "One minute. Get it all out. Please. Just promise me that will be the end of it. Okay? Okay, go!"

Hey, well, now it would be cruel *not* to tell him, so I let it rip. I start to jump up and down and kick my legs and point at him and spin, spin, spin.

"I told you so!" I say. "I told you so. I told you Chip was evil, but you were like, 'Oh no, not my glorious Chipward, he calls us *lads*, and he's so cool,' and I TOLD YOU SO, I TOLD YOU SO. I mean, I full-on told you soooooo."

Too much? Oh well, there's no stopping me now. I put on my radio voice. "You're listening to I TOLD YOU SO RADIO, where we play all the hits, like 'I Told You So' by I Told You and the Soes.

"Oh, and here's some breaking news, President Reagan is having a meeting at the White House with AyaTOLDYOUSO Khomeini. . . . Now back to the hits." Then I start to sing and clap out the beat. "I don't know, but I've been told! Actually, I do know: you got told. Sound off! Told you!"

Beep beep. Tez's Casio sounds off the minute. "Aaand that concludes the longest sixty seconds of my life," Tez says, cutting me off, tapping the face of his wristwatch. "I guess we better get to the Rec Barn."

"Or," I say, "we can *skip*."

There's just something so unbearably dopey about aerobics, if you ask me. It's all about corny music and synchronized leg kicks. And leg warmers! What are they for? Why do they believe legs are inherently so cold? They already invented something to keep your legs warm, and they're called *pants*.

We swing open the heavy door to the Rec Barn and are hit with a humid wall. It's body odor, and the red paint on the walls and the acrid evil undertone of everything in this place.

Rows of happy campers stand arm's length apart. And leading everyone in this sweaty activity is . . . definitely not Winnie Shacklehoff. What the Hoff? I nudge Tez with my elbow and point my eyes in her direction. He looks back at me; his eyes go big. He mouths, "I knew it," or something like it.

I grab him by the good arm. Should we get out of here or . . . But Tez is already inching toward the front of the room. Is he in the thrall of some new evil?

"I always wanted to try aerobics," he says loudly. "I totally know this routine. I'm going to hop in real quick."

I don't know why Tez says he knows how to do this. The new counselor is mambo-march-step-changing her skinny booty all over the Rec Barn. Meanwhile, Tez is trip-trippy-tripptripping and trying not to fall into anyone else. While he struggles, I march my eyes at the new counselor. Who the heck is this person?

She's short and tanned and something about her facial structure, her coloring . . . There's nothing specifically wrong about her appearance—camp shirt, short shorts, tube socks—but it's unsettling. . . .

Then it hits me. Duh.

I'm not saying she's Cherry's clone, but if you told me they were cousins I'd believe you. Her hair is a little browner, her eyes a little wider. But they definitely came from the same tree. Or hatched from the same nest. The same snake nest.

Every single normal counselor—replaced. By an army of evil. I feel like I've been socked in the gut. I can't believe I was salivating over French toast just this morning. Now I don't think I ever want to eat again.

So if all the counselors get replaced and they want to suck the life out of the campers, when exactly do they . . . ?

Color war . . .

Oh no. Now, I really want to ralph all over this rancid-smelling pit they have the gall to call a Rec Barn. Color war is going to be a full-on massacre.

"Come on in, friends," the Not-Hoff says. She's decked out with sweatbands on her forehead and her wrists, because everybody knows you lose most of your sweat from your wrists. Not.

Planting her feet on the ground, she sticks her arms out like a zombie. But instead of shuffling toward us, looking for brains, she squats. Then stands. Then squats. Then stands.

"We're working our rears!" she shouts enthusiastically. "You should feel that pull in your derriere and all the way down your thighs. All the way to your knees. That's it, that's good, keep it coming. You can do it!"

Here's the thing. She hasn't met me. I probably can't do it and wouldn't even if I could. I stand there with my arms out, but I barely bend my knees.

"And now we're up!" Not-Hoff shouts, panting between words. "Lift those knees! Turn left! Let's go. Loving this sweat! Loving our bodies!"

I snicker, but I'm the only one. Because everybody else is actually *doing* this stuff. The whole room is bouncing and loving it and sweating, and here comes Tez, right in the middle of it!

"What the heck is all this about?" I say when he high-knees/stumbles in my general direction. "You're not supposed to be doing physical stuff. Also, you're the worst aerobics-er I've ever seen."

He puffs a dismissive breath out of the side of his mouth. "It's not exactly the Ironman Triathlon."

"But you're not supposed to—"

"It's aerobics, Corryn. It's for old ladies." Just to be careful, I guess, he puts two fingers to the side of his neck just under his jawbone to check his pulse. "I wanted to get a closer look at her."

"Guess what?" I say as the record player bops out its psychotic beat. "Her face is visible from here, too. And it's a real familiar one."

"Aimee? The new activity counselor?" asks Hairspray, who is shimmying up next to us after eavesdropping, apparently. "She looks just like Cherry, right?"

"Yes, because she practically is Cherry," says Braids, who keeps looking back up at Aimee so she doesn't miss a step. When Aimee calls it out, Braids reaches into the air in front of her and pretends to pull it back to her chest. Reach! And pull! Reach! And pull!

"Okay, yes," I say, then I change the subject to what's important around here. "Listen," I say. "We have big news."

"Aaand grapevine, 2-3-4!" shouts Aimee from the stage.

What happened to one?

"Okay, where are the rest of the Murderfaces?" I ask. My stomach turns 2-3-4. I have news for Aimee: there's no way I'm turning around and bending over to touch the ground. I don't trust these shorts to hide my underpants.

"Our new name is so rad," says Knees, clapping 2-3-4.

"You know it," says Hairspray, 2-3-4. They high-five and spin.

"Look," Tez says, "we can't trust anybody but us. Chip's one of them. He has crazy fire powers. He destroyed all of our mail, on Winchelhauser's order!"

When she hears that, Hairspray hulks out. Like, she really seems to get bigger as she sucks in all the stale air in the Rec Barn. "They *what*?"

"You heard me," Tez says. "That means, trust no one. Lips zipped around everybody over the age of sixteen, got it?"

1 and 2, and they all nod in time to the music. The change in Tez is visible. There's a grimness I haven't seen in a couple of weeks. And you know what? I hate that. I didn't want him to be oblivious. But it makes me ache seeing all that happiness going away. The Tezbot deserves better. That's all I'm saying.

Bowl Cut is breathing hard, his normally pasty face

bright red. "All right, then, what next?"

I swear the music keeps getting louder and louder. Does Uncanny Aimee have magic volume hands? Maybe she can volume-boost annoying pop songs with her mind, the way Chip can turn his hands into flame-throwers.

"Group meeting during mandatory swim!" I shout over the din.

The music is too loud to talk about it. Mouths are moving like it's a kung fu movie, but the only thing we hear is exercise-friendly synth beats.

Tez points at everybody, one by one. Thumbs-up? Yeah. A thumbs-up from everybody, so we're meeting during swim time. We'll all be together; that'll be the perfect time to tell them the plan.

Hopefully, that'll give me and Tez a chance to come up with one.

31
Hypnosis in the Boys' Room

Tez

Now that we know the only way we're getting a save from outside camp is through the radio station, that clarifies our options completely. Corryn and I hide in the latrines before swim to talk. On the boys' side.

"Because if a boy comes in the girls' room, it's creepy," Corryn says. "But if a girl comes in the boys' room, she probably has a good reason."

I don't question her judgment on this proclamation. My book on *Things I Know About Girls* is very, very short. It has only four headings: Mom, Sister, Corryn, Camp Girls. (I put Nana Jones and Mimi Williams under "Mom" and all my aunts under "Sister." Taxonomically efficient!)

Since there's no water to shower, and everybody changes for swimming in the cabins, the latrines are the ideal place to meet. The daddy longlegs aren't venomous, and the stink keeps lurkers away. Plus, we're supposed to go to them in pairs, so it doesn't raise any suspicion.

Corryn sits on the counter, and I lean against the wall in front of her. I can see the back of her head in the mirror. She can see me and the battered hand-towel case at my shoulder. It's not a dispenser. It just has one long cotton towel on a loop that everybody uses.

"We sent a message to Chief Wolpaw," I say, scratching an itchy shoulder on the wall. "And we know Mr. Ferdle is listening in to our radio station. He seemed pretty concerned. If stuff goes super south, we can get a message to him, too. We just have to code it."

"The problem is, we still don't know what's going to happen. Ew's dream wasn't really specific, you know? We're all just getting in the water."

"True," I say. "But! We didn't know what we would find when we went to the Mechants' Lodge on the other side of the lake in the middle of the night either. We just knew we had to go there." I fold my arms across my chest. "On the other hand, we fell into a ravenous bone pit and almost died, so maybe that's not a point in our favor."

Corryn swings her legs, leaning forward to peer at me. "Do you know what kills snakes?"

My face squinches up on its own. I catch a glance at myself in the mirror. Is that really what I look like when I'm thinking? "A garden shovel? A machete? They're not like werewolves; there's no silver bullet for battling giant human-snake hybrids."

"WRONG!" Corryn crows. Her smile is gotcha wide, and she shakes her shoulders in delight. "A mongoose. Mongeese? Mongooses kill snakes. Didn't anybody ever read you *Rikki-Tikki-Tavi*?"

Amused, I nod. "Fair enough, mongooses kill snakes. Do you happen to have one in your pocket?"

Our laughter breaks the seriousness for a moment. Outside, the sun must slip behind a cloud because the light in here dims. That, and the smell of a latrine, cuts the giddiness down by half.

"So, let's say that the crazy French vampire devils

still want souls. Or blood. They're real big on blood," Corryn muses. "They can't devour the whole camp. Somebody would notice."

Sadly, I point out, "Yeah, but by the time anyone *would* notice, we'd all be devoured."

"Okay, how does this grab you?" Corryn says, tossing her hair out of her eyes. "They're getting everybody numbed up and dumbed up with the water for a reason. You don't have to control breakfast, man. You just eat it. I think they're gonna keep most of us alive. For something."

A thorny little tendril blooms in my chest. The pain is real, but the prospects are existential. "Eat some and enslave the rest?"

Corryn touches her nose with the tip of her finger, then reaches out and flips my nose, too. Gently. She's gotten a lot better about Corryn-handling me in a way that's playful like she means it but painless, like I requested. My brain offers up a bloobly little acknowledgment of that, and those feelings are slightly kinda soppy.

But no time for soppy feelings now. Clapping my hands together, I say, "Okay. Eat some, enslave the rest. And color war seems to be reeeeeally important. So this is the plan."

"I'm all ears," Corryn says, sounding ready to jump in, in case my plan is dumb.

Trying not to take a deep breath, because the latrines are pretty pungent, I wave one hand. "We have today and most of tomorrow to finish collecting weapons and stuff. That's part one. Some bows and arrows, that big paddle they use to stir the bug juice from the kitchen, maybe trash can lids for shields . . ."

Corryn's listened for long enough. "We can probably snag a couple of shovels like we did before."

"Right. And then we can use Nature Encounter time to store that stuff in strategic locations."

"Maybe we should all have stomachaches at dinner so we can skip it," Corryn says, though her stomach literally groans in protest. "It's supposed to be soup and grilled cheese! They're probably making the soup with the water, and we need clear eyes and clear minds, soldier!"

I bark a little laugh. And I nod, "Fair. No eating anything that might have water in it." Missing out on grilled cheese would have been a hard sell, but we mostly ignore the thin tomato soup they serve with them, anyway.

Outside, the sun shifts again. The latrines darken.

There aren't any electric lights in there—it's ambient or nothing. It's one of the reasons that you're supposed to have a buddy.

Buddy One points a flashlight at the ceiling while Buddy Two does their business, and then they trade off. (Or, if you're in my cabin, Buddy One points the flashlight down in the pit or in your face or turns it off as soon as you get your pants down.)

Since it's daylight, neither of us has a flashlight. We just have to deal with the new shadows in the corners. Shadows that seem to creep from the outside in, which is impossible. A shiver rushes down the back of my neck. That's probably psychosomatic. In other words, I'm probably just imagining that. So, where were we?

Oh yeah.

"Okay, so we distribute the weapons. I taught Bantam Camp some things, just in case."

"What things?" Corryn asks.

I wave her off. "Not important. We need to get this plan down solid."

"Should we get other cabins in on this?" Corryn asks. She raises a hand to scratch the back of her head. "There's only eight of us, and we're down one arm."

I'm not sure why I'm so fascinated at the way Corryn's

fingers skim through her own hair. I can't stop watching, but fortunately, I can talk at the same time. "Better not. There's not enough time, and we don't know who we can trust."

"Yeah, there might be some Elm Camp garter snakes in disguise."

Gesturing between us, I agree. "It takes a while to catch up with this much cool."

"Fair, fair," Corryn says. Her fingers dig deeper. She's scratching now like she's digging for gold. Maybe she has a tick? "So we get all our stuff ready and we—"

Completely distracted now, I stare into the mirror. Corryn has pretty thick hair, I guess, but it's starting to look like her whole hand is buried in it. What the heck? She says my name, normal like, and I don't look away, but I do reply, "Wait for something to happen."

"And what if we all die?"

"Uh," I say. Is Corryn's hair getting darker?

Wait.

What did she just say to me?

"We're not going to die. We're ready this time. Readier, anyway. And there's more of us. We needed one guy to help us last time. Now we have six."

Corryn's voice sounds low and croaky. "What if it's

not enough?" Her hand disappears in a bad way. It looks like she's dug into her brain wrist-deep. Darker hair. It's darker—not because the light shifted. Because she's dug through her flesh, and she's bleeding.

"Corryn, stop," I say, and I go to grab her arm.

But when I do, her whole face comes into view. It bulges out. Her eyes are bloodshot and bruised and open so wide I can see the orbs of them. Her lips are purple and swollen. Her tongue lolls out, thick and fat like a slug.

No, no, no no no no no!

I yank on her arm, trying to pull it out of her head. The world around me is falling apart. I hear someone screaming as I try to put Corryn's head back together. The latrines grow darker around us. When I grab the hand towel, I leave dark handprints on it all the way around.

Whipping back to Corryn, I squeeze my eyes closed. *This isn't real, this is impossible, this isn't happening, we just have to get out.* Maybe I'm screaming that instead of thinking it. I just don't know. It takes all of my strength to pull Corryn off the counter.

Her body is heavy as lead. I crash into the wall with her against my chest. My feet slip on the floor. It's damp (with blood, oh no, it's Corryn's, it's—), and I start to sink under her.

My throat burns. I thought I was so smart. I thought we could take on some ancient evil!

"Don't be dead," I whimper, wrapping my arm around Corryn. Through tears, I look up as the light shifts again. A bright beam comes through the vents. It dances on the battered metal mirror. Then the mirror fogs up slowly, like someone's breathing on it.

A single line streaks through the fog. Something squeaks against the mirror, but it's nothing I can see. Only its track. It's hideously, terribly slow track that spells out:

SOON

"No!" I scream, wet and hot and sticky, and I don't want to think about what that is, I don't, I can't. "No, Corryn, no!"

Suddenly, everything resets.

Corryn's back on the sink counter, only now she's staring at me like I'm a total goob. Her face is perfectly normal. It's tanned and freckled, and her brown eyes are baffled but exactly where they should be. Sliding to her feet, she offers a hand to me. A clean, dry hand.

"Dude," Corryn says, hefting me to my feet. "You look like you saw a ghost."

I shake my head, then realize my knees are about to buckle. I throw my arms around her, hugging her tight to keep from hitting the ground.

"Worse," I tell her, squeezing her. It was an illusion. Or a hallucination. It's the same thing that happened to me in the infirmary the last time, when the building went wonky and the nurse turned into a . . . a thing. It wasn't real. *This* isn't real. Just the evil trying to psych me out.

Relief almost chokes me. Corryn is okay.

"O-kay, so now we hug a lot?" she asks, and she doesn't sound like she's thrilled at the prospect. Corryn's sort of stiff, but she does hold me up. As soon as I'm sure I won't flop on the ground, I take a deep breath and step back.

"Sorry. Sorry. I'm just glad you're okay."

"You're a weirdo," Corryn says fondly, pushing me toward the latrine exit. "And I'm more than okay. I'm *epic.*"

I don't tell her that, classically, epics don't end well for the heroes. Instead, I nod and agree, and I force myself to stare at the ground as we go. I'm afraid I'll see the worst-case scenario all over Corryn's face again, and I don't think I can handle that.

For the first time, I wonder if we're just delaying the inevitable. If the evil has been playing with us since the beginning. There's a very real possibility that we're the trapped mice and they're the bored cats, keeping us alive until it suits them. I'll never say it out loud, but . . .

Whatever we're up against, I'm not sure we can beat it.

32
An Extraordinary Feat

Corryn

"Okay, switch!" Ew yells.

And like a big dumb ballet, we do. The boys' cabin sloshes out of the lake, and the girls slosh in. We keep talking, to keep our heads as clear as possible. And we keep switching to keep our counselors out of our hair. So far, it's working!

The sad thing is, the weather is great! Sunny with a chance of vultures but great! It's warm but not too hot. It's bright but not blinding. . . . It's perfect weather to be outside. But instead of enjoying it, we're setting up for a war we don't even know if we can win.

"We need a complete inventory," Tez says. "That

way we can place everything effectively. All we can go on are Ew's dreams. So we should expect to be forced to the lake and then into it. Whatever's behind this—the Winch, evil French dudes, vampire devils—who knows for sure? All we know is that it's all leading us to the lake."

"Easy," Knees says. "We just drain the lake."

Nostrils laughs, and Knees looks a little hurt. Wow, way to step in it, dude. even *I* knew he was being sincere.

Hairspray dips her head back in the water. Her hair slicks over her shoulders when she rises back up, and Braids immediately reaches in and starts plaiting it. Braids says, "The fireworks are under our cabin, so we have those. We put some in each backpack."

Shuffling on the shore, Nostrils paces like a caged rabbit. He has too much energy and no way to blow it all off right now, so he's twitching with possibility. "I did a thing."

"What?" Bowl Cut asks. He stands in shin-deep water, as close to Ew as he can possibly get.

They're not even pretending to be just friends anymore. They sit together, they walk together, and even when we're shifting in and out of the lake to minimize its effects, Bowlie and Ew stick together. I'm tempted to yell, *JUST KISS*, at them. Buuut I didn't like it when they did it to me and Tez, so I'll just yell it in my heart.

Nostrils rubs his palms together, eyes shifty as he lowers his voice. "I stole the juice."

"What?" I ask. "And why?"

Drawing on the sand with his gnarly big toe, Nostrils says, "The cans of the bug juice powder. I went to snag that paddle, right? But the kitchen doors were wide open. Nobody was in there. And the mix was sitting right there! So I got both! The paddle and the juice!"

Excitement starts doing jumping jacks in my stomach. "Nuh-uh!"

"Uh-huh," he replies.

Thoughtful, Ew says, "That's going to tip them off."

Nostrils puffs up. "Nope. I left one can. They're just gonna think they ran out."

Tez starts to laugh. Like, a happy laugh, which is nice to hear. He claps his hands and says, "Nostrils, that was a stroke of genius! Well done!"

Knees must feel left out, because he chimes in, "I got bows and quivers! And the arrows to go in them."

"That reminds me," Braids says lazily. "You know all those firestarter things we made in Arts and Crafts?"

How could I forget? We got to wrap shaved wood in linen, put in a wick, and then coat the bundle in wax. It was even more boring than making lanyards. And the lanyards, at least, we got to keep. The firestarters, we weren't allowed to take out of the building. Like, what was the point?

"Well, I swiped them," Braids says. She's so casual, French-braiding all around Hairspray's head and discussing petty larceny. I love it! "And all that macramé twine. What if we need to tie somebody up?"

Holy spinnoli, my heart is singing love songs to these doofy goofs. They've been plotting and planning and breaking into every building in camp to get the stuff we need to fight this fight. I seriously want to bow down to all of them. But I won't because I don't want to get my face close to the water.

"This is all fantastic," Tez says. He looks around at us, one by one. "Now we have to assume that every counselor is compromised. They have powers, and we don't. We have to play this smart."

Ew's expression is dire as she chimes in. "Seriously. Do not get close to them. We've already seen them do some crazy stuff, and we still don't know what happened to Bubbles in the woods. Assume if they can see you, they can hurt you."

"And whatever you do," Tez says, "stay out of the water."

Knees interrupts, "What happens after?"

Puzzled, Tez says, "After we win? Um . . . finish camp, I guess."

"With no counselors?" Knees arches a brow. "How's that gonna work?"

"Bowl Cut's gonna send a message to the chief of police, and he's gonna figure it out for us." I shrug, because that's the best answer we've got. There's a grown-up cavalry out there. Yeah, it's just two old dudes, but the librarian knows everything, and Wolpaw is in charge of everything. It's a solid strategy.

The lukewarm water kissing my shins is getting warmer, like a bath. It feels really nice, actually. That warm feeling spreads all through me, but it feels incomplete. I should just sit down for a minute and—

"SWITCH!" Tez bellows, and grabs my arm. He pulls me to dry land and looks me over. "What's your name?"

"Corryn Quinn, Bubbles," I say dreamily. "DJ CQ on the mic."

Tez gives me a tiny pinch. So small, it feels like a bee sting. It still hurts. Then he says, "What were we just talking about?"

It takes me a moment. I roll my eyes all around, trying to wake up my hazy brain. Then suddenly, I remember. Dropping a hand on Tez's shoulder, I fix him in my gaze and I say, "Battle plans."

Relief washes over his tight face. "Good. Everybody? You saw how fast that happened. Sharp minds. Buddy system. Do not let the lake win."

Still a little fuzzy, I raise a fist to the sky. "Not today, lake!"

And when the sky replies with a rumble of thunder, we shudder.

Tez

It's an extraordinary feat of acting that I can be in the same cabin as Chip now.

Now that I know who he is—what he's done—I can barely look at his face. And really, is that even his face? Ew and Corryn said that Cherry transformed partway, that her mouth opened on a hinge to reveal giant fangs. And her eyes turned yellow with a slit of a pupil.

All we saw from Chip was fire spill from regular

human palms. Like that isn't enough! I edge away from him as we prepare for bed. The last night of sleep before color war starts.

"Now, you will all notice that you have tabards on your bunks," Chip says cheerfully, sweeping up the cabin floor as we change into pajamas. "All of Oak Camp will be wearing these—anybody in green will be your ally."

That's what Chip thinks. The lake has been calling us all summer, and there are only eight of us who realize that. Peeling off my T-shirt, I fold it neatly and put it in my cubby. Ordinarily, dirty clothes would go in my duffel bag. Not tonight. It's under this cabin right now, stuffed with supplies.

Carefully circling the feet of the bunks, Chip draws out dirt and dust bunnies, still talking. "You're going to meet up with the other Oakies at our designated bonfire and decide where to hide the flag. After that, it's going to be a heckuva fun day."

The four of us are remarkably quiet. Not me; I can spend extremely long periods in quietude (for example, in a library). The things that have happened to Bowl Cut have left him much more introspective. But Nostrils and Knees are unusually still, as well. They don't jockey for position. Knees is not trying to do a backflip from the frame of the bunk. They don't compete for the loudest burp. It's unnerving, and not just for me.

Chip stops sweeping. He leans on the top of the broom handle, looking around at us. "Now, call me kooky, but none of you are feeling the camp spirit tonight. What's the matter?"

Knees shrugs, melting his pomade in his hands before massaging it into his hair. It smells sweet and coconutty, almost like suntan lotion. "Nothing. We've got our heads in the game."

"Oh?"

Nostrils sprawls on his bunk. "Yep. Elm and the seniors are going down."

"You mean Orange and Blue," Chip corrects cheerfully.

There's lava in my stomach. It boils with Chip's every word. There he is, wearing that lying smile. All that lying *concern* in his voice. I look away when I sense he's about to turn to me. I pretend to straighten my cubby. I say, "We take competition very seriously."

Chip starts sweeping again, brushing in my direction. "It's supposed to be fun. And I wouldn't be doing my job if you all weren't having fun!"

The bunk creaks when Bowl Cut gets up. He

wanders in my direction, then reaches over my head to open his cubby. As he rummages, Bowl Cut says, "We take our *fun* seriously, too."

The pause after Bowl Cut says that is not significant. It's barely a blip. Other people might not have even noticed it. But it's there, just like the weight in the air.

"Okiedoke. Whatever crumbles your cookies, lads!"

Ducking around Bowl Cut, I climb up to my bunk. My sleeping bag is slick, and I skid right up against the wall. Chip had better not come any closer, that's all I have to say. I've never been a fan of violence, but my fist itches to punch him. Over and over, for every time he lied to me. A pop in the nose for every time he was a fake friend. And two or three punches for fooling me.

Also, I wish I could punch myself. I wasted so much time following Chip around like a dumb little pet—time I could have spent with Corryn. And another punch for being so credulous (the opposite of incredulous, which means, *Wow, I can't believe my nice new counselor turned out to be a snake in the grass.* Possibly literally.).

My stomach hurts. It twists into a hot, compact knot that just pulls and grinds in my gut. Above me, the roof of the cabin hunches like a vulture. It's dark up in the middle.

It's dark inside my head, too. My whole life, the one thing I had going for me was being smart. But when it really mattered, I was about as dumb as it gets.

"All right," Chip says, making himself sound rueful. "If everybody's ready to turn in, I guess I'll turn off the lights."

"Night," Bowl Cut says curtly.

Nostrils concurs with a grunt. Knees is a "whatever" man. And me? I answer with silence. Because I have nothing to say to Chip until I vanquish him.

And then it will be too late for words.

33
The Battle Begins

Corryn

Get up. Gear up. Shorts on, shirt on. Tabard on, check.

Socks on: pull 'em up, pull 'em up higher. Shoes on: tie 'em tight. Hands in fists ready to fight. Knuckle crack, hair tied back, I feel the fight song blaring on the stereo of my heart. *Ba da da da da da da daaaaaa*, let's go! Tonight, we fight.

But first: breakfast.

I meet the Murderfaces at the breakfast table and I'm ready to slap the drinks out of their hands. Then I realize it's just milk, and though, yes, milk has water in it, I don't think the cows were supping at Lake Sweetwater.

What if they were, though?

What if this water gets pumped into the town water supply? The state! The country! The evil flows like water and water flows everywhere. How far can one drop go? Does it matter how diluted it is? We can't take any chances!

Just to be safe I smack the milk out of Nostrils' hand.

"What the heck, Bubbles?" he says.

"We can't be too safe," I say, pounding the breakfast table like a general preparing for war. "Milk has water in it."

"Everything has water in it," Ew says. "People are like sixty percent water."

"Maybe you are," Knees says, waggling his eyebrows. "I'm one hundred percent sugar."

Barf. Now I'm really off my feed.

"Hey, here's something I'm wondering. Why doesn't anyone eat chicken for breakfast?" Nostrils says, grumpily recovered from losing his milk by poking at his scrambled eggs. "We eat chicken, like, all the time but never for breakfast. Is it because we already eat eggs for breakfast? Like, you can't eat chickens *and* eggs together because it's rude to the chickens?"

"What are you talking about?" Braids says.

"Chickens already gave us the eggs; haven't they done enough?" he says, waving his fork. He sounds really exasperated.

I slap the eggs off his fork. "Don't eat chicken. Don't eat eggs. Don't eat anything. They could make those eggs with water." No one is listening, so I repeat it. "Don't eat anything and don't drink anything."

"But I'm hungry," Hairspray says with a little whine.

"Good," I say. "Be hungry. Let the hunger fuel you."

"I'd rather have Cap'n Crunch fuel me," Knees says. "It's part of a nutritious breakfast."

Tez, who has been quiet until now, bursts to life. He says, "Corryn is right. We have to be cautious. One false move and we're not sitting with a participation trophy. We're *dead* underneath a pile of bones, forever!"

"Intense," Knees says.

"Today, it's war!" Tez says, pounding his fist on the sticky table. "The Battle for Camp Sweetwater begins!"

I see Örn eyeing us from across the room. Bowl Cut whispers at us, "You might want to tone it down so we don't get the attention-ay of the ounselors-cay."

We lower our voices to, if not quite whispers, then at least the normal level so we don't look like generals rallying the troops.

"Okay, guys, for real," I say. "We have to be on guard. Heads on a swivel! Beady eyed and bat eared! The danger is real. We know for sure that they killed three campers a whole bunch of years ago, and we're pretty sure they're going to kill more if we don't stop them."

"Gulp," says Nostrils.

"What we're going up against?" Tez says in a voice that resembles a growl. "They're. Not. People." His eyes are wildfire. He leans in and says, "Does everybody know where their supplies are?"

Nods all around the table.

"We don't know when or where this all starts," I tell them, "so be ready!"

"Awake!" Nostrils shouts.

Knees yells, "Alert!"

"ALIVE!" we all shout, and now everybody in the Great Hall is looking at us like we're weirdos. But they don't look at us for long. Outside, there's a scream. Then a couple of shouts. From here, I see a bunch of seniors rushing toward the lake.

THIS IS IT! FULL SPEED AHEAD!

Except the next sounds aren't carnage or unearthly voices. It's a bunch of regular people whooping with

303

excitement. Everybody in the Great Hall, us included, get up and rush toward the yells. The press of bodies feels dangerous, like an unstoppable wave. We spill onto the lawn between the Great Hall and the lake.

Now that we're outside, I see a thick circle of vultures over the middle of the lake. Up until now, it's been just four of them swooping and flapping along. But now, there's gotta be ten of them, easily. Even though the sky is a bright blue, the vultures darken it.

And there, beneath the center of the vulture-go-round, the lake bubbles. It gleams—it's too bright outside for glowing. But me and Tez, we've seen this before. When we rowed away from the bone pit, the lake glowed an eerie blue. It's happening again.

Then something breaks the water. A couple of people shriek. The anticipation is crazy thick. Everybody starts to murmur at once. It's like the crowd has one voice, and that voice is going, "What the what?!"

Pressing against Tez's side, I say, "What if it's time?"

Tez doesn't look at me. He's staring at the lake so hard, a little vein pops out at his temple. "What if it's *the vampire devils?*"

Nostrils drags a hand through his hair. "Oh dang. I

was really kinda hoping this was all a game, but look at that."

Oh, we're looking at it. The water foams in a ring on the surface of the lake. And then a blackwood tree rises up out of the center. Its wide spindly arms drip heavily with water. Blackwood. We've only found twigs of it, here and there. We burned it when we first got here and got the vision of the missing campers from way long ago! This is a whole tree made up of it—and it is massive.

And it's still moving. It glides up and up, and then the water breaks. A hump, followed by more trees and—

"It's an island," Ew says, clutching my shoulder with her tiny fingers.

Nostrils curses, and I agree with him. This is some horror-movie kind of stuff, and we're living in it. It takes only a minute for the entire island to rise out of the lake. It's *covered* with blackwood trees. The vultures swoop down, with their knobby wings and narrow necks. They perch in those trees. I swear—I swear to every god there ever was—that their eyes glow red.

Just the sight of it turns my stomach, and I've got a cast-iron stomach, according to my dad. I'll eat almost anything just to try it. And I'll eat anything if you give me a dollar. It all stays down, even if I ride the teacups three times after.

But this gags me. And not with a spoon.

The worst part is the sound they make. It's not that dinosaur screech you hear in Westerns when the buzzards show up. No. It's this low raspy growl. It sounds like . . . it sounds like . . .

Well, I can't say it with authority. But I think it's the same sound you'd hear if you were dragging a dead body across the floor.

34

Everything Is Terrible, and Nothing Is Good

Tez

We tried to get the rest of Oak Camp to let us guard the flag so we could be free to armor up at a moment's notice. (We didn't tell them that, but that was why.) Unfortunately, we were outvoted by Cabin Groups B and D. They put two girls from B on guard because they both have yellow belts in karate and two boys from D because they're in wrestling at school.

Fine. They picked people who were qualified to guard a flag, but come on! We need a win today! More accurately, we need *to* win today! I don't want to become, to borrow a phrase from Corryn, vampire chow. And I don't want anybody else to either!

And yet, it's feeling more and more inevitable. That new island in the lake is completely disconcerting. Every time I glance at it, my stomach flips upside down. The vultures hang in the trees; everything there seems to radiate darkness. And that shouldn't be possible, but there it is!

Despite the new and terrifying terrain in camp, color war battles on! The events are spread all over camp. Bright flags mark their locations. The seniors are already running an obstacle course under Day-Glo-orange flags.

My Bantams are climbing into burlap sacks underneath bright yellow banners. I wave to them, but they don't see me. Minefield waits for the counselor to look away and promptly climbs into Soft Shoes' bag with him.

My chest fills with a fierce anger. Those are *my* little guys over there, and they're in danger. Everyone is, but it seems especially unfair for them. They're just babies. They haven't even had peanut butter and chocolate-covered-banana sandwiches yet.

Oak keeps tromping toward our destination. Everybody in our cabin group is heading to our first field event like it's a walk to the gallows. BECAUSE IT IS.

ANYWAY.

When we arrive beneath the bright orange pennants, Aimee, from the Rec Barn, smiles so wide, you can see the shadows of her molars. Bouncing toward us, she claps her hands.

"All right, all right, all right, welcome to the . . . three-legged race!" she shouts with glee. "Let me count you—two, three, six, eighteen, twenty—okay! We'll have four heats so everybody can play! The winners move on to the next station! And the losers . . ."

Some kid from A makes a sad trombone sound: *wah wah*. Everyone around us laughs; Aimee does, too.

"The losers," she says after the giggles die down, "are going to wish they had worn their swimsuits, because you're getting *dunked*!"

Again, around us, people laugh. The Murderfaces share uneasy glances. But we have to participate. We don't know when evil plans to attack, so we have to stay in the thick of it. I wonder if my mom, back at home, would be proud of me for all this.

Probably not. She'd probably be scared out of her Reeboks if she found out how much action I'm seeing this summer. I'd be restricted to home, library, and museums for weeks, I think. My dad would agree with her. *You can't be irresponsible with your health, Tez*, he'd say.

But there's exactly eight of us against who knows what. The odds aren't in our favor, but we have to *try*. I move toward Corryn, so we can work together. She's the only one who knows I can't race for real. Between that and my sling, we're definitely going to lose. First guinea pigs into the water.

"Now, let's see," Aimee says. "I'm going to pair you up by size so no one gets hurt."

Corryn raises her hand. "Can we do it?"

Aimee's smile only grows. "Oh no. That would be wildly irresponsible of me! In fact, Bubbles, I'm going to pair you up with Bowl Cut."

They look at each other with undisguised horror. They don't move, so Aimee has to grab their arms and gently-not-so-gently pull them together. My stomach turns over again. I wonder what kind of evil Aimee is hiding beneath her preppy clone exterior. I wonder it hard while she ties Corryn's left leg to Bowl Cut's right.

"Um, ma'am," Hairspray says, "um, excuse me, but I'm the same height as Knees. That would be a good matchup."

Aimee eyes them both, a little too long. But then

she says, "Right you are!" Next, Nostrils gets lashed to Braids, which leaves me and Ew. And I will admit, I'm not the tallest guy in the room, but I am, at least, a little taller than her.

"Hmmm," Aimee says, looking at my sling, "Why don't you sit out, Chickenlips? I can pair Ew up with someone from the other cabins."

No! No way! We can't get separated!

Quickly, I pull the strap over my head. Valiantly, I don't wince when I free my arm from the sling. I toss it over my shoulder and move my arm around a little bit. Inside, it's grinding with crazy bursts of pain, but I keep it light with Aimee. "I'm all better, see?"

She regards me with suspicion. "I don't know. . . ."

"Seriously," I say, breaking into a cold, hard sweat as I lift my arm to prove it's fine. "I was still wearing it out of habit."

Corryn shoots me a look, along with a shake of her head. I know exactly what she's telling me. I need to quit being a dork and put my arm back in the sling. But I can't. I can't risk getting the Murderfaces separated. We're a team. No man left behind.

"All right," Aimee says, totally believing that it's okay for me to just ditch my medical device in the middle of a war. She has all the indifference of two British camp counselors set loose on an unsuspecting cabin group. "You and Ew it is!"

Miraculously, the Murderface team on each heat manages to win. I don't know how, I really don't. But somehow, we all come together to beat the pants off everybody in the three-legged race. That's probably not something to brag about in the civilian world, but at Camp Sweetwater, it totally is.

Panting as we untie ourselves, I watch as two more counselors I've never seen before collect the teams in last place for their dunking. They're laughing and bumping into each other, chattering with excitement.

They have no idea that, when they hit that water, they're going to get numb and dumb—easy pickings for the things that go bump in the night.

Or the vultures, who spread their ragged wings and watch in silence.

35
It's Time

Corryn

The sun is just beginning to set, painting the sky in ominous streaks of bloodred and flame orange.

And the fire for Oak Camp is already looking like it will be a good one, too. Probably not that hard to get her lit when one of your counselors happens to be Preppy Lord Pyro, scourge of camp mail everywhere. No wonder I always preferred Silver Surfer.

There are four roaring fires around the lake—one for us (Oak Camp), one for Elm, one for the Bantam babies, and one for the seniors. All around the lake—except for the horns at the far shore—bonfires blaze and gatherings gather.

All of a sudden, all I can think about is my dad. His goofy faces, and his Sunday morning pancake failures. An ache fills me. Now is not the time to get homesick, but I can't help it. What is it about incinerated wood that can make me so . . . emotional? It's not the smell, of course. It's the memories.

Bonfires mean camping, and camping means time together with my mom and dad in better days. Better days, man. Better days. I haven't thought about Mom and Dad in a while now. Their fights, the divorce . . . all of it seems like it happened to another person on another planet a million years ago.

Does that world even exist anymore, or is it gone forever? How am I even able to think of them, with everything going on? "Everything going on"—ha, what an understatement. What a way to describe *this*.

As I walk closer to our fire, little explosions ring out. I leap into a defensive stance . . . then stop when the girls from D Group give me a dirty look. Ugh. It was just popcorn. They should choose a less violent snack when tensions are so high. Or at least give a girl some warning.

In spite of the sounds, the popcorn smells good— people are happy, the air smells nice, and there's howls of laughter coming from the little ones. I hear someone yell, "Minefield!" and there is more laughter.

I decide to wait a bit to grab a seat by our fire, to see if I can find Tez with his Bantam buds. Walking down that way, I feel something pricking in the back of my brain. I don't know what it is. It really feels like there's a straight pin being poked right through my skull and into the brain meats. I just can't place it. Uneasy, I look around as I make my way down the hill.

I pass the Elmsters; it smells like they got hot dogs from somewhere. No fair. We never have delicious meat by-products at our fire. Shaking that off, I peel my eyes and look out for Tez.

And there he is—a horde of little ones chasing him around, throwing leaves at him. He's trying to flee but not so hard that they can't catch him. The little ones laugh *so hard*, somebody might need to check their diapers.

Tez is like 90 percent leaves at this point. When he shakes off his new coat, he's smiling like a goon at the littles. And when the littles crash into him, they get big happy hugs from him.

In spite of my state of high alert, I smile at the sight. Tez is slow, but he's kind and smart, and braver than anyone knows. Even though he was slow to get back on the defeating-evil wagon, he's been a good dude since the first moments of camp.

And you know what? I'd take half a Tez over a hundred BMX dweebs back at home.

"Hey, Tez," I call to him, after his last duckling runs back to their fire. "Are you coming or what?"

Shaking off the rest of the leaves, Tez starts toward me. His arm is back in the sling; I know he's hurting, man. He probably didn't take his pain medicine either. I don't like him being an arm down for the battle royale, but what can I do about it?

When he reaches me, he says, "Sorry. I had to talk to Minefield and Soft Shoes, and it turned into—" He waves a hand to fill in the rest.

"Yeah, I saw," I say with a grin. "You're a popular guy with the kindergarten set."

He blushes.

"So, the fire's already going."

Tez nods. "Yeah, I figured."

"They stacked the wood all stupid," I tell him, even though I have no idea how the wood was stacked.

"I figured Chip, or whoever he really is, had it covered."

Man, Tez is taking this hard. I knew he was, but for Tez, those are some fighting words. We walk up the hill together, passing through the other campers from other cabins. That pin in my brain is back. Slowly, I look around, and . . . Wait. I think I know what it is! I ask Tez, "Does it seem like we're down some people?"

"What do you mean?" he asks, but immediately surveys the area. "Huh. I don't see Side Pony Girl or Scruff. You know, that guy who thinks his beard is coming in?"

Yeah. Neither do I. In fact, by the time we arrive at the bonfire, I can name (sort of) at least ten kids who are missing. People are thin on the ground up in here. There's dancing and laughing and marshmallow roasting going on like everything's fine. And everything is *not* fine.

We walk up to Ew first, and I nudge her. "Hey. Is it just us, or do we have some missing campers?"

Standing together, we all study the people around us. It's not just me and Tez. Ew agrees there are people missing. And then she adds a piece we hadn't noticed.

"The losers," she says. "Not all of them, but look. Everybody that's here won at least one event."

Realization hits me in the head like a meteor. "They took them to the lake."

"And they never came back," Tez finishes.

DANG IT!

The battle has already started, and we didn't even know! We saw the losers being led off to the lake, but we just kept chucking on through our field day events. The evil started taking kids right out from under our noses! What kind of heroes are we?

"Where's Bowl Cut?" I ask. "He needs to get to the radio station—now. And we need to suit up!"

"I'll get Nostrils and Knees," Tez says. "You get Hairspray and Braids. And Ew, you go get Bowl Cut."

We split up, rounding the fire as fast as we can without arousing suspicion. This is easy for Tez, because he's just waddle-walking. I, however, have sudden adrenaline power! Because my body wants to go fast and my brain wants to slow down, I trip over my own dumb feet.

Panic explodes in me like fireworks. For a second, I feel like I'm going to fall into the blazing bonfire. Fortunately (?), I just hit the dirt, face-first. All the breath wooshes out of me. My stomach does that thing when you go high on the swings. Heat from the fire grows until it feels like my scalp will catch fire.

Suddenly, a hand grabs my arm. I look up. It's Cherry. Of course.

And it's Cherry wearing some stupid grim reaper robe. I don't know what that's about, but it seems a little too on the nose, as my dad would say.

Ugh, Cherry Cumberland, the lady snake herself, leader of the clones. As the fire hisses and spits, so does she. With her reddened cheeks peeking out just under the black robe, she says two words. "It's time."

There's laughter, maybe the kind of laughter that's less about something being funny and more about pretending not to be scared to death. Tight-jawed laughter. *Ahahaha haha. Ha.* Welp.

Here we go. Now or never, time to saddle up, rock and roll, let's get this show on the road. (How many phrases did Dad have for starting something? I'm realizing now, a lot.)

"Let's take a dip, Bubbles," Cherry says. I swear to dog, a little forked tongue flickers between her lips. "You could use a bath."

No no no no no! I struggle against her grip, but she's like iron. All I manage to do is swing around at the end of her grip. One bad wobble sends me perilously close to the fire. I'm not escaping at all; I'm trapped.

Chip appears beside Cherry, grinning his stupid, okily-dokily smile. "Need some help, baby sister?"

"Sure do, big brother!"

Without warning, Chip swings a leg. I crumple when he hits me in the back of the knees. He just did that! Like it was no big deal! And he grabs my feet, so now I'm strung up between the devil twins of Cabin Group A.

"SCRAMBLE!" I yell, signaling the crew. "SCRAMBLE. SCRAMBLE!"

"Shhhhhh," Cherry says. Or it could just be a hiss. She and Chip haul me down into the trees, their claw-like hands digging into my flesh. I hear water. We're headed to the lake, and my brain starts chanting, *Don't forget, don't forget, don't forget!*

Almost to the shore, Chip and Cherry are unstoppable. They shouldn't be able to move through the woods this fast. It's unnatural. My stomach curdles, and I squeeze my eyes closed. This is happening, I tell myself. And I have to remember it when I get out of the water.

Or if?

I scream, hot tears splashing in my eyes. A piercing whistle joins my cry. And then a bang. Chip, that faking faker, curses, and Cherry shrieks. She sounds kind of like the laser guns on Battlestar. Both of them drop me. *Whup!*

I roll over to look. Another sharp whistle rips through the air. The bang comes again, and I finally recognize the sound. Bottle rockets! Somebody's shooting Chip and Cherry with bottle rockets! I'm saved!

Then I realize: kids are running, falling. Counselors in robes drag them back to the fires. Bodies on the shore, all around the lake, sprawl helplessly, just like me. They scream and scream, and I do, too. It rips out of me, unexpectedly and high-pitched.

The moon hangs ominously above us, bright enough that I can make out colors. Bright enough that I can see—

The lake is red.

The lake . . . is blood.

36
Devilwood Rising

Tez

Stuffing matches into my pocket, I help Corryn to her feet. Gunpowder and smoke linger in the air. The smell is sharp and sweet, and it should remind me of the Fourth of July. But this isn't any parade. It's war.

"You okay?" I ask, pulling Corryn up with my good hand.

"Nope," she says, and points.

I turn in time to see Chip drop his grim reaper robe. At first, I think he's just pulling it off because he's smoldering from my bottle rocket attack. But no.

His chest bulges. His polo shirt swells. Tighter.

Tighter. The buttons pop like popcorn! The shirt splits down the middle. Shreds of teal cotton cling to reptilian skin. Green, overlapping scales run down his chest. His pressed khaki shorts peel off, to make room for his tail. HIS TAIL.

"Holy—"

"Joe Piscopoly," Corryn breathes.

Cherry slithers up next to him. I almost fall down from shock. She has a human head and human arms, but the rest of her is all cobra. For a moment, my brain feels glitchy and broken. Yes, we saw ghosts before. Yes, we got attacked by a library. But our counselors turning into naga before our eyes? IMPOSSIBLE.

"I sssseeee two cutiessssssss about to get brand-new attitudiesssssss," Cherry hisses.

Chip shakes his head, his eyes now bright green with slit pupils. "That'sss for sssure, sisssster!"

"Ssssoooooon," they intone together, "issssss nowwwwwww!"

Booms explode over the lake. The sound waves echo. They prickle the hair on the back of my neck. The night sounds like a single scream. One that claws through the woods and digs into our bones.

Corryn clamps a hand on the back of my neck and pushes me toward the woods. "Run, Tez. For real this time!"

I grab back with my good hand and yell the same thing. I'm not about to leave her behind, and I think she feels exactly the same way.

"Oh no you don't," Chip say. He rises on his tail and zooms right at us.

Corryn grabs a tree branch, long and flexible. She lets it go after we run past. It slaps snakeskin with a vicious snap. Chip yelps. We don't look back.

We escape through the trees, doubling back around Elm Camp to get to our cabins. Hisses fill the darkness. Shrieks sear through it. I don't know what they're doing. But I don't have time to wonder.

Stumbling into the clearing between our cabins, the Murderfaces are assembled as planned. And armed. When Corryn and I appear, everybody turns toward us, brandishing their weapons. Ew sets off the flash, and a strobe burns through the dark.

Behind us, we hear shrieky, snakey screams. It sounds like they tried to slink through the raspberry brambles out there. Good. Let them get punctured!

"We just lost Cherry and Chip," I say, blinking at

the reverse flash that's still burned in my eyes. "They're evil, both of them!"

"No kidding, Sherlock," Knees says. "Catch!"

I duck. Corryn sticks out a hand in front of me and catches the shovel with one hand. She may still be a little out of it, but her reflexes are sharp as ever. She hands me the shovel, then catches the rake when Nostrils throws that. I don't know why we're throwing garden tools, but there's no time to discuss that.

"They all turned," I say. I'm not sure whether everybody saw Chip and Cherry's transformation. "They're all snake people."

Ew steps up, furious. "I told you guys!"

"We be-*lieved* you," Nostrils says, holding up his paddle. "One zillion percent."

After catching her breath, Corryn rallies. Dirt is smeared across her cheek, but that just makes her look fierce.

"Okay, Murderfaces," she says, her voice soft at first. "We need to stick together. Whatever's in charge of this, it's gotta be on that island. We're gonna have to fight whatever we find. Did Bowlie make it to his station?"

With a distant sort of look, Ew says, "He headed

that way. We hope he made it."

"All right," Corryn says. "We need to move out. We're gonna take that island!"

Braids asks, "How are we supposed to get there?"

I raise my good hand. "Canoes."

We haven't been allowed to take them out yet this summer. But that doesn't mean the boathouse isn't *right there*, just west of our cabins.

The dingy red canoes bump in their stalls. The wooden walls amplify their hollow thumps, plaintive calls reminding us that they're waiting. Waiting to be used. Sometimes, when the wind is right, I hear them at night. Tonight? We sail against evil.

There's no argument. We move together.

The screams are changing. The shock seems gone. Now it's all fear. Fear as thick as smoke. It's thick in the air; it's bitter to taste. The water warps everything. As we hurry toward the lake, kids sob behind us. They moan. It's almost a song. A song of agony.

The underbrush claws at our ankles as we move. I try to beat the ground in front of me with the shovel to clear the way. Braids is doing better with the kitchen paddle. She whacks a path through, grimly determined.

A greenness freshens the air with each broken branch and brush.

Then Corryn screams.

Vines from the ground wriggle up her ankle. They slither and hiss; thorns dig into her flesh. The ground is alive under her. It's like this place has a horror made for each one of us.

Corryn tries to beat at the vines with the handle of her rake. "No, no, no, not again!"

"Hold still," Hairspray says, remarkably calm. She sinks down and pulls out a tiny pair of scissors. Moonlight bounces off the sharp blades. They glint silver. With a quick twist of her wrist, snip-snip-snip, Hairspray cuts through the vines.

Knees looks to Nostrils and whispers, "Wicked."

"Yeah," I say, "but let's go. Something wickeder this way comes."

Nostril shakes his head. "Dang, Chickenlips. You always know what to say to make things worse."

37
Sending Out an SOS

Corryn

We stumble out of the woods together.

Knees and Nostrils lunge toward the shore and fall to the ground. My cabinmates burst from the tree line but stay on their feet. Even Tez manages to recover before he trips. He looks kinda pale, too, but that's probably from the running.

"Ahhhhhhh . . . ," Nostrils says, along with an elegant cuss. Sprawled on his back, he's the first one to see what we all turn to look at.

Vultures. Not just five or ten now. Hundreds of them. Flapping their big ragged wings, growling like zombies over the lake. They circle so close to each other, there's barely any sky between them.

And I don't need Tez Jones, Professor of Birdology, to tell me that ain't right. Because Braids takes one look at the black spiral above us and says, "Oh no, not today, devil birds."

Knees and Nostrils get to their feet, and we huddle closer together. For a minute, we're quiet. But the night isn't. Across the lake, the senior camp is on fire. Like, actual fire. The flames lick up from cabin roofs, and the sky starts to glow a dark red. Kids run in every direction. Snake counselors try to herd them toward the shore.

Snake counselors. All the replacements—the cheery, preppy, pastel-sweater set—are slithering around, dragging kids toward the lake. There's way too many of them. More than the number of counselors in the whole camp. Bodies hit the water, and I realize now.

The eggs.

The extra snake counselors had to have hatched out of the eggs! I want to stop and tell everybody, but I can't. We have one goal. Charge that island in Lake Sweetwater and strike down whatever we find there. There's carnage in every direction. We're the only ones who can save the camp now.

I sure hope Bowl Cut is getting our message out. That was his one job. Get to the radio station and play one request, over and over. I can practically hear his nasally voice on the mic.

"All your requests from Camp Sweetwater, sending out an SOS to watch the Winch, and this one's for you, Fan du Lac!"

And then, if he's doing it right, he drops the needle on that *Edmund Fitzgerald* song. It drones for about a thousand years (actually, six minutes and thirty-two seconds), and then he's supposed to start all over again.

It's so loud in my head, I feel like I can hear it *outside* my head. I have the stupid thing memorized at this point. That's why it's so vivid. That's why I'm sure I hear those immortal lines about the shores of Gitche Gumee and November coming early.

"Somebody's playing the radio," Tez says. He's paler than ever.

Nostrils cusses. "They're gonna know!"

With a set jaw, Braids says, "It doesn't matter. He got the message out. We just have to hope somebody heard it!"

"I have an idea," I say, my voice accidentally breaking with fear. "How about we get to a stinking boat and murderface some vampire devils?"

When we get to the boathouse, we find it locked. Of course! Nostrils and Knees take kung fu turns, kicking at the door. They bounce like flies off a bug zapper. But they keep at it.

"Hurry, hurry, hurry," Braids says. For the first time tonight, she pulls the bow off her back and brandishes it. Her hands shake a little. But she gets an arrow notched on the string and holds it steady. "I don't wanna shoot something with a face, but I'm gonna have to if you don't get that door open."

Okay. Dumb-fu kicks aren't doing anything except cracking the wood. Stuff's about to get real up in here. So, here comes Cannonball Quinn! I can wreck anything. Just ask my aunt Melody about her hallway table.

I get a running start and smash my shoulder against the door. Splinters fly everywhere. The door moans, but it doesn't fall down. I do, though. Ow, ow, ow, it's not like the movies. Running into a door full-force feels like taking a header into an empty koi pond (Aunt Melody's again).

As Tez tries to help me up one-handed, Knees takes another mighty kick at the door and . . . he ends up on the ground, too.

There's a *twanggggg* and then a whoosh. I'm up just in time to see Braids' first arrow fly at a naga headed our way. Braids' aim is true. I don't know what she hit, but the naga drops. It lies in the dirt, twitching.

Holy sheep shears, that was hard-core. I'm gonna have nightmares for *months*.

Because behind that snake chick is a whole swarm of them, headed this way. I can't tell if Chip and Cherry are among them. What does it matter, anyway? They're not people. They're unholy monsters, and I'm pretty sure they want to see us dead.

Ew runs up next to Braids with her camera flash in her hand. She raises it over her head and hits the button. The burning white light floods the forest. It makes the naga line scream in one devil voice. They slow, just a little.

When the flash burns away, it's dark out here. Everything reflects flame and lake in weird red shadows. I know the Murderfaces are scattered around me. Digging into Braids' stash bag, I pull out a Roman candle. I yell over the din, "Tez, light me up!"

He strikes a match, and the fuse sizzles.

"INCOMING!" I yell.

Fat balls of colored fire spit from the firework in my hand. I can't see what I'm shooting at, really. I just point it away from us. With each flaming ball, a whistle rips through the air. I can feel the Roman candle getting hot in my hand, but I hold on tight.

Screaming. There's just so much *screaming*. And underneath, or maybe over it, Bowl Cut intones, "All your requests from Camp Sweetwater, sending out an SOS to watch the Winch, and this one's for you, Chief Wolpaw!"

Come on, Chief, you gotta be hearing this. You gotta.

"Stop kicking the door, you dinks!"

Until I hear her voice, I don't know where Hairspray is. It startles me, actually, because it comes from *inside* the boathouse.

Jeez Louise! She climbed around the outside of the boathouse! She full-on primate-climbed that thing and got herself inside. Nostrils and Knees fall back.

The door shakes from the inside. Something wood hammers against wood. Then suddenly, Hairspray throws the boathouse door open and shouts, "We're in, let's go!"

Another piercing wash of white light floods the sky as Ew strobes the naga again, blinding them long enough for us to get inside and get onto the water in a boat.

Tonight, we sail the seas of blood, toward the dark and wooded island. Toward the eye of the vulture storm.

Toward destiny.

38
A Blazing Message

Corryn

Crossing Lake Sweetwater feels too easy.

The last time me and Tez were in a boat on this lake, it churned with a strange glow; it wanted to pull us down. Tonight, the water is blood red. It bubbles around the sides of our boat, but nothing rises from the deep. The vultures remain shadows above us, circling, circling. . . . It's literally smooth sailing, and I don't like that one bit.

"Land ho!" Nostrils yells when we reach the new island.

Knees snickers, then jumps out to pull us onto shore. Our feet squelch when we jump out. The ground (or

335

whatever this is) actually splashes. It sucks at my Converse and that's not okay. It feels like walking on wet carpet. I shudder a little.

Once the boat is secure, we open our bags of supplies. Somebody purloined soft helmets from the confidence course. There are a couple of chest protectors like a baseball umpire would wear—I grab one of those right away and foist it on Tez. He needs the extra armor in the chestal region.

Pretty soon, we're all wearing a mishmash of sports gear. It looks like some sort of foot/base/basket/hodgepodge ball game is about to break out, but it feels like safety. Everybody gets armed; everybody has a flashlight. Everybody is ready. Heck yeah, this is what an A Team looks like!

Then Hairspray asks, "Are those trees . . . moving?"

We all turn at the same time. Gnarled trunks hunch around us. The wood is black and barkless, just like the stuff we found around the lake when we first got here. Except these branches are attached. And they *are* moving.

"It's the birds," Ew says. She sets off the flash. Vultures, tons of them, suddenly flap their wings. They cling to the trees with knobby claws. They fill the air with a low, body-dragging growl. Red spills around their dark beaks. It's blood, my brain tells me. They've been killing things. They're gonna kill you.

For a second, I feel like I'm a little kid again. I want to cry; I want my mommy and daddy. I don't care about the divorce. I just want them close to me again.

"Let's go," Ew says gently. She plants her hand in the middle of my back and pushes. The first couple steps are by force. But I shake my head and get it back in the game. Of course they want to kill us! This whole camp wants to kill us! But I've got news for them! We're the ones doing the murderfacing today, suckers! Because I need to get back to my parents!

We move through the trees like a crack band of commandos. Nostrils and Braids lead with their bows out. Knees and Hairspray bring up the rear with a pugil stick and the bug juice paddle. I can't wait for Knees to break out the pugil action. Whacking vampire devils with a giant Q-tip is my kind of fun.

The middle of the party, that's me with a baseball bat, Ew with her flash and the matches, and Tez with fireworks. I'm glad he ditched the shovel. The way he was waving that thing one-handed, there was a good chance he'd take off one of *our* heads.

"What are we looking for?" Knees asks.

"We'll know it when we see it," I say confidently.

"Uhhh, I see it," Braids says, stopping abruptly.

Tez and I stop, too; Nostrils runs right into us. Okay, when I said a crack team of commandos, maybe I meant *cracked*.

Knees holds his flashlight over his head. It creates a big, but dim, circle of light. It's all we need, though.

"Uh, you guys," Ew says. "Like, is that a *coffin*?" So that's bad. But not as bad as the question that follows. "And, um. Am I wack, or is it empty?"

At the same time, Ew hits her flash, and Knees lowers his flashlight. Not just *like* a coffin, an actual coffin. And not just one coffin. Lots of coffins. Six, at least. Their sides are carved all fancy. They're black and open (did I mention open?), with the lids tossed aside.

Tez squishes next to Ew to get a closer look. When he does, he lets out a low whistle. "Just as I thought," he says, tapping on one of the coffins, which makes a dull thud. "They're made of lead."

"Lead? That means they're *definitely* vampires, man," Knees says, pacing furiously. "You put flipping vampires in flipping lead coffins so they can cross the ocean!"

"It gets worse," Tez says.

Then the sky explodes.

Kind of a weird time for fireworks. But it's a whole sky full of them. Instead of big booming blasts of bright color against the night sky, they're all red. Red and orange, like blood and fire.

The spiral of birds breaks; some land around us. Others swoop to the opposite shore. Kids scream as the birds dive toward them.

As soon as the birds clear off, the low crimson sky swirls with more explosions. Whistles and pops and bangs. More flash than Ew, and louder than Bowl Cut blasting ol' Gordo.

The sparks shake and start to form shapes. The shapes of letters. A blazing message forms from the red embers of the fireworks.

IT IS TIME, ASTRID

It's as clear as the blocky print of black Sharpie on the waistband of your underwear. "Who is Astrid?" I wonder out loud.

"Astrid Mechant," Tez says, like he's connecting one last dot.

The name Mechant is never followed by something good. Neither followed nor preceded by anything the least bit good. They're the ones who cursed this place, who brought the vampire devils from France. And if the vampy Ds are warning *her*, they're not talking to *us*. They're talking to the one who's supposed to feed them.

Yeah, it's two seconds later than Tez's dot connects, but, oh my dog, Gladys Winchelhauser is the last Mechant.

There is the loud scratch of a needle on a record. The Gordon Lightfoot marathon has finally come to an end. I'm hoping to hear the voice of Bowl Cut, maybe saying the police are here. Would *really* love to hear him telling us reinforcements are on the way.

But the voice I hear broadcast loud and clear across Lake Sweetwater is most definitely not Bowlie's.

"Oh hello, dears," it purrs, in a voice humming with evil. "I see you out there. Hi! I hope you're having a nice time."

Yep. There she is. The Winch. She stands on the main beach, surrounded by snake-counselors and little kids. The blaze from the bonfire illuminates her off-putting smile, casting demonic shadows on her eyes.

As if it's a regular camp get-together, she speaks

340

directly to us. Without a microphone. Through some kind of terrible magic, her voice booms across the lake, rolling like canned peaches in the kitchen.

"Well! I don't know about you, but I have had enough folk music for one day," she says. "Had to put an end to that. And your friend's message. Really, very cute. 'Watch the Winch.' Is that what you call me? The Winch? You were hoping someone would rescue you, I take it? Charming."

"Yeah!" I yell from our spot on the island. I cup my hands around my mouth. I'm so mad, my voice gets all ropey, and it's almost as loud as the Winch's. "The chief is coming, and then you're in trouble!"

"Ah yes, our old friend Chief Wolpaw," she says. "Wouldn't it be lovely to see him right about now? Just lovely." She turns slowly, waving at something just out of sight.

Not something. Someone.

It's Chief Wolpaw.

And it seems the Winch got to him before he could get to her.

39
Meeting Astrid Mechant

Tez

There's a distinct possibility that we have been out-planned.

Something that used to be in coffins is loose, and Mrs. Winchelhauser doesn't seem to mind that all of her counselors have turned into snake people. That's something I would mind—if they weren't on my side.

So, obviously, they are. On the Winch's side. Duh.

"You're probably thinking to yourself," Mrs. Winchelhauser says, leaning against Chief Wolpaw lazily, "what on earth is going on? And since it's the very last thing you'll ever hear, darlings, I'm going to tell you."

Nostrils shoves Knees. "She's going to monologue! It's the villain's monologue!"

"Shhh, shut up, man," Nostrils replies, shoving him back. "We need to hear this!"

For once, Nostrils is right. The sky is still on fire. Our fellow campers are still screaming in terror. The villain's monologue might be our only chance to gain the upper hand. We *definitely* need to listen.

Mrs. Winchelhauser reaches down. I recoil, because she's stroking Soft Shoes' head as if he's a pet. Bristling all over, I clench my jaw. She needs to get her hands off my Bantam campers. Like, yesterday.

"If you're gonna talk, talk!" Corryn yells. Right! Exactly what I was thinking!

"Tsk tsk tsk, always in such a hurry. And so very nosy." Mrs. Winchelhauser shakes her head. "Everyone should know, what happens tonight, well, it's all your fault. Tez. Corryn. Emily. Antonio. Dayvi. Jake."

All of us on the island look to each other, confused. Who the heck are—?

Mrs. Winchelhauser continues. "I always knew that a few children might be sensitive to the power here, that they might notice this place is more than a summer camp. But how much trouble could a few children out of hundreds cause?"

From the senior camp shore, a boy yells, "You're about to find out!"

Then, from Elm Camp, a girl. "We know your game, Winchelhauser! And we're gonna take you down!"

"Hey, wait," Braids says, looking to me. "Who the heck are they?"

I shake my head, baffled as anybody. Is it . . . is it possible Mrs. Winchelhauser is telling the truth? That we Murderfaces aren't the only ones fighting this battle? My uneasy heart does a loopty-loop, and lands squarely in the pit of my stomach. It feels a little like hope.

We're not alone.

Mrs. Winchelhauser booms out, "Ah, lovely. A demonstration of just how much trouble they can be. I tried to play it nice. I tried to get what I needed without arousing too much suspicion, but alas. The best-laid plans of mice and men!"

"AND SNAKES!" Hairspray yells.

"Children," Mrs. Winchelhauser growls. The vultures all around the lake growl with her. "It's very rude to interrupt. Very rude indeed. But after tonight, that won't be my problem. I, Astrid Mechant, last of the Mechant line, will finally sate the appetites of the ghouls that have held my family captive for one hundred and thirty years!"

Nostrils kicks the ground and looks at us in disbelief. "First, we've got bugs, then ghosts, then snakes, then vampire devils, and now we've got ghouls?"

"Ghouls just want to have fun," Corryn mutters.

That's not very helpful, so I tell Nostrils, "She means the vampire devils. Those are the ghouls."

"Then why didn't she just *say* that?"

Ew shrugs. "Poetic license."

"Well, I'm revoking that license," Nostrils says. He brandishes his paddle with a grim determination. "Officer Nostrils doesn't give out warnings! Revoked!"

I shush him. There's motion on the beach with Mrs. Winchelhauser . . . or, I guess, *Madame* Mechant or *Ms.* Some ladies like to be called Ms.

The point is, an unholy crimson glow surrounds Mrs. Winchelhauser, and she rises off the ground.

Hairspray squares her shoulders, ready for battle. "Well, that's not good."

"They promised us everlasting life! But what good is everlasting life if we CAN'T EVER LEAVE? We come back again and again, we make our sacrifices again and again, but it's NEVER ENOUGH!"

Ordinarily, I'd say the enemy of my enemy is my friend, but since it looks like the Mechants have been feeding little kids to the vampire devils for more than a century, I think we just have two enemies to fight. Maybe the enemy of my enemy is my enemy squared. Carry the one.

My chest is tight; it squeezes my heart and makes me a little dizzy. It's okay. If we have to fight two battles, then that's what we'll do!

"This year, it *will* be enough! This year, it will be *all of you*! And I will be free!" She throws her head back and laughs, a strange, grating sound. It carries over the water but not well.

Corryn shakes her head. "Not the best villain laugh. She really should work on that."

Nostrils agrees. "She sounds like my dad's old Buick when the alternator went out."

And then Mrs. Winchelhauser explodes in a blaze of fire. Great flames leap toward the sky. My Bantam campers scream and try to run away. What seems like a whole army of snake-counselors herds the kids back together.

The fire rises, rises, off the ground. It flares,

changing color, blue flame to golden to scarlet, and then an explosion! The shock wave reaches us on the island. The Bantams fall on the beach, helpless. Helpless, as Gladys "Astrid Mechant" Winchelhauser reveals her true form.

The sensible shoes, the khaki shorts, even the color war T-shirt explode in a cloud of embers. All that's left is golden, glowing, scaly skin, a cobra hood as rich as King Tut's, and luminous red eyes. Devilwood's own Monstress, forever and ever, but not amen, Astrid Mechant . . . the Queen Cobra.

And that's my cue. I cup my hands around my mouth, and I yell to the little kids littering the beach around her. Actually, to two specific little kids. "MINEFIELD! SOFT SHOES! ATTACK!"

All at once, my Bantam campers, the ones that Corryn and everybody else just brushed aside, reach into their pockets and pull out the slingshots I taught them to make during Arts & Crafts. They pull back, and stones fly!

"What the what?" Corryn mutters in shock.

Hairspray laughs. "Omigod, Chickenlips. You trained the diaper babies!"

"They're . . . the diaper *assassins*," Ew says.

I feel a flare of pride in my chest. But I also know the diaper babies can't take Mrs. Winchelhauser down with slingshots. That's up to us. Raising my good arm, I call out to my campmates, my team, my *friends*.

"LET SLIP THE DOGS OF WAR!"

With a sigh in my direction, Braids says, "I don't know what we're gonna do with you, boy," but she sure knows what she's gonna do with that bow and arrow. Knees flicks a match, and the wad of beach towel wrapped around the arrow lights up like a torch. She fires, a glorious arc headed right for Mrs. Winchelhauser.

To my surprise, more arrows fly, from Elm Camp and the senior camp. The other rebels! Our comrades-in-arms, our unknown allies! Buuuut, I have to say, our preparations are a little bit better. Because Corryn stuffs a mortar down a tube, and Nostrils leans in to light it.

There's a crackle, then a *FOOMP*.

The fist-sized ball flies out of the tube, right toward Mrs. Winchelhauser. It speeds across the lake. It leaves a perfect, scarlet arc as it flies. Then it hits Mrs. Winchelhauser in the chest—and explodes! Bright whistles pierce the air. Sparks in all the colors blaze out around her. She drops, and the Bantams flee! YES!

When Mrs. Winchelhauser rises again, it's on a thick serpent's tail. Her face is completely transformed with fury. She raises her hands and screeches—the sound I had expected the vultures to make, actually.

"GET THEM!" she howls. And I'm not sure who she's talking to. We're alone on this island. Those coffins are empty.

But the skies aren't. Black vultures, eyes glowing a vicious red, take flight. They dive-bomb us. The rush of their wings whistles through the air, and I throw my arm up to protect Corryn. I think I even yell, "No!" but it's chaos now, and hard to tell.

What's not hard to tell is that Hairspray just unholstered a can of Aqua Net and set the spray on fire with the matches. "Swiped it from Cherry!" she shouts.

"Flamethrower!" Nostrils yells.

Knees yells, "I LOVE YOU, HAIRSPRAY!"

The huge cone of fire passes over our heads, chasing the vultures away. We start to regroup for another volley on Mrs. Winchelhauser. Unfortunately, that attack is going to have to wait.

Because two of the snake people—Chip and Cherry, who else?—rush full speed onto the water. On. Not in!

Their bodies leave waves in their wake. They're

speeding across the surface like Jesus Lizards and heading right for us. It's fascinating; they shouldn't be able to stay afloat like that. And yet, they are. Top speed, right in our direction.

40
A Three-To-Four-Armed Fighting Machine

Corryn

"Incoming!" I yell, and back up to Tez's back.

I'm like a head taller than him, so it's more like back to butt. Whatever. We're a lean, mean, three-to-four-armed fighting machine. Tez lights a volley of bottle rockets.

Bwee bwee bwee! They rip through the air. A flash of sparks! They explode. Cherry hisses and spreads out her snakey hood. She looks like a giant cobra with a lady face, and that lady face is *maaaaaaad.*

No time to enjoy that! I light another Roman candle. Big balls of blue and red and white *foom* from the firework. Chip throws up his arms and recoils. That's right, deathsnakes! It's barbecue time! I think it's Chip making that screaming sound. Hard to tell. There's a lot of crispy serpent going on right now.

"They're coming!" Braids yells, lighting up her next volley of arrows.

Hairspray yells, "I do NOT have TIME for this!" then grabs the pugil stick lying on the ground. She douses it with Aqua Net and *WOO*! Who knew that leather stuffed with horsehair would go up like a torch? Hairspray did! She leaps off to one side with a roar.

Tez yelps, and my heart leaps.

"You okay?"

His fingers are stuffed in his mouth. "Bunned my hand!"

"Less fire on you," I advise, scrabbling to light another firework. "More on them!"

Reloading paused us long enough for Chip and Cherry to rush us from the beach. Cherry stops dead and waves her hand. What the heck is that all about?

Chip, though, knows what to do. He flings out both hands. Fireballs fly from them. Right at us!

"Watch out!" I yell to Tez, and push him back. It's not till the fire passes us that I feel the heat. My cheek sizzles like barbecue. Smoke and the smell of burned hair fill the air around us. That better be somebody else's hair. Bowl Cut has a lock on bald this summer.

The surface of the lake ripples. Snake-counselors skim toward us at top speed. But you know what? That's fine! We Murderfaces have enough hurt to go around!

Off to Tez's left, Braids lights up the sky with another flaming arrow. I don't see it land, but I hear the snakey scream. Nice! Then, to the right of me, *socka-sock POW!* Ew swings the bug juice paddle. Splat, right in the serpent puss!

"Nostrils," Tez yells, "think fast!"

I can't tell what Tez throws. All I know is that, after he does, Nostrils does the Tarzan yell. He beats his chest, then races toward the incoming snakes with a canoe paddle in hand.

"WAKE-'EM-UP DROPS!" he bellows, and knocks a naga into next Sunday.

YES! We're winning this! We're turning them back! A long string of firecrackers arcs in the air. The rat-a-tat explosions are like war cries. I feel them in my gut. I'm all punch-drunk and ready for more. Digging into the bag, I pull out a rocket. Oh yeahhhhhhh!

This is better than a bonfire! This is good over evil! This is Murderfaces saving the day! More bottle rockets fly. Somebody, Knees, I think, lights another mortar. The *FOOM* it makes is my favorite sound! And I light my rocket, pointing it straight at Cherry Cumberland's perky, evil face.

A viney hand shoots up from the ground. It grabs the rocket *out of the air.* It gnarls and curls. The rocket crumples in its grip. No fire. No earth-shattering kaboom.

This is what she made me forget the night Ew and I followed her. The fact that she can control the forest. The fact that she turns it deadly.

Cherry raises her hands, and the ground explodes between us. Twisted vines and roots shoot up. Conducting, Cherry laughs as more roots punch into the air. They deflect our bottle rockets. They grab Ew's paddle.

Ew yanks at it, wood splintering with each tug. But another viney hand grabs, then another. Ew kicks, and that works. On one. The next one grabs Ew's ankles. Her arms flail as the root-hands yank her off her feet. She groans.

"STOP CHERRY!" I scream. I can't even tell if anybody hears me. The air is full of booms and whistles and screeches. It's full of vultures. It's full of the arrows and the smells of burned hair and scales.

Tez pushes against my back. "Move, move, move!"

I toss a look over my shoulder. "It's clear this way!"

My heart drums in my head. It's like crazy bongos: beat, beat, beat! My legs are moving. I know that because my body is moving. The thing is, I feel floaty. Like I'm here but not here; like something else is in charge. Something that's awakening.

My inner BMX Monster. Yeah!

It bursts through my conscious brain, flooding me with adrenaline.

I'm radder than Danny Stark right now, dragging a bag of fireworks away from the brambles of doom. I shouldn't enjoy this. I know I shouldn't! This is a battle for our very lives! But I was born for this! I was born to take the Winch and her minions down, I just know it.

Hairspray shrieks, and not in a good way. "There's more!"

"We can do this!" Braids yells back. Then she cusses. A lot.

Snake people spill onto the shore, and I drop my bag. No time to regroup or carry by one or whatever it's called when you stop in the middle of a fight and start again.

Plunging my hand into the duffel, I feel around for

a rocket. A mortar. A sparkler, anything! It's empty! All my ammunition lays in the squishy dirt, spilled out of a hole in the bottom of my bag.

No time to worry about that, though! I pick up the bag and shake it out. Shake, shake, nothing. I'm baffled for a second. Then I'm ticked. Because the baseball bat, *my* backup baseball bat, is in Chip's stupid serpent hands! Like he even knows what to do with it!

"Give that back!" I shout.

"Shushh," Chip says, flicking his tongue in my direction. It waves like a blade of glass. "I never did like you."

He raises the bat over his head like a swordfighter. Fire glints off his scales and his fangs. His stupid, stupid, snakey fangs. What does he think he's gonna do with that pose? Dork us to death?

"You hold that bat like a dummy," I say. I mean, what? The only weapon I have left right now is my wit!

Chip raises the bat against the vulture-dark sky and slithers toward me. All that adrenaline I had a minute ago bails. Coward adrenaline! I throw my arms up to protect my head. He swings—

"No!" Tez yells. I tense. I squeeze my eyes shut.

WHUP.

It sounds like a rotten melon, squished. It takes me a second to realize it's not *my* melon that took the hit. I drop my arms and look around. It's craziness out here. I'm in the eye of it, surrounded by a lunatic hurricane. It's me and Chip and . . . me and Chip?

With a jaunty swing, Chip tosses the bat into the air and sets it on fire. "Glad that's over with. That kid was a real pain in my rump."

The bat seems to hang in the air. The fight around me drags to slow motion. It feels like I'm breathing through a straw. Because I look down and there's Tez. Embers float down and land on his face. He doesn't move. Not even a flinch. His head is fine, but his head was never the problem, was it?

Tez's hand lays lifelessly on his chest. Over his heart. His stupid, weak heart.

No, Tez. Wake up.

No.

41
I Think I'm a Ghost Now

Tez

I think I'm on the ground. And I shouldn't be on the ground.

Sounds and light warp around me. The last thing I remember is Chip going for Corryn, and now I'm down. And I can't catch my breath. Strange shadows and lights swirl around me. It's like the world is a snow globe. Someone just shook it, very, very hard.

Corryn's voice winds around me. She sounds like a backward record at first. Then her words speed up and coalesce. They become English again. And English words I never expected to hear Corryn say in my lifetime. She huddles over me—yes, okay, that's up, and those are her brown eyes. Filled with tears?

"Don't be dead!" she yells. "You can't be dead!"

I try to tell her I'm not. It's weird, though, because I feel a buzzing where my lips should meet. My tongue is hazy; I still can't catch my breath.

"Two birds, one stone," Chip hisses cheerfully. He glides away from us, calling to one of the other dread counselors, "Be there in a jiff!"

Corryn drops her head, sobbing an order at me. "Wake up right now, you goob! *You don't get to be dead!*"

That sends a jolt through me. All of a sudden, I'm standing over Corryn. That's weird because she's taller than I am. And also, because she's sprawled on the ground, hunched over my body. The battle rages on around us.

Hairspray thwacks a serpent-preppy with the remains of her pugil stick. Behind her, Braids is out of arrows and has moved on to serving flaming tennis balls at the incoming hordes. And, honest to Pete, Knees and Nostrils are using their fake karate and actually kicking snake faces. But I can't help but come back to Corryn clutching my body as I float above her. How is that even poss—

Oh.

I raise my hands in front of my face. They look like mist, vaguely hand-shaped but indistinct. My legs fade into nothing; my lips still don't meet when I try to say Corryn's name.

I'm . . . dead?

The big thing that scared my parents happened. And after I promised I'd be careful at camp. That it would be okay. That I wouldn't do anything dangerous. But when I made those promises, the most dangerous things at camp were square dancing or leftovers for dinner or girls.

"This fight isn't over!" Corryn yells. Then, less yelly, she says, "We never even kissed!"

"Whoa, wait, what?"

Corryn's head jerks up. "Tez?"

Yes! I managed to talk. "I'm here. I'm okay."

"Bloody well ain't," a familiar voice says behind me.

Whipping around, I stare when I see Gavin and Scary Mary floating in front of me. They look just like they did the last time I saw them: Gavin bored and Scary Mary soaking wet. Well, except they're a lot more translucent. A cold tickle ripples through me, and I say the first thing that comes to mind. "You died, too?"

"Innit?" Gavin agrees.

Scary Mary drifts toward me. "Threw us into a pit of bones, the Winch did."

With a jerk of his head, Gavin looks behind himself. There are more counselors there. Floppy Hat Guy and Whoa Whoa Whoa and all the others. Everybody Mrs. Winchelhauser replaced with a preppy naga. They float there, a virtual army of ghosts. Among them, a slight glow rises. It moves toward me. When it breaks through the crowd, I turn into soda bubbles—at least, it feels that way.

"Thought I told you two to beware the deep," Finchy says.

Our Old Lifeguard, our friend! The one who finally got to go to his peace with his sister when we set free her and two other missing campers. That seems like a million years ago, but it was mere weeks. I try to walk toward Finchy, but I don't have the hang of it yet.

On the ground, Corryn stands up. Tears run down her dirt-smeared face. A quiver overtakes her lower lip, but she doesn't give in to it. She demands, "Tez? Are you there? You better not be messing with me, or I'm gonna frog you into next week!"

"Some things never change." Scary Mary moans, rolling her eyes beneath her seaweedy hair. "Whinge, whinge, whinge."

"It's okay, Corryn, I'm here. With friends."

A scream cuts through the night. Hairspray beats at her own head, running in circles. At first, I think there's a wolf on her shoulders, but there are no wolves in Ohio. It's a vulture, and its talons drag Hairspray into the arms of two snake-counselors. Mrs. Winchelhauser's voice booms out.

"We've had ever so much fun tonight," she says as vultures drop from the sky all around the lake. "But it's getting a tad late, and I don't want to miss my rerun of *Dallas*! Time to stop playing with the food!"

Finchy reaches out to me. "Come on, Tez. You don't want to see this."

"No, I don't," I agree, furiously. "That's why we're going to do something about it."

"Do what?" he asks. "I waited a hundred years for somebody to stumble along and help set my sister, Virginia, free. Do you think I did all that waiting for my health? It's because I couldn't do it myself! The dead have no power here. All we can do is watch."

Squinting at him, or I guess having the feeling of

squinting at someone when you don't have a body, I say, "You did a lot. You were a lifeguard. You rowed a boat. You pulled us to safety."

Exasperated, Finchy says, "That was different! You were two dumb kids, and I pulled you out of a hole. I couldn't do a darned thing about Virginia, once that pit swallowed her up. You go in there, and you're done for."

As soon as he says that, I feel . . . warm. Like I'm glowing. I point at Finchy, and I yell, "Perfect!"

Wiping her face, and a little annoyed, Corryn says, "Will you tell me what the heck you're talking about? You're not making any sense!"

Corryn can see only me. But that's fine. She doesn't need to see more.

I point to her, and I say, "You need to take the fight to Mrs. Winchelhauser. Distract her. I have an idea, but it's not gonna work without you."

Grabbing the shoulder of her T-shirt, Corryn drags it across her face. She comes back up clean and determined. "Okay. Then what?"

This is where I'd take a deep breath if I were alive. Instead, my mist sort of gets bigger, and I say, "Then? You guys get out alive."

"What about you?"

"Get to the canoe, okay? You need to get across the lake. Fast. We'll help."

Corryn looks suspicious. And when she gets suspicious, she gets stubborn. "We *who*?"

No time for explanations. I reach out to put my hand on Corryn's face. But I don't have a hand. I just have mist, and Corryn shivers when my touch passes right through her. No matter how brave I'm pretending to be, I'm not okay. I'm dead. I'm dead in a Camp Sweetwater T-shirt and color war tabard, lying at Corryn's feet. I got a best friend and lost her, all in one summer.

"Just do it," I say croakily, then drift away.

No wonder spirits just stick around and watch. It turns out that ghosts can't cry, no matter how much they want to.

42

Not on My Swatch

Corryn

Maybe I'm cracking up. Or maybe I'm just getting started.

I know I heard Tez's voice. Maybe it was an inside voice. Maybe he spoke from the not-too-far beyond. Doesn't matter. It's heavy destruction time. I keep my chin up. I won't look down. I refuse to see Tez's ashy face. Not looking at his still body. Nope.

Nobody's paying attention to me. Chip left me crying, and now, it's like I'm a little bit invisible. Awesome. Snatching some of the scattered fireworks, I tuck in my shirt and dump my haul down the neck of it. Keeping low, I circle the edge of the island. The snake crowd has thinned out a lot. A whole bunch of campers are holding their own.

Thwock! One of Braids' flaming tennis balls bounces off Cherry's head. Good! I hope Braids serves some up for her monster of a brother. I made a promise, and I'm gonna keep it.

The spongy ground grabs at my shoes, so you know what? I turn back to the melee and kick those suckers off. I'm not sure which snake-o just took two size fives to the back of the head, but it was very satisfying! Now that the sludge is squishing between my toes, I haul butt and get into the canoe.

It's almost too easy to shove it off the shore. I have only one oar. But she glides right out, silently. Maneuvering around, I get the boat turned toward the Winch and start for her. This thing moves like a dream. My paddle barely hits the water, and I slice forward effortlessly. It reminds me of the boat ride Tez and I took after we escaped the bone pit. . . .

Stop. Cannot think about Tez right now. On a mission. Eyes forward! Head down! I'm far enough into the water that I can see the battle all around me. The senior camp, cabins and all—everything is on fire. Snake silhouettes are dragging people shadows down to the water.

In Elm and Oak, there's only the bonfire. I can't really see what's going on over there, but I can hear it: the grind-grind-grind of the vultures, the sounds of kids being chucked in the lake. I shudder and point my peepers at my destination. The beach. The dock where the wicked Winch watches as the diaper babies get rounded up.

"Not on my watch," I whisper.

The wind whispers in a thick British accent, "Shut it, You."

Inside, I shiver. Outside, I prepare my attack. First, I get under the diving platform, on the ledge where the seniors usually lounge like manatees. I don't think anybody can see me there. Once I'm set up, I'll tie all the fuses together on my stash. Then I'll light the whole thing, and *kablam*: a direct hit on the Winch and a grade A+++ distraction.

The waves slosh against the sides of the boat, white foam on red. With my head down, I keep the front of my boat pointed right at the diving platform. I still see the Winch in the corner of my eye. Hear her, too. She laughs like a tipsy aunt, watching the Bantam shrimpsters get dunked in the drink.

This is all on me now.

I'm gonna stop the Winch in her grimy, despicable tracks.

The canoe bumps against the back of the diving platform. It seems like it steadies itself, so I can climb off safely and unseen. The underside of the platform is slick. It smells like algae and old rubber. It bobs with the waves, and my heart ripples with fear each time I slip a little. Water splashes over my feet. My foot bones ache with the cold.

A gentle fog drifts into my brain. Wouldn't it be nice to just lay down right now? Just lay on the platform forever and look at the stars and never go home again . . .

I slap my own cheek. Snap out of it, Quinn! I don't need a notebook to realize this lake is trying to kill me. Actually, correction. The Winch is trying to kill me. The lake is just her sloshy accomplice!

With another slap, just to even out my face, I crawl into the frame of the diving platform and glare at my nemesis across the water. Every bad thing that happened this summer is her fault. The bugs, the hauntings, the bad dreams, the missing mail, the murderous forest:

all Winch's fault. No. Worse.

All her *plan*.

When she opened this place back up, she wasn't just some old hippie with a good idea and bad management plan. She opened it up planning to feed kids to an ancient evil. The Winch wrote some murder checks and thought she'd get away with us cashing them for her.

She thinks she's gonna feed everybody to the vampy Ds? Not in this lifetime, Astrid.

Careful to keep them dry, I pull the fireworks out of my shirt one by one. They smell sweet and smoky. That's what I focus on as I thread them together. Fireworks and victory, singing some good ol' Gordo Lightfoot as the dawn breaks on a new day and Tez dead on that island—

Nope. No time for that. Do not think about that. Don't think about telling his parents that he died a hero. Especially don't think about telling his little sister he's not coming back. Or the Bantam kids. Do *not* wonder how big his coffin will be.

Stop it, stop it!

Stop thinking about his gravestone or the memories buried there with him. Kids shouldn't die. They should never die!

Suddenly, I realize my sight is blurry. And it's not because the lake is kicking up. Hot, snotty tears run down my face, and I only have my T-shirt to wipe with. So gross, but I gotta see what I'm doing. I'm the distraction. I have to believe, one last time, that Tez has a plan.

Cry later. Kick diabolical booty now.

I finish lacing the fireworks together and reach for my matches. It's time to close this camp down for good.

43

A Little Help from the Other Side

Tez

I don't have time to miss my body. I have a war to fight.

And it's pretty cool fighting it on the other side. The ghosts have spread out—the whole lake is dotted with them. They make an eerie, undead fog. The cries and shouts on the shores change. There's confusion mixed with terror and—dare I say it?—a little hope.

Here, on the island, I have Gavin and Winnie and Örn on my side. Somehow, Örn has a spectral racket. On his backswing, he whacks a naga counselor so hard, they go flying. It actually takes a moment to hear the splash. Örn disappears completely. Blinked out of existence, he reappears a moment later.

"Nice shot," Winnie says.

Örn winks at her. "I'm a pro."

He barely gets the words out before she punches her misty arm right through a serpent's chest. Its eyes go wide, its tongue slithers out, and then its eyes glaze. When Winnie pulls her hand out, the naga hits the ground. Dead? Unconscious? I don't know, but it's effective. Winnie fades out, tipping her beret to Örn. Her voice is a whisper on the wind. "Me, too."

Gavin just Gavins his way across the island, the same way he did when he was alive. He curses with luxurious fluency, grabbing snake tails and flipping them onto their backs. Each time he does, he flickers. Nostrils and Knees think they're suddenly masters of karate. And hey, maybe they are. Their kicks just have a little help from the other side.

When I get to the island's shore, I pick up a big branch of blackwood. And I stagger a little. The effort to move something physical burns. It's a fever that steals my strength. I fight to swing the stick at all the vultures, but it drops through my grasp almost immediately. My vision fades; I think I'm sinking. . . .

Finchy grabs me by the collar and hauls me back up. "You gotta conserve your strength, kid. It took me a hundred years to get as good as I am, and I still end up in the Nowhere Place."

If I had skin, I'd shudder. "What's the Nowhere Place?"

"Exactly what it sounds like," Finchy says, then squints out over the water. When he speaks again, he changes the subject. "Looks like Mary and that nurse got Corryn to the platform."

"Then we should get moving."

I step off the beach and onto the water. Even though I can't really feel it, I do sense the cold. It's like an ache, waiting to reach up and grab me. To curl into my bones and drag me into the dark.

Determined, I keep walking. I raise a hand and shout, "Corryn's in place. You know what to do after the boom!"

My voice sounds like a wail. It's not me at all. It's the call of the banshee in the middle of the night. The harbinger before the doom. If I'd ever heard that sound before, I would have cried and crawled under my bunk. I'm not ashamed to say that. Especially because, now, it'll never happen.

I think Mrs. Winchelhauser hears it. She pauses and looks out onto the water. Finchy and I stop, waiting for her gaze to pass us. The threatening cold rises. It's the dead of summer, but it feels like winter to me. Are we vaporous? Is there water in us? Could we literally freeze, like statues, on the surface of the lake?

I don't wanna find out. As soon as her gaze moves back to the chaos at her feet, we move on. Under my breath, I ask Finchy, "Is Virginia here?"

He shakes his head. "Her business was done."

"Then why are you here?" I ask. We had set him free, too, Corryn and I.

With a shrug, he says, "Guess I had a little bit more to do."

With that, we head for the beach. My Bantam campers are still giving it their all. I don't see a lot of slingshots left. But I do see them breaking all the rules at once. Throwing rocks, throwing sand, going under the dock, biting . . . They're the best.

Across the lake, the ghosts flow toward the beach with me. There are *so* many. I recognize this year's counselors, but I see other faces, too. Counselors from the twenties and thirties, their hairstyles unmistakable.

Some even older than that. A few trappers, with their buckskins and beaver hats. A couple of Continental soldiers with bayonets. Two teenagers dressed for a formal dance, his tie missing, her skirt tattered. There's even one Native man in his long shirt and leggings, deer rattles shaking silently on his hems as he walks.

It's a hazy parade of innocents, fed to a malevolent evil for centuries. Well, you know what? Whatever deal the Mechants made with the vampire devils, it ends tonight.

A spark appears beneath the diving platform. It's just one match, but it's like a spotlight. A fizzing, anxious moment passes. Will it work? Is it going to be enough?

Suddenly, a single bottle rocket flares into the air. It whistles, it spins, then pops with a faint explosion. It's not enough to turn Mrs. Winchelhauser's head. We really need Corryn to knock her off her game, so we can do this right. So we can do this at all. I still don't know how much power she has. She can apparently spawn a hundred snake babies in one summer while also organizing lanyard-making supplies. I wouldn't put anything past her!

Behind us, a wail rises. I look back in time to see some of the darkwood on the island going up in flames. The devilwood spits and sputters green fire. Vultures flap high into the sky, shrieking their bone-grinding calls.

Then, in front of us, another kind of shriek cuts in.

It's beautiful, the cacophony of too many fireworks exploding all at once. A massive ball of fire flies across the breach. Balls of green and blue shoot in every direction. They scatter the Bantam campers, good! Now they're away from the cursed lake—out of the line of fire!

White, whistling sparks fly off in spirals. Two snake people streak into the lake, trying to douse themselves.

The rockets reach Mrs. Winchelhauser, and *FWOOM!* The biggest, baddest boom of them all goes off. Her arms flail, and she stumbles back on her thick, reticulated tail. Yellow and gold and scarlet explode right on top of her. The blast knocks Chief Wolpaw onto his backside. From beneath the dock, baby cheers rise up.

"NOW!" I say, pushing myself forward. None of us is strong enough to do this alone, but together . . . just maybe we can end this curse once and for all.

I HOPE CORRYN CAN FEEL HOW HAPPY I AM RIGHT NOW.

She gave us the perfect distraction. Mrs. Winchelhauser is stunned!

Summoning all my strength, I lift the Winch into the air. Not with my hands—with some otherworldly power that I have now. Me and all the other victims of Camp Murderface. We form a line. Winch bobbles, but I pass her off to Finchy just before everything goes black.

44
The Nowhere Place

Tez

I'm there only a second, but I recognize it.

The Nowhere Place. The Nothing. It's the whole universe telescoping closed. A never-ending cold surrounds me. I start to forget names and faces and moments. It's like my mom never taught me PEMDAS and my dad never sang Gregorian chants to me.

I don't have a body anymore; what does a hug feel like? Did I ever have a friend? Wait . . . do I have a name? Everything seems to spin but remains still at the same time. Goodbye family, goodbye friends, goodbye girl with brown eyes and brown hair. Did I know her? I'm sure I did. . . .

At once, a voice cuts through the nothing—

"UNHAND ME!" Mrs. Winchelhauser howls, dangling like bait on a fishhook.

Shaking off the Nowhere Place, I turn to orient myself.

Maybe Winch doesn't want to bodysurf across Lake Sweetwater on a sea of angry spirits, but that's what's happening! Ghost after ghost carries her above the waves, each one flickering out after they expend their energy. But the chain is unbroken. And somehow, midway across the lake, the radios in camp blare to life again.

"—uys and ghouls," Bowl Cut says. "Guess who's back on the air! That's right, your one, your only, SOS DJ! We're taking this camp back from the inside! The senior side is burning to the ground, and it looks like our camp director is floating through the air. I wouldn't believe it if I hadn't seen it myself, but that's the news, folks. And here we go, getting ready to spin another Watch the Winch hit—"

There's a groan across the camp, just underneath all the yelling and battling. We're all a little Gordon Lightfooted out. I swear, even Mrs. Winchelhauser yelps, "Not again!"

"Here's a little KISS from me to you!" Bowl Cut shouts, and I can hear the glee in his voice. "With ROCK AND ROLL ALL NIGHT!"

Jangly electric guitars and booming bass spill out from our humble radio station. The atmosphere changes. It's like air comes back into a stuffy room, like sunshine after a week of rain. As a rock singer shout-sings through the trees, kids break into song on the shores.

The snake-counselors bail: they see what's happening to their leader, they don't want to end up with her. Serpentine bodies bleed into the woods. Campers emerge from hiding spots and fighting posts. They shout and punch at the air! They watch, we all watch, as unsettled souls carry the camp evil back to its source!

I'm so high above the lake, I feel like I'm looking at a map. At the map Corryn and I stole together. After the Nowhere Place, I taste that memory so vividly. Our laughter and fear, all mingling together. The warmth of her hug. Her friendship. The way she smelled like grass and sweat and soap.

I see Corryn now, standing on the diving platform, watching with her jaw dropped. On the island, Knees and Nostrils high-five, and the girls clutch each other in a tight, screaming knot of hugs and elation. The more Mrs. Winchelhauser protests, the louder the celebration gets.

When the ghosts get her to the other side of the lake, a new, rumbling growl fills the air.

"You have failed, Astrid," it says.

"I fed you more this summer than you had in twenty years," Mrs. Winchelhauser shrieks. "You owe me! You promised me!"

But apparently, a primeval darkness can't be bargained with. Three phantasmal campers take Mrs. Winchelhauser the last few feet. From the jaunty pitch of their hats and their neatly pressed sashes, I'm guessing they're campers from the 1940s. They've been waiting for this for a while.

Without a flinch, or a hesitation, they open their ghostly hands and drop Mrs. Winchelhauser into the bone pit.

She disappears from sight. And then nothing— I mean, I know what happens down there. The hands drag you down into the bones. The sound of a thousand teeth chattering fills your ears. And nobody's going to throw Mrs. Winchelhauser a life ring.

Then red light explodes from the ground. It points

straight up, cutting through the forest. Its glare blasts away the last few vultures lingering. It even seems to burn away the clouds. The glow bathes the entire camp in red light.

The ground rumbles. I can't feel it. I don't know if it's quaking. But I see what's happening. The remains of the Mechants' Lodge sink into the ground. The senior cabins, too. It's like the earth opens up, hungry, and devours them all. Kids run from the destruction, gathering on the shores of Lake Sweetwater.

Elm and Oak camp collapse next. Though I can't make out our camp group, I see smoke and dust rising through the trees. It's a good thing none of us were allowed to bring anything important to camp this summer, because I'm pretty sure we're not getting our luggage back.

All through camp, buildings crack and crumble. The Rec Barn falls like a house of cards. The band shell rolls on its back and cracks like an egg. About halfway through the second chorus of the KISS song, the radio station cuts off. This is proof. Quantifiable, measurable proof that the evil that settled here all those centuries ago is devouring itself.

The only thing that doesn't collapse is the Great

Hall. Kids from all around the camp move toward it. My Bantam campers run into the arms of senior campers, who pick them up even if they stagger a little under their weight. I see sooty, sweaty, bruised-up kids of all ages coming together.

And I grin when I see Soft Shoes take one look at Chief Wolpaw and then step onto his chest.

"WAKE UP!" he yells.

Minefield hears him and comes to yell, "GOOD MORNING!" in the chief's other ear. Sirens echo on the log drive that leads to camp. Headlights spill through the dark. Leading the pack is a woody station wagon. When it stops, Mr. Ferdle rolls out of the driver's seat.

Right behind him, an unmarked car with a bubble light skids in the gravel. The two detectives who came after we saved the girls from the bone pit step out. They're a little late for the big show, but that's all right.

No more evil French guys. No more midnight possessions. No more missing campers or counselors. No more blackwood or poisoned bug juice. No more wicked anything in these woods. Once the Mechants came here, this place was poisoned. Nothing good could come of it. And now, nothing bad will happen here again.

Well, maybe one thing.

Braids just noticed my body. And the fact that I'm not in it. I start to float that way, semicurious if anyone learned anything from our haphazard first-aid training the first week of camp. Something soft and cool stops me. Finchy. His ethereal hand on my noncorporeal shoulder.

"I wouldn't, kid," he says.

With a shrug, I slip away from him. "Those are my best friends down there."

Finchy replies with a shrug. "Suit yourself. But I'm warning you. Your own funeral? It's not as fun as it sounds like it should be."

"Well, then it'll be just like summer camp, then, huh?"

45
Vic-Vic-Victorious

Corryn

You know how people say when things get wild, everything's a blur?

I think that's because their brains would leak out of their ears if they had to take everything in at the same time. Because color war is over, and we won! But color war is over, and Tez is gone. We sent our SOS, and people came to save the day! But they just now showed up, too late to save my best friend.

The A Team loads Tez into one of the canoes left behind. Then they paddle out, like one of those depressing poems about sad ladies in rivers we have to read in English class. (What is *that* about?) A light mist hangs over the lake, stripped of evil, drained back to a normal shade of greenish-gray in the night.

When everybody reaches the diving platform, I can't look down.

"I'm really sorry," Hairspray starts, but I put up my shushing hand.

"Nope."

Against my better judgment, I take Knees' sweaty hand and step into the boat. I look everywhere but down. I can't face Ew. She's got a certain, shall we say, package lying across her lap, and she sniffles softly as we push off for shore. I have stuff to do. I have stuff to remember.

Like, I need to make sure that whatever they write about Tez in the newspaper, it doesn't say anything about a charnel house. That got him pretty steamed last time, when they claimed the bone bit was just full of animal parts. Definitely, they have to mention at least sixteen vocabulary words and encyclopedia facts, or it's just not accurate.

Before the newspaper, we're gonna have to talk to the police. And the park rangers. And the town librarian. Wait, what? Mr. Ferdle stands on the beach, a beacon for a bunch of the mighty weenie babies. They gather around him, calmed by the presence of a grown-up, I guess. But what the heck is *he* doing here?

I shake my head as we hit the silty beach shore where Tez once chundered his whole breakfast.

Other grown-ups, people I don't know, drag the boat all the way onto the sand. They swarm around it; we all jump out. Well, except Ew and Tez.

Mr. Ferdle runs over to me, clapping his hands to my shoulders. "Are you guys all right?"

I slide out of his grip. For a guy who does nothing but read information all day, that's a pretty foolish question. Everything inside me snaps, like a fishing line pulled too tight. My voice goes high when I yell, "Does it look like we're all right?"

This is one of those questions that people ask and are all annoying because they don't want you to answer them. I'm doing it on purpose, because it's my turn to be annoyed. More than annoyed. Furious. Enraged!

"Our camp director has been feeding kids to an ancient evil for WHO KNOWS HOW LONG! We just spent all summer being brainwashed by a poison lake, and our counselors all turned into snakes! Does that sound all right to you?"

I jerk my thumb over my shoulder, and the words

just keep on coming. "You see that big ol' red light over there? That's what happens when you feed evil to evil and SAVE THE DAY. And by you, I mean WE. US! By ourselves!

"Did you notice that the aforementioned day is already saved, and you guys are just now showing up? Bowl Cut probably played ol' Gordo about a hundred times! THAT'S SIX HUNDRED FIFTY-THREE MINUTES, FERD!"

My throat croaks, and my tongue trips over the "aforementioned." Because that's Tez in my brain. That's this dweebo, goonfaced, know-it-all kid who never, ever shuts up. It hits me again that he's shut up pretty good now, huh? Just when I was finally getting him to be less dorktastic! Just when we finally made up and—

"And you know what else?" I continue. People are gathering, and I don't give a hoot. Let them gather! Let them hear the truth! My face stings, so hot, and my chest is so tight. "The vampire devils up in here haven't even been, like, sneaky! They've been here forEVER, and did you do anything about it? NOOOOOO."

Swinging around, I gesture at my A Team. Braids and Hairspray clutch each other, and Knees is actually resting his head on Nostrils' shoulder. Ew's still in the canoe, just standing there.

I don't know where Tez is. They must have taken his bod—nope. I squeeze my eyes closed and start again. "We're the ones who took care of it! All these guys here! And those itty-bitty beasts! And the weird guys with the caterpillar mustaches in senior camp! WE did it! Not you! Not any of you. US!"

"Corryn," the woman detective says, like she's trying to shush a horse. Well, this horse is not going to shush!

I hear a kid I don't know clear her throat. "She's right," she says, stepping forward. She's one of the senior campers, holding a lacrosse stick. "Nobody helped us."

It strikes me—this must be one of the other kids who felt *something*, who saw things about this place no one else did. Like us. A secret A Team leader.

Another one, a dark-haired boy from Elm Camp, puts his arm around the girl with the cool crutches. "Not when we wrote home. Not when we snuck into town to get help—"

"I mean." Another one of the older kids. A dude? A girl? Can't quite tell; they're just cool. "Federal agents were out here because those little weirdos from junior camp found body parts, and you still didn't do anything."

We're not weirdos, but they're on our side, so I'll take it.

Turning back to the Ferd, I say, "So you don't get to come in here and act like you did anything! You stand there and be sorry! You stand there and apologize because a SNAKE MAN tried to kill me, and that kid right there took a bat to the chest to save me. You didn't do ANYTHING!"

Tears start to fall, and I don't even care! And then somebody comes up from behind me and puts an arm around me. What the wha— It's Bowlie. He's gleaming with sweat, so he probably hoofed it up here from the station. I'm just glad to see he's alive. (And is that something you should think about a kid at summer camp? Let me spell it out for you: N! O!)

He squashes me awkwardly against his side. Ew steps out of the canoe, like somebody switched her back on. She runs over and throws her arms around me, too. Hairspray follows, then Braids. Nostrils and Knees come in to fill out the huddle.

Before I know it, we're all hugged up together.

Snorfing. Sniffling. Even some sobbing. We don't have to act tough right now. We're in this together. We always have been.

Oak Camp, Cabin Group A.

Victorious, but one man down.

46

Okkameedees

Corryn

In the quiet after the storm, I realize something.

I had to be bribed to come to camp this summer. But for the first time, all summer, I wish I could have gotten to know these dorks a lot sooner. Look at what we did when we barely had any time at all.

You know what? I don't even feel like a numpty—whatever that is; it was one of Gavin's favorite insults—crying here with them. Because we went to war and back together. And not all of us made it home.

Gasps break out around us. Still hanging on to my cabin posse, I look up to see what's got their attention. Actually, I don't have to look up. I just have to open my eyes all the way. Even though everything's smeary, I see soft, blue lights appear on the lake.

Murmurs pass around me: "Is that?" and "No way" and a lot of "Whoa." After I wipe my face with my shirt, my eyes widen. The lights are people—were people. They're ghosts. Probably a hundred, probably more.

They're wearing all kinds of old-timey clothes, wearing old-timey hairdos. Some of their glow is joy, smiles plastered on all their misty faces.

Ohhh, ohhh.

I get it. I *did* hear Tez. And he *was* talking to someone else, too. It all makes sense now, how the Winch got carried down to heck by invisible hands. All the fantoms du the lac were in on it. All of them . . . and Tez.

Mr. Ferdle and the detectives look like they got clobbered with Thor's hammer as the blue glow brightens. It's not every day you see a couple hundred years' worth of former Ohio residents floating above a formerly vampire-tainted lake.

Hope feels like a soda bubble in my chest. I crane my neck, searching for Tez. The bubble swells, almost light enough to lift me off my feet. Finchy's here! Standing (floating?) at the edge of the water, he tips his head to me, and I tip mine back. Respect for the dude, but also, he feels like a good omen.

If he's back, then Tez should be, too! Eagerly, I search for him. My heart is panting like a puppy dog; where is he? I know he's kinda short, but come on. He's gotta be here.

All around me are familiar faces, worn-out faces— not to imitate Scary Mary, but this world is mad, innit? Speak of the specter, there she is, with Gavin—she rolls her eyes, and he stands there and looks like a dope. I *almost* miss them for a minute.

But if they're here and Finchy's here, come on! That plan was Tez's idea! He's gotta be here. He has to be. HE BETTER BE.

Ew watches my face, then hugs me again. I think she knows who I'm trying to find. And failing. Where did he go? Why is Pierre LePet over there ghost chatting with a lady in a hoopskirt, but Tez is nowhere to be seen? Before I can get my rage on again, a blinding light pierces the haze.

We all turn to look. It's one of the ghosts by the island! The light is like a halo around her. Her hair is kinda floaty, and she looks up toward the sky. With a crazy happy smile, she shoots into the air.

When she slows, she breaks apart in a shower of

blue fire, a whole new kind of firework. White diamond lights sprinkle down, a shower of sparks that fades before it hits the water. There's nothing left of her, but it feels like it's a good thing.

She's barely gone, and another ghost lights up the night. I swear to dog that the sparks swirl into the shape of a heart before fluttering away. One by one, these souls, trapped for so long, fly free.

"We did that," Hairspray says softly.

Knees murmurs, "Heck yeah, we did."

I feel that, I do. But I feel something else, too. Deep and heavy, like an anchor on my heart. We tip our heads back to watch them fly, and Ew squeezes me tighter and whispers, "I'm really sorry."

See? Ew gets it.

"I never even found out his stupid middle name," I say, weeping.

A little hand tugs on mine, and I untangle enough to look down. It's Minefield, one of Tezzerino's faves. She crooks her little finger at me, to make me come closer. So I do. I bend down to hear what she has to say. Her face is serious and also wet, so I'm not the only one cutting onions out here.

Minefield cups her hands around her mouth, and

says to me, "Okkameedees."

"What?"

A weird, croaky voice rises from the ground. "She said Archimedes. It's Tesla Archimedes Jones."

"What kind of middle name is *that*?" I demand, then turn around to whip off some top-notch middle-name slams. I've got a million of them (especially because mine is Dawn), and they're almost to my lips when I realize I'm about to play a game of snaps with— Wait, what?

Sprawled on the ground between a dude in scrubs and a lady with a stethoscope, Tez is still browny-gray like oatmeal, but his eyes are open. One arm hangs limply, and he holds the other across his chest. His lips are the color you get when you suck on a pen in school and it accidentally breaks and then you get ink in your mouth and you have to spit it out but you're not supposed to spit in the water fountains, so—

Oh my dog! The weight holding my heart down releases. At the same time, my knees are too weak to hold me up. I drop onto the ground next to him and grab his (good) shoulder.

There may be tears dripping off my face. There might be snot dripping from my nose. But I'm so happy to see Tez blinking and staring and giving me that doofy Tez look that I don't care. "You're alive!"

With a grunt, Tez struggles to sit up. Stethoscope lady supports his back but warns him to take it easy. I have news for her. Tesla Archimedes Jones doesn't know the meaning.

Wincing, he lets go of his chest and tugs my hand off his shoulder. But he doesn't push it away. He holds it.

"Ooooooooooooooooh," Knees singsongs behind me. Then I hear him go, "Oof," which means Braids probably just socked him good.

"Sorry I died on you out there."

I'm too happy to yell at him. Heck, I'm so happy, I might even ask him about corpse facts— later. After a respectful amount of time passes.

This whole night swirls in my head like a crazy tornado, and I don't know when all the pieces are going to land. My stomach quivers with used-up adrenaline and brand-new happiness.

I want to tell him so much, but I can't find the right words at all. And I want to ask him everything, but for once, he doesn't look up to giving a lecture. So instead, I rub his clammy hand and say, "You're pretty good at taking a dive."

He grins. "Thanks."

"I'm probably gonna hug you," I warn him, but he shakes his head quickly.

"Maybe not yet," the dude in scrubs says. "He's got a couple of broken ribs."

"Whoa, okay," I say. "Maybe not."

The high-pitched call of an ambulance breaks through the murmuring dark. Once again, red and blue flashers bathe the Great Hall, and all the kids who came to Camp Murderface this year. But this time, it's for good. It's to take my best friend in the world to get fixed up. It's to shut this place down forever.

I feel like I should come up with something better to say. Or do. Unfortunately, all my think-fast is thought out for the night. Maybe for the rest of the summer. And I'm not about to kiss him on his grimy cheek, not in front of this barrel of monkeys. So I do the next best thing, before I have to get out of the way and let the professionals do their jobs.

I give my best friend, my ALIVE best friend, a Corryn Quinn name-brand wet willie.

Yeah. That feels right.

47
Local Legends

Tez

It wouldn't be a celebration at the Fan du Lac public library without Grodo the clown.

He stands on the front walk, bothering people with his competent balloon animals. I watch him from the Local Legends section (Knees' idea) wanly presenting a cobra hat to Minefield. I can't condone her kick to his shins, but I can absolutely empathize.

Balloons hang in the air inside the library. By the reference desk, there are long tables heavy with snacks and cookies and drinks. A radio plays quietly in the children's section, barely audible over all the campers packed inside and soaking up the AC.

It's festive outside, too—aside from the clown, I mean. In the closed street out front, there are tables and chairs, a massive boom box, and party streamers hanging from street signs.

The senior campers lean at various angles, sipping from party cups and trying to look cool. The junior camp kids huddle in masses, lurking over the assigned dance area. The only kids actually dancing in the sunlight are my Bantam campers. Those little guys are party monsters, and they're running the volunteer chaperones ragged.

They just have to make it through today. After Camp Sweetwater alternately collapsed into sinkholes and/or burned to the ground, the locals packed us up and brought us into town. The school principal opened the gym to give us somewhere to sleep while the police contacted all our parents.

I missed the gym shenanigans (Braids beat Nostrils in rope climbing; Knees and Hairspray raided the cafeteria and instantly became Snack Czars) because I stayed the night in the hospital. I wasn't alone; there were probably twenty other campers there with me. We were less lively overnight, but we also got Happy Meals. I'd call that a win-win.

400

After a nice, *normal* breakfast, they brought us here. To the library, the best place in the world. The sum of human knowledge lives here, even if I am sitting next to a display of books titled IT AIN'T SWAMP GAS: A Tour of Fan du Lac Folklore. Every time Bowl Cut sees it, he shoves a hand in his armpit. The sound he makes when he pumps his arm isn't swamp gas either.

"Hey," Corryn says, sliding in the chair next to me. She lowers her voice, but not out of respect for the library. Slyly opening her canvas bag, she grins. "Check it out, I scammed us some water in those Summer Reading squeezy bottles."

"Exxxcellent," I say, reaching for one. I take a deep swig and sink into my chair. It's one of the soft ones, but I can't get too comfortable. My shoulder is immobilized, my chest is bruised, and the doctors taped up my ribs. It hurts if I breathe too deep, and I love it. It's proof I'm alive.

Checking to make sure no one's watching, Corryn slowly opens her squeezy bottle. Then she tips her head back and sprays a stream into her mouth. Mostly. It also splashes on her cheek and on her T-shirt, so I do what any friend would do. I point and laugh. "I think there's a hole in your lip."

With a shrug, she brushes the water into her jeans. "My bad," she says carelessly, then laughs. "Chief Wolpaw drove all the way to Cleveland for this sweet, sweet plastic jug water. I can't get enough!"

She's not lying either. Gallon jugs of purified water stand sentry under the snack tables. Nobody's taking their chances with the local water just yet. I can't say I blame them. Why should they, when there's a ready supply of fresh, bloodless, ghost-free water right there?

"So," Corryn says, heaving a deep breath. "When are your mom and dad getting here?"

I glance at the clock. "Any time now. They left before the sun came up."

"Mine, too," she says.

"I can't believe we live in different states."

"I can't believe we're not allowed to kick Ohio out and just sew Pennsylvania and Indiana together so we can live closer."

"That would be catastrophic for native flora and fauna."

Corryn claps her hands over her face, then drags them down. She stares at me over her fingertips, baring the underside of her eyes. "Oh nooo, the fauna . . . Just, dude, why are you such a dork?"

"Lucky, I guess."

I want to tell Corryn so many things. I started to write them down last night, but the nurse took away the stationery and pen. She said I needed rest, which was true. But my brain also had to start figuring out what happens next.

Camp is gone. We're going home. I won't be there to see Corryn chug Fruity Pebbles from a box at breakfast. Or get to get lost in the woods with her anymore. No more square dancing or sneaking into the camp van. It's gonna be farewell to everything we've done together. Probably I'll never ride another tandem bike again in my life.

I take a deep breath, twinge, then say, "I'm gonna miss you."

"Shut up," she replies.

Turning my chair to her, I lean into her personal space. "I am. You're smart and brave. A little bit mean, but you mean well . . . and I know you have a soft spot, too. You're interesting and a great speller—"

Corryn's face darkens from dusky peach to kind of a sunset rose. Her blushes aren't ordinary, and neither is she. I can tell her hand itches to give me a frog. I can also tell that her brain is telling her hand to shut up.

Finally, she says, prompting me, "The best BMXer you've ever met."

My laughter spills out. "Definitely that. Basically, you're fearless."

"Yeah right," she says sarcastically.

"And I . . . I like your freckles," I somehow manage to say. Then my throat snaps closed. My face is on fire; those words tricked me! They snuck past my brain and right onto my mouth.

Before Corryn can reply, we hear a commotion outside. It's high-pitched and coming right this way. It takes a second to make out what's happening, but when I do, my heart does a weird jelly flip in my chest.

"TEZ!" yells my little sister, Hi, bursting through the library doors. Her dark, curly hair bounces with every running step she takes. She's at least two inches taller, and she barrels through the crowd like she's made of rubber. I'm gonna have to introduce her to Minefield and Soft Shoes. The three of them could probably figure out how to power North America with their energy, if they put their minds to it.

With Corryn's help, I stand up. And with Corryn as a bodyguard, Hi doesn't crash into me full-speed. Instead, she crashes into Corryn first. *Then* makes a softer landing, throwing her arms around my waist and looking up at me.

"Did you know that clown outside hasn't registered his *face*?" Hi asks me incredulously. She's crazy about clowns. It's borderline obsessive, honestly. She goes on, "He didn't even know about the egg registry in London. How is that possible? I suspect he's some kind of clown impersonator, don't you?"

Corryn starts to cackle. Like, throw her head back, full-on hyena-barking laughing. I can tell it's not a mean sound, but Hi might not be as attuned to subtle social signals as I am. I slip my good arm around Hypatia's little shoulders and ask Corryn, "What's so funny?"

"She's a mini Tez," Corryn crows.

Hi considers her. Then she looks up to me. "This is the girl you wrote home about, isn't it? She *does* look like she could punch the face off a wolverine."

Puffing up, Corryn says, "Thanks, squirt! That's the nicest thing anybody ever said to me!"

The front doors jangle open again. This time, my parents come through. They look a little harried. Mom's hair is usually in a smooth, neat ponytail, and Dad doesn't usually speedwalk. No doubt, Hi gave them a scare when she lost them in a strange town. I tell her,

"You really shouldn't run ahead, just for the record."

"An interesting proposition," Hi says, in a way that tells me she's already ignoring it. But it doesn't matter. The air stirs with the warm scent of home when my parents get to me. They form a hugging cage around me. They've had to cuddle me in a sling before; they know the drill.

In theory, this display of affection could be embarrassing. But in practice, I want to sink into it forever. Relief trembles through me. Even though Corryn and I made sure everybody else was okay, finally, the ground is solid beneath me. We don't have to face anything else alone.

"We're so glad you're okay," Mom says, stepping back and catching my face between her hands. Usually, I hate this, because it means she's worried I'm sick or hurt or both. Her skin is cool and soft and familiar. "But you're going to have to explain what happened again. The caller last night didn't make a lot of sense. Something about a snake infestation at the camp? And then there was a fire? I mean, my gosh, honey!"

Dad combs a hand through my hair, worry furrowing on his brow. He has the darkest, brownest eyes in the world. I didn't know I missed grown-ups looking at me like that, with care and concern, until just now. "I was afraid this would happen."

Baffled, Hi interjects. "You were afraid Tez's camp would be full of snakes and fire?"

Corryn chokes back a laugh. That's when Mom and Dad's laser focus softens a little. They both turn to look at her. Mom has this strange secretive smile on her face. Dad just looks curious. I'm not sure I like either of those looks, but what can I do?

"Sorry, guys, yeah," I say. "This is my best friend, Corryn Quinn."

"Ohh," Mom says, with a little singsong in her voice. For a second, she sounds a tiny bit like Hairspray. "It's so nice to meet you, Corryn. We've heard so much about you."

With gusto, Dad agrees. "Until Tez stopped writing, he mentioned you in about . . . every single letter!"

Now Corryn and I both flush. I plead with her, with my eyes. We're trapped here, and when adults trap Corryn, weird stuff happens. Gah! I just want my mom and dad to like her enough to say hi and then to leave it alone!

"He told me a lot about you, too," Corryn says, and reaches out to . . . shake their hands? Then, even more politely, she says, "It's really nice to meet you. Thanks for letting Tez come to camp this year."

And just like that, my parents melt. I see stars in their eyes. They look at Corryn like she's treasure. And she is. She completely is, but this is—to put it in the vernacular—totally blowing my mind.

"Corryn!" a woman yells as she comes in the front door. We're all pretty loosey-goosey with the noise level in the library today, not that I expect anything less. Corryn turns and recognizes the lady.

"Mom!" she yells back, and then runs to her. They crash together in a massive hug, right in front of the snack tables. They rock back and forth so hard, I'm a little concerned they might tip over.

But I also can't stop smiling. Because that lady looks and hugs just like I imagined Corryn's mom would. I didn't know it was possible to feel the love and warmth from somebody else's hug. But my heart is kindled warm and bright right now. At least until Corryn leans back. Looks uncertain.

Then says, "Dad's not coming, is he?"

48
Hello

Corryn

I'm not gonna cry.

I say that because I'm really not gonna cry. All of a sudden, boom, pow! Real life is back! Things can't be crazy when your mom's around! I bet if she'd come to camp with me, this whole summer would have been a bummer! I'd like to see the Winch try to back Rachel Quinn down!

Squashing my face against her shoulder, I breathe deep. She smells so clean! There's fabric softener on her shirt! Her hug is softer than a summer cloud. I don't know how I went two months without one mom hug. Never again, quote me on it.

AND YOU KNOW WHAT ELSE YOU CAN QUOTE ME ON?

I made it out of this summer awake, alert, *and* alive, so it's gonna be okay if my parents get divorced. I don't want it to happen. I don't like it. But I can get used to seeing them one at a time. Dad's still my dad, even if he's not standing right—

"CORY!" Dad yells when he busts into the library.

Okay, I burst into tears. I'll burst something else if somebody gives me a hard time about it.

My dad is here! He's here. He comes over and wraps his arms around me *and* my mom. That's just a big old miracle.

"I'm glad you're both here," I say, not blubbering. Okay, blubbering a little. "And I'm not mad at you guys anymore. I understand why you had to send me away. And I'm okay with it!"

Dad pushes his glasses up and squints at me. "Did I miss something?"

"Who am I going to live with?" I ask. "Can I paint my walls orange?"

From who knows where, Mom produces a tissue and swabs my face. There's concern in her voice as she says,

"We can discuss the walls, but what do you mean? You live with us."

"Right," I say. I'm trying here, people. Work with me! "But Dad has to move out if you're getting divorced, right?"

Dad rears his head back. "Why would *I* have to move out?" he asks, at the exact same time Mom boggles at me and exclaims, "We are *not* getting divorced!"

Okay. Look. I just spent nine weeks in Camp Murderface. I literally watched my best friend get killed by a giant snake man. Last night, I slept in a school gym that wasn't even my school, and I let Braids put three braids in my hair while I brushed Ew's hair, who brushed Hairspray's hair—it was a whole thing.

I made my peace with all of it! I was going to be OKAY. And now, what the what? I stare at my parents, and I just want everything to make sense again.

"I heard you guys talking through the vent in my room. I'm not a dingus! You said that you didn't need Dad's input; you were really mad!" I look to Dad. "And *you* were all glad you could make these big changes while I was at camp!"

They look at each other, doing their weird parent

telepathy. Will that go away when they're divorced? But then Dad smiles, and he squishes me against his side. "Honey, we're not getting a divorce. We're pregnant!"

"*I'm* pregnant," Mom says, then leans her brow against mine. "*We're* having a baby. Oh sweetheart. It was too early to say anything yet. And we wanted a chance to look for a bigger house, and get some things settled—"

"We thought you'd be bored, because we wouldn't have as much time for our usual summer fun, kiddo."

Oh.

What?

Ohhhhhhhh!

There's a little bit of my origami heart that just unfolds. Just like that. Because I was ready to be okay, but this is *so much better.* I can teach a new baby to do all kinds of rad stuff. They'll be the coolest kid in school because they went to DJ Bubbles's boot camp! And they'll have tiny little hands to help get into places I can't get to anymore! (Like, the water jug full of quarters by the back door, for example.)

And finally, if something *happens* to break in the house, it's not automatically me!

"But we can talk about all that later," Mom says,

stealing a kiss when she leans back. "We want to hear about you. And camp. What happened? What started the fire? Is everyone okay? Oh, did you ever make friends with the girls in your cabin?"

Dad follows that up with a laugh. "Did your pukey little buddy ever pass his swim test?"

Whoa. Okay. This is gonna take a while. I nod toward the Local Legends section, where Tez is sitting with his family. "Meet me over there, okay? I'm gonna get some Chips Ahoy! and introduce you to Tez, and then we'll tell you all kinds of stuff."

I mean. We're going to lie our butts off. But they're going to get one heck of a story.

Tez

All summer long, I kept waiting for the best camp day ever.

Well, it finally got here. All day long, grown-ups showed up for their kids. All day long, we got to eat real food and share real laughs. All day long, we got to remember the good stuff that happened. The bad stuff? Eh. We were kind of over that.

As the sun starts to set, there aren't that many of us left. Luckily for us, because Oak Camp, Cabin Group

A, is still here. The street in front of the library cleared out a while ago, but we took over.

Music plays from the boom box, although Bowl Cut points out to his mom that he learned to be a way better DJ at camp. Debatable, but it's awesome that he's smiling again.

Knees and Nostrils take full advantage of the empty pavement. They've been doing a karate show for six years, or a few minutes. Not sure which. But I sit next to Corryn, and we ooh and ahh for them anyway. Since they don't kick anyone's face off, they deserve the praise.

"Most improved dorks," Corryn whispers to me, grading their performance.

Gently, I nudge her, but we both smile.

My sister and Braids' little brother color the street with fat sticks of chalk. They had to start entertaining themselves, because they exhausted Glummo the Clown into quitting early. The minute Hairspray found out that Mrs. Quinn was having a baby, she plopped down next to her to ask a million questions. That's how I find out that she wants to be a teacher. Hairspray! A teacher!

After a dinner donated by the diner, Ew's family say it's time for them to hit the road.

"Wait, wait," Mr. Quinn says. "We have something special for Corryn. We thought she might want to share it with you all."

"Is it edible?" Nostrils asks.

"Is it a wolf?" Knees inquires.

All of us shout out at once in glee, "IS IT A BUG?" and we all laugh our heads off until our parents start to look worried.

So we put ourselves back together, and Corryn clears her throat. "Is it a million dollars?"

"Actually," her mom says, popping a melon square into her mouth, "we thought Corryn might like to introduce you all to Elliot."

Somehow, I'd forgotten all about Corryn's back-home boyfriend. It was a detail that got lost in all the chaos. The first chaos and then the second chaos, both. But now the chaoses are over, and boy, do I feel sheepish. I wish I hadn't said what I said about her freckles, but . . . well. I did. Now it's time be a good *friend*, because that's what I am.

I mean, it would be nice if Corryn would stop doing that wacky dance of jubilation, right in the road. But I smile! And I say, "Yay." Just like that!

"Here comes Elliot," Mr. Quinn calls. We all turn

to look. He's probably taller than me. And stronger. And rad. And all the things that I, Tez Jones, am not. But no matter what he is, I'm still the one who saved Camp Sweetwater at Corryn's side.

And . . . I don't see Elliot. But I do see that "borrowing" runs in the Quinn family, because her dad is rolling a bike this way.

"Elliot!" Corryn yells, and runs over to him. She smears the handlebars with kisses, and hugs the seat. Of a bike. Then she actually sprawls on the ground and pets the tires, like they're the softest kitten in the free world.

Ew leans over my shoulder and says, "You should see your face right now."

I bet I look like a doofus. My smile feels pretty doofy. I cup my good hand around my mouth and call down to Corryn, "Show us some tricks!"

As soon as I say that, Hi lifts her head. "Tricks?"

Braids' little brother jumps to his feet. "Bike tricks?"

Every Oak Group camper left on the street yells, "YES," to bike tricks. Corryn doesn't have to be begged or anything.

She leaps on Elliot and tears up and down the street. The wind pulls her hair, and the speed puts color in her cheeks. She goes with no hands. Then no feet. Then no hands and no feet. She stands on the seat until her mom tells her to get down.

There's wheelies and bunny hops and one-eighties and three-sixties, and at the end, Corryn even balances on the front wheel and bounces around in a circle. It reminds me of a trained poodle trick, except better, because it's Corryn.

Finally, she skids to a stop in front of me, spraying tiny gravel beneath her tires. She's out of breath and about as happy as I've ever seen her. "Whatcha think?"

I think I'm going to miss her. I think I'm going to have to force her to write postcards. It's okay. I'll send them, already stamped and addressed, in my letters. I think if her parents like my parents, that we might be able to convince them to meet in the middle next summer and all go camping.

I walk with Corryn back to her parents' car, to put Elliot away.

"Hey," Corryn says, leaning Elliot against the car. "I'm glad you didn't die for good last night."

Shuffling my feet, I grin. "I'm glad you didn't die at all."

Gruff, Corryn says, "Okay, come here. I'm not

hugging you in front of the geek squad back there, but you're not getting out of here without one."

I can only offer one arm's worth of a hug. Three total arms are plenty, and we hold on long enough that it starts to feel just a little weird. She pulls back and wipes her whole hand down the middle of my face. Just like old times. I start to say that, but she darts in and drops a peck on the corner of my mouth.

"Nope," she says loudly, her face bright red. "Chickens still don't have lips. Come on before they start gossiping about us."

Corryn takes a couple steps, then waits for me to catch up. Then she walks at my pace all the way back.

You know, that first day on the bus didn't seem promising. Introductions made by underpants rarely are, I imagine. But somebody pretty smart once told me that summer doesn't start until you can't see your parents wave goodbye. Therefore, the corollary rule would be, summer doesn't end if you don't stop saying hello.

So I already know how I'll start my first letter to her. I'm going to say hello.

The buildings are gone, the camp is closed.
No more tennis, no more swim,
No more Mechants to prowl the night.

No more ghosts. No more monsters.
No more bugs (than usual).
Things should stay quiet around here now.

Summer's over, autumn comes.
And one covered, black, lead coffin bobs to the surface
of a lake that is still a little red at the edges.

Acknowledgments

This one is for KPez and Jedward. The eagle flies at midnight.